K L COLE

Rose and Gate Publishing

Exit Darcus
First Edition 2013

Author: K L Cole
© K L Cole 2013

Cover Design:
Cornerstone Vision, www.cornerstonevision.com
Based on artwork 'Daring to Believe' by Billy, www.billyart.co.uk

Published by
Rose and Gate Publishing
Cornerstone House
28 Old Park Road
Peverell
Plymouth
PL3 4PY

ISBN 978-0-9927911-1-7

DEDICATION

Chris, your spirit of faithfulness runs
like a Celtic knot through these pages.

Inside all of us there is a door.

Who, or what, we let in makes all the difference.

Chapter One

TRESPASSING

A LICE RESTED ON the grass verge. The tall, wild stems cushioned her weary body.

She flinched as a large spider scurried through the layers of her black organza skirt.

Squelch. Her nimble fingers crushed its fat body between the netting. Grasping a nearby dock leaf she brushed off the gooey mass. Time was unimportant. She was heading nowhere in particular.

She ran her pale hand over a poisonous bouquet of toxic wildflowers. They lay beside her, loosely tied in a velvet ribbon taken from her raven hair.

Oh, the delight of picking them along the wayside.

Hemlock, foxgloves, nightshades – Alice smiled to herself as she studied them. Having deliberately searched for the deadly flora, they made a fine collection of all she had been forbidden to touch as a child.

Sighing, she fell back onto the verdant carpet and into a troubled sleep.

A shrill, piercing cry broke the silence.

She awoke, startled and anxious.

A barn owl screeched eerily into the midnight air. Bright, stark moonlight made the limbs of the surrounding trees appear as spindly bones.

Her dreams had been bizarre and oppressive. The caustic voice of her mum's boyfriend burnt like acid in her ears.

"Get the hell out of here, Alice! Get lost!"

And that's exactly what she had done.

Allowing herself brief reflection, she questioned her mother's sanity.

Where was Mum's head at, bringing that weak, stupid loser into their lives?

Curse the night he had staggered back from the Three Castles and wormed his way into Mum's bed!

When Alice had gone down to breakfast the following morning, she had been shocked to discover this scruffy, bleary-eyed biker slurping black coffee from her favourite mug. He smelled of stale lager and dope, fused with cheap, greasy bacon.

Jimmy Griffin. She nursed the hatred she felt towards him with great relish.

In less than three months he had completely taken over the cottage that she had called home for eighteen years. It was not only his jungle of pot plants that had forced their way in. His domineering ways held a choke hold over her mother. Somehow, he had captured her affections so tightly that she'd become oblivious to everything and everyone else around her. It was as if she'd been hypnotised by him.

Alice suddenly felt a deep pang of gnawing hunger. It wasn't just for food.

The loneliness within her had driven her to forage into dark realms for comfort and companionship. Fumbling for her flowers, she arose and hastened down to the brook where Vanda, her Irish Cob, stood tethered to an old oak tree. She mounted the steps of her gypsy caravan and carefully opened the lid of a small, glazed jar. Reaching in, she lifted out some weed. Presently a waft of marijuana smoke rose into the night air. A short-lived sense of peace and wellbeing calmed Alice's aggravated thoughts as she sat in the doorway counting the fading stars.

The misty morning caused a veil to hang over the brook.

Alice untangled the leather thongs of her bohemian sandals and dipped her feet into the cool water. She glanced down at her right ankle. It had been feeling itchy and dry. Two weeks had passed since the hot scratching of the tattoo artist's needle had etched in her birth sign. Now it encircled her flesh as a delicate bracelet of calligraphy, laced with tiny ivy leaves.

She gathered a handful of comfrey and tossed the broad foliage into Vanda's wooden bucket. The herbs would relieve her horse's tired legs.

Assessing her circumstances, she decided to linger indefinitely, safely concealed within a wooded area on the vast grounds of the Beulah estate.

She had wilfully driven her caravan beyond the ancient, granite boundary stones and through the gateway, despite the sign clearly indicating that trespassers were prohibited. Melantha, the manager at the Three Castles, had often gossiped about the fact that Mr Brunswick, the owner of Beulah, was absent and many believed he would never return. His large property had fallen into disrepair and the men he had hired to maintain his grounds were unaccountable and seldom there.

Stringing a piece of rope between two silver birch trees, Alice created a washing line. The distinctive, white, peeling bark reminded her of times when she had walked for miles through the countryside with her mother. Always educating her in the ways of myth and folklore, she had laughed, saying, "Alice, your grandma told me birch protects us from evil spirits, but I believe it symbolises *love!*"

Anger arose as she lamented her mother's dippy, irrational behaviour. When it came to the affairs of the heart she was absurdly impulsive, dragging any old bloke into her illusion of romance.

Soon a striking array of quirky garments spread artfully out across the rope. It made for a pretty sight. Vintage fabrics with lace trim, soft pastel chiffons, dark purple cottons and a black net petticoat hung in the warm breeze.

The rest of the day was spent knitting and baking chapattis on the small wood-burner in the caravan.

As evening fell, Alice sat outside eating a truckle of cheese and drinking a bottle of Jimmy's home-made wine.

The fact that she had stolen it from him made it taste all the sweeter.

It was mid-summer, and a solar-powered Moroccan lantern had been soaking up the day's heat. Its stained glass panels transformed the captured sunlight into a mesmerising display. Lifting it off a metal stake, she climbed over the ledge of the van.

In the warm glow of the lamp, she undressed and put on a satin chemise. A double bed lay, chest-height, across the back of the wagon. It was accessed by a short ladder. Alice hopped up and sank into the welcoming mattress. Dried bunches of lavender hung overhead and provided an instant calming effect. For a few precious hours, her inner turmoil was relieved as she drifted off to sleep.

Early dawn rays filtered through voile panels and danced around the rustic wooden chamber. Stirring, Alice parted the canopy and clambered down from the bunk. It wasn't long before the aroma of fresh coffee started to revive her.

Having washed in the brook, she returned to plan the day ahead.

Today she would explore.

Lifting an antique hand mirror, she smudged kohl around her hazel eyes. A touch of gloss softened her lips. She pulled her organza skirt over her slender form and threaded the eyelets of her corset-styled blouse. Fastening her sandals, she slipped out into the morning sunshine.

A simple bridge of thirteen stepping stones allowed her safe passage across a natural watercourse. In front of her rose a steep grassy slope. Multitudes of emerald blades moved in the breeze like soft rippling waves.

Slowly ascending, she breathed in shallow gulps of flowery air.

The challenge of reaching the top was generously rewarded by the vista that opened up before her: sweet meadows, rolling hills, and a long way in the distance, the faint grey roof of the House of Beulah.

As she came across an old track, Alice's tired legs welcomed the level ground.

A wooded area on one side provided shade in its cool shadows, but the glimpse of Beulah had unnerved her. Anxious thoughts began to spiral. An accelerating panic forced a strong image to the forefront of her mind. There, as if seated upon a throne, sat *Melantha*.

Melantha. Quick-witted yet mysterious, the resident manager of the Three Castles had led an eclectic life. A skilled musician with a fine, haunting voice, she had performed at many festivals with her folk band, *Fairy Fay*.

Her exquisite needlework had earned her much acclaim and led to her opening a small, exclusive city boutique, clothing the rich and famous.

A long string of broken relationships had driven her to seek refuge in a more concealed rural lifestyle. Damaged and bruised, no one ever gained access into the vault in which she'd buried her heart. Although on the surface she quipped and played along with the locals who frequented the pub, she secretly despised them.

Chapter Two

DARK ARTS

ALICE RECALLED THE first night she had ever met
Melantha.

The long bar rolled the entire length of the old pub. Never
more animated than when there was a full line of customers
seated on its rattan stools, Melantha plied her captive
audience with her charms. As their minds slowly blurred
under the haze of alcohol, the dark, spiritual forces that
operated from deep within her, spun their enchanting web.

Melantha was aptly named after a parasitic vine; her
spellbinding personality coiled around, and suckered into,
that which was exposed and vulnerable. A strange, loose

energy connected with their lostness and then – *clunk* – the powerful magnet locked tight.

The live music had been good that evening. Several musicians with their fiddles, flutes and mandolins had gathered. They sang songs of full moons, bygone heroes and lost love.

An assortment of occupied chairs and tatty benches were arrayed across the oak-plank floor. As last orders were called, most of the revellers disappeared into the cold night air. Several lingered behind, as if caught up in some unspoken anticipation.

It was then, that *it* had happened.

Like lemmings being led over the edge of a cliff, they followed as Melantha beckoned them into the adjoining room. Tobacco-stained walls released a stale, earthy fragrance into a wooden cavern of snugs. Dimly lit, it possessed a dark interior. The covert atmosphere enhanced the love of secrecy and all things hidden.

Having locked the front door and shut down the main pub, Melantha appeared in the doorway. She exuded an aberrant, hypnotic beauty. All eyes were upon her as she skilfully led those gathered into a long night of occult practice.

Until 3 am they drank deeply of the cabalistic, then, dragging their bodies like ruined monasteries, they returned to their earthly homes filled to the brim with darkness.

Alice had been a willing participant, and waking the following day, instinctively knew that the heaviness she felt within was not *just* the symptoms of a hangover.

Something fundamental had changed inside her.

Somehow a door had opened in her soul.

An invisible entity had been allowed to take root, burying itself in the essence of her being. During the coming months, she became increasingly aware of its presence invading her personality, intellect and will.

Rapidly, depression set in.

She was often assailed with an overwhelming sense of unease. Destructive imaginings would wash over her like a churning sea. They would start as inklings, whispers, suggestions that would grow into cruel urges towards self-annihilation.

Once bright, her countenance was often cheerless and gloomy. Anti-depressants only masked the underlying bleakness. Heightened feelings of desolation and fretfulness never left her and she became aware of a *guide* – an attendant force flowing through her, influencing her actions with its ever-present genius.

Although very wary of Melantha, Alice became increasingly obsessed with her. Fuelled by a cocktail of fear and fascination, she was drawn to her, and a powerful, unseen manacle enforced the attachment.

There were alarming stories circulating the village – mishaps, accidents and strange happenings. All of these had beset the other eleven attendees of that fateful night in the Three Castles. Something profoundly disturbing was going on.

Attracted to her mastery of the dark arts, Alice sought the counsel of Melantha, looking to her as an expert in all things spiritual. This came at a price, raising more questions than answers. Confusion set in, as perplexing conundrums were presented as enlightenment. Astrological enigmas were demonstrated and practised, introducing uncanny experiences into ordinary life.

The domination and control exerted by her tutor was subtle. Alice soon emulated the woman in ways of dress, eating habits and lifestyle. She made frequent visits to the apartment under the old pub's thatch. There, sipping potent wine, Alice would listen to tales of festivals, sacred narratives and all things paranormal. On one such occasion, the subject of the ancient estate of Beulah was raised. Alice had been intrigued by Melantha's account of how she had broken into the house with Ethan Jacobs, the handsome heir to a brewery fortune and owner of several licensed premises: desiring to shield them from prying eyes, Ethan had driven Melantha in his open top sports car for miles along the winding estate road. Reasoning it to be unoccupied, they had found themselves circling the large stately home. Although rumoured to be abandoned, Beulah exhibited a certain magnificence that demanded investigation. Spurred on by legends of vintage wines worth many thousands of pounds, Ethan's desire to explore was further aroused by the hope of a chance find from deep down in the cellars.

They tumbled out of the car, laughing in a carefree manner. Melantha draped her arm across his shoulder, and they playfully staggered towards the imposing steps.

Ethan had long banished his conscience from interfering with the immense pleasure he received from his casual, occasional 'business' trips to the Three Castles.

Melantha conveniently lived by herself, and knowing full well their relationship was illicit, he only ever stayed at the apartment when he could go undercover in the dead of night. Ethan was married to a lovely woman with whom he had two young children. His pretty wife, Adele, doted on him. With her sweet-nature, warm heart, and petite elfin looks, she was a beautiful treasure waiting to be discovered. His fiercely independent and self-reliant temperament curbed any expression of tender sensitivity. Many a lonely night, she cried herself to sleep, desperate to connect with him emotionally. Denying access to those who truly loved him, he sustained his need for worth by drawing on the admiration of those with whom he had shallow dealings. He surrounded himself with people who looked up to his status and position, feeding off their attraction to his perceived power and influence. To them, he appeared highly successful and charismatic. His wife witnessed another side: a man driven by an earnest desire for achievement and distinction. Always striving, his need to impress others was the forceful, underlying motivation in all he did.

At home, when he let down his defences, the thin veneer of niceness dissipated easily under pressure. Beneath his manly bravado and heavy drinking, Adele recognised his glaring insecurity and lack of peace. The son of an authoritarian, distant father, he had grown up closed and distrustful. His longing for praise and approval made him effortless prey to feminine seduction.

The outer packaging of his handsome features concealed a broken man. With such storms raging beneath his calm

11

exterior, it was almost inevitable that he would seek respite in the arms of a woman who had few emotional demands. Melantha's coldness suited him.

It had been two years since they had first encountered one another.

Arriving at lunchtime on a warm day in spring, he had strolled into the pub dressed in an oyster linen suit.

Instantly standing out from the casually attired locals, his striking good looks had prompted a stirring in Melantha. The meeting had long been arranged to discuss her tenancy and the ongoing running of the establishment.

Signalling to a young bartender to cover her responsibilities, she stepped out from behind the heavy oak counter and directed Ethan towards a door marked 'private'.

A quaint wooden staircase led to her living quarters. Although well aware of the layout, *nothing* could have prepared him for the sight that met his eyes on reaching the small landing.

The whole upstairs had been painted in dramatic dark colours with shades of purple and berry-reds. The main lounge was dominated by a black accent wall, on which hung an ornate, medieval mirror. Either side were two wrought iron candle sconces. Damson velvet curtains, edged with black lace, pooled onto the dark wooden floor, giving a luxurious feel. A scattering of old-styled traditional furniture and curiosities added to the whimsical look. The smell of joss sticks hung in the air.

"Every woman's desire is to live in the house of her dreams, Ethan," she mused. At first he was taken aback with her boldness, immediately sensing her saucy over-familiarity with him. After all, he was her boss and this was *his* property. He remained silent as he absorbed his surroundings. It certainly had an elegant, romantic ambience but the black stencilling gave it all an edgy feel. Ignoring his discomfort, she led him along the passage. One room had been turned into an open wardrobe. Like a mini boutique, clothes hung on shop-style rails. A hat stand displayed a vast collection of necklaces, beads and scarves. A huge variety of shoes stood neatly aligned.

Knowing what he was thinking, she gibed, "I don't have too many shoes, Ethan. I just have too many places to go in *different* shoes. A woman has to be equipped." Picking up a pair of very high, slim-heeled, black sandals, she stroked them affectionately. "Flip-flops for the sand between my toes, wellies for muddy festivals, wedges for shopping, and *these*, Ethan, *these* are for playing footsie under candle-lit tables." She passed him a little wink and continued down the hall.

He swallowed hard as she brought him into a small bedroom.

It had been converted into a cramped office. A cut glass vase of dried red roses centred the mahogany desk. Gaudy plum walls were smothered with images of her, some taken alongside the *Fairy Fay* band members. Uninhibited and non-traditional, they obviously indulged in life's excesses.

As he stared at the photographs, an appealing sense of something unrestrained swept into his mind. Suggestions of freedom confronted the routines that enslaved him, stirring his dissatisfaction with all that had become mundane and predictable.

Scrutinising a pile of documents, his trained eye didn't take long to ascertain that things were being kept in good order. Melantha presented him with meticulous accounts and her knowledge of the business immediately filled him with confidence.

When she left the room to fetch him some refreshments, he felt safe to study the photos of her more closely.

The epitome of hippy chic, she certainly had the look of a leggy model.

There was one image that particularly drew his attention. Framed by a psychedelic background, she stood decked out in a floaty belted dress. The way it was hitched on one side added softness to her skinny jeans and cowboy boots. Her face, beautiful in features, was surrounded by long, straight hennaed hair. A blunt fringe reached down to the very edge of her smoky, sullen eyes.

Disturbed by the sound of her footsteps, he glanced down at the paperwork.

"It's all looking good," he affirmed, "I won't need to stay long."

He pushed back his chair and turned towards her.

Leaning against the desk, Melantha bit into a firm cherry, staring deeply into his eyes. As she discarded the stone, she offered him the bowl of fruit.

"There's an aura around you, Ethan. Have you ever had your fortune read?"

He ended up staying much longer than he'd planned. He even cancelled his next appointment. Within hours he had become putty in her hands. Another soul hooked into her cunning schemes.

Chapter Three

BREAKING INTO BEULAH

MELANTHA'S BLOCK HEELED boots crunched into the weedy gravel as they approached Beulah's grand frontage.

Two marble statues of lions, standing on all fours, were stationed either side of the steps. They would have made an imposing statement had one of them not lost its head. Lying in the pebbles, alongside a concrete plinth, was evidence of the decapitation. Expertly chiselled, the strong noble face, with its distinctive mane, was turned upwards.

As Ethan stood staring down at its handsome contours, something tugged deeply within him.

He felt sorry for the beast.

This symbol of dominion and stateliness had forfeited its dignity. No longer could it stand tall, hold its head high, and courageously guard the home.

Ethan's phone rang. Glancing down, he saw Adele's name appear on the screen.

Gesturing to Melantha by placing a finger over his lips, he took the call.

Drumming up a bright enthusiastic tone, he greeted his wife warmly.

"Oh, hi love, how you doing…? Yes, the meetings are going fine thanks. I've had three so far, only two to go and I'll be home for the weekend."

He hesitated. Adele spoke for a long time.

Melantha threw him agitated glances, signalling with her hands for him to hurry up.

Wheedling his way out of the conversation, he ended the call.

"Oh, don't worry, hun, it'll all be fine. Catch you soon. Love you. I can't wait to see you. Get a babysitter and I'll take you out on Saturday night."

He pressed extra hard on the 'end call' button.

"One of the kids is ill," he murmured.

Threatened by whatever he couldn't fix, he hated anything to do with family sickness. It didn't fit into his neat, controlled world. Instead of being able to give support and empathy, he just felt anger and frustration.

Melantha rolled her eyes. She really wasn't interested in his problems and she certainly couldn't deal with him getting all mopey. She ran her manicured fingernails through the back of his thick, dark hair, smoothing the nape of his neck with her palm.

Normally he liked it but today he felt uneasy.

Lingering by the headless statue, she brushed her left hand across the broken plane of the marble.

An arrogant disdain surged inside of her – silly, stupid Ethan, didn't he realise how weak he was? His authority was so easily usurped. A little flattery, a few choice words, a tiny hint of seduction and she had managed to steer him away from all the riches he didn't know he had. A boss in the boardroom maybe, but he wasn't able to govern his own soul.

Absorbing the enormity of the house, they gazed up at its four storeys. Established on an ancient foundation, it had been added to over the centuries, each different era contributing a unique quality and form.

Although evoking thoughts of a castle, its gracious style suggested that it had not been designed for defence. The mellow brick exterior was topped with an ornate marble balustrade. An assemblage of columns, turreted towers and chimneys crowned the roof. They appeared to mirror the skyline of a resplendent city. At the very centre was a large, domed belfry with an oculus window.

Having once dated an architect, Melantha was well informed about the obscure meanings behind certain structures. "The eye of god is on us," she mocked disparagingly. "He's watching our every move. He knows you're cheating on your wife, Eth!"

Ethan didn't need some cheap reference to a bit of architecture to make him feel any more uncomfortable.

Looking bemused, he frowned at her. "Then we'd better get out of view," he retorted, still troubled by the phone call.

Wandering around the perimeter of the great mansion, they contemplated ways to enter. Ethan had thought it would have been easy, but on close inspection, all the entrances looked strong and sound.

The window panes were intact.

Nothing, apart from the lion, was in the state of disrepair that he'd been led to believe. It bothered him that perhaps the property might well be inhabited after all.

Weary from so much trudging about, Melantha leant up against some railings.

She sneered at his failed mission. The inflection in her voice was scathing. "I'm not going to trail endlessly after you, Ethan. So much for your great expedition! Instead of being exciting, the day's turned out to be as dull as dishwater."

Rummaging in her velvet shoulder bag, she drew out a silver cigarette case. The scorpion emblem on the front of it attracted Ethan's attention.

His eyes widened as he teased her, "Ugly box for an ugly habit, babe."

Glowering defiantly, she shrugged her shoulders and puffed smoke in his direction.

Evening was beginning to draw in. Glancing down at his watch, he nuzzled up to her.

"We could head back to your place soon," he whispered, brushing her neck with his mouth.

She cast her lipstick-stained stub to the ground and reciprocated his advances.

As they frolicked around, her cigarette case fell loose from the top of her bag and tumbled down a stone stairwell. Ethan went to retrieve it.

On bending down, he noticed that a small sash window beneath him didn't have its catch lock fastened. Calling for Melantha to join him, he pressed hard against the wooden frame. Once he'd gained leverage, the lower section of the window slowly separated and slid up.

Head first, Ethan clambered through the gap. Turning to assist her, he received the full pelt of her bag as she swung it through the opening. It whacked him squarely in the face. Slightly dazed, he aided her clumsy entrance.

He dared a joke about her weight. Her eyes raged with scorn as she dusted herself down and rearranged her clothes.

Ethan cautiously took in their surroundings. His heart pounded, knowing they were unwelcome. Having landed in a large, empty room, he stepped tentatively through a bare doorframe. Melantha brashly followed, striding heavily across the exposed floorboards. She loved the illegality of it all.

With only one direction in which to turn, they proceeded along a narrow corridor. A timber staircase descended towards the basement.

Ethan grinned, convinced the legendary cellars of Beulah were almost within his reach.

As they hastened down the winding stairs they came to a beautiful arched doorway on which hung a heavy oak door. Fastened either side, a fine pair of Gothic, torch-shaped lanterns accentuated the entrance. Melantha instinctively tugged at them to see how securely they were fixed to the wall.

Ethan observed the metalware on the door. An ornate brass faceplate was decorated with minute bunches of grapes. It surrounded a heavy matching door knob. His firm grasp caused it to slowly give way.

Using the torch from his phone, he pressed forward and found himself on a small landing, looking down into a great circular room. An exploratory flick of a switch yielded a soft golden glow, further rousing his fear of inhabitants. This place certainly displayed signs of maintenance and care.

The light revealed a carved sandstone basement, steeped in an atmosphere of power and mystery. A rib-vaulted ceiling arched over the space – its grandeur the evidence of a skilled master mason.

Ethan sensed something sacred about the place. Melantha also picked up on the special ambience. She lit another cigarette in an attempt to befoul it.

Engineered beyond the reach of sunlight, the tawny cave opened up before them. A cool distinct chill in the air helped to drive them forward. The gentle hues from the honeyed stone provided the only warmth.

Recognising the perfect conditions for wine storage, Ethan keenly eyed the rock face for nooks and crevices. The sight of four limestone pillars abruptly delayed his search. Set within the perfect frame stood a stunning, wooden table.

Melantha started to shake. "Oh Ethan, I'm really freezing. Can I borrow your jacket?"

She sounded like a petulant child.

As he relinquished the garment, she pulled it on and strolled around the beautiful piece of furniture.

She counted seating for twelve.

The cedar table top was inlaid with a long central panel, formed out of polished stones. Each individual jewel was set in metal.

Using Ethan's jacket cuff, Melantha gently dusted the surface and a dozen beautiful shades began to emerge – pale grey-pink, orange, sapphire, red, lavender, violet, gold, and five varying shades of green.

Turning from the find, Ethan gasped with delight at discovering row upon row of old wooden racks. Every slot contained a bottle of wine. There were no gaps. He lifted one up. The immense thrill of coming across such treasure was heightened as he observed the handsome crest of the House of Beulah. He ran his finger across the classic, refined label. Heraldic, it displayed a crowned shield with an embossed winged lion in prominent upright stance.

Melantha placed her hand upon one of the heavy wooden chairs. As she attempted to drag it out, an overwhelming sense of nausea welled up within the pit of her stomach. A crazed fiery look appeared in her eyes and she lunged back, feeling a violent urge to vomit. Staring down at the floor she noticed a dark, blackish stain beneath the seat. Feeling a berserk compulsion to search, as if hunting for something, she hauled out each of the other eleven chairs. A similar stain lay beneath all but one.

As she crouched down, she slowly drew her finger around the outline of a discoloured patch. She didn't dare touch it.

"I *hate* this place, Ethan, we must leave now," she muttered.

Accustomed to her bizarre behaviour, yet still surprised and annoyed, he complied with her demand. She was always cranky, but her bad temper was prone to very sudden flare-ups.

He could only ever handle her in small, infrequent doses. Not wanting to leave the house, he attempted to exit via a different route than the old arched door.

He walked forward, carrying one of the bottles of vintage red wine. A pool of natural light came from a rounded stairway. Its historic artistry fascinated him. "I reckon this could be the belfry. Let's try it out anyway and see where it goes."

Chapter Four

REBELLION

MELANTHA BARGED ANGRILY in front, leading the ascent up the cramped stone steps. Eventually, calming a little, she revived as an influx of fresh air streamed down the main shaft. In spite of the vast stair count, she pressed on.

Mid-way up, a small wooden door led out of the tower. Ethan paused, desiring to investigate what lay beyond it. Melantha overruled him. Driven on by a frantic compulsion, she demanded that he follow her to the top.

Upon reaching the upper platform, they found themselves in a heptagonal turret, with seven open, stone windows.

Melantha slowly paced around them, her eyes fixed upon what was hanging beneath the domed oculus window. For there, attached to a wooden yoke hung a great cast metal bell.

She breathed in deeply and passionately proclaimed the inscription around its girth, *"Rebellis Maleficentia Magus."* As the utterance flowed from her lips, Ethan felt an unearthly chill pass throughout his body.

Disturbed by the impending sense of what she was about to do, he growled at her, "Don't you dare attempt to ring it!"

She silently stared back at him, a callous smirk spreading across her lips. Her defiant black eyes pierced into him. From a deep, dark place within her, an answer formed, inaudible to anyone but Melantha: "Oh, but I have already rung it, Ethan. I ring this bell every day of my life. I thrive on its reverberation. My very life force marches to its sound!"

With that she sank into a sombre trance.

Ethan reeled under the atmosphere of evil that emanated from her. He sat on the top step with his head in his hands.

In an ethereal vision, Melantha heard the bell peal out a thunderous summons. Symbolic of arrogant rebellion, its cry caused a mobilisation of unhallowed demonic forces. Appearing swiftly as great clouds of gross darkness, their heaviness spoke of an inevitable deluge of hostility upon mankind.

Connecting with the lack of peace within the hearts of men, the mutinous clamour baptised multitudes of people with viciousness. Their minds were filled with all manner of iniquity.

The earth was violently jolted with an almighty quake. It shook off every drop of bloodshed that had soaked into the ground since the very first murder.

Each succession of conflict throughout the ages crashed forwards in a turbulent sea of warmongering. Melantha saw herself standing on a high cliff looking down upon a beach of scorched, blackened sand. An enormous tsunami of death and destruction rushed towards her.

This monstrous wave carried with it the full force of every sorrow, affliction and catastrophe known to the human race. A mighty wind drove it on, fuelled by the love of money, pride, fear, hatred, jealousy and wickedness.

Energised by tiny childish squabbles, whispered playground taunts, screaming household conflicts, drunken street brawls, torturous drug cartel punishments and ravaging genocides, it gathered momentum.

Wreaking havoc, it left in its path grief, vexation, anxiety and mourning.

Melantha drank it in, arms outstretched to the sky, invoking its strength into the essence of her. She was at one with the spirit of the bell. Having wilfully surrendered her whole being to its authority, she manifested its character of unrestrained evil.

"Rebellion is as witchcraft!" she cried, awakening from the stupor.

Ethan groaned. He had been held in an abhorrent daze. Images of his family being dragged into the vortex of a heinous tornado left him severely alarmed.

As Melantha walked towards him in all her lustful attractiveness, he began to discern her with different eyes.

Outwardly she was stunning, but the woman embodied an immense ugliness.

In silence they departed. Mid-way down the stairwell, Ethan tried the handle of the little arched door. To his great satisfaction, it yielded.

Slowly creaking open, it led into a well proportioned circular chamber.

There was nothing on show apart from a four-poster bed. Displaying notable craftsmanship, it stood in the centre of the room. Hand carved in walnut, it exuded regal warmth and a musky, sweet fragrance. Within the frame lay a thick feathered mattress. Once covered with pure white linen, several unsightly stains now blemished its beauty.

Chapter Five

THE UGLY TRAVESTY

O N DISCOVERING ANOTHER staircase spiralling
down beyond the bedroom, they passed through into
a long corridor. Ahead of them were two ancient doors that
led into a grand hall. Ethan edged his way in, wary and
nervous. He eyed the room carefully, taking in its vastness
and splendour. Melantha casually plonked herself down on
the floor amidst a large pile of old paint cans. Picking one
up, she marvelled at its soldered lid and label. She could
just make out the date – 1859. A rusty can opener lay beside
a bucket. Holding up an antique paint card, she called out
to Ethan, "Look at the dull colours they had back then."
Laughing she read out some of the shades, "Ugh, they used

olive, hazel, oxide red, and fawn."

Ethan, not a bit interested in her find, was impressed with the museum style gallery. Bathed in fading evening light, it was washed with an ecclesiastical air. The softly highlighted walls displayed six large decorative frescos. On close inspection, he detected a sophisticated ploy to deface all of the underlying images.

Modern amoebic shapes had been deliberately smothered over the originals in an attempt to obliterate their genuine beauty and authenticity. Priceless pieces had been distorted and ruined with thick encrusted paint.

The Greek mythological sea-god, Proteus, was emerging from single cellular forms. His versatile, mutable shape assumed many guises as it advanced across the six pictures. Ethan knew the fable of this elusive god, answerable only to the one that could capture him – he changed his anatomy from one creature to the next. This old man of the sea adapted himself by becoming different animals. The ugly travesty evolved across the wall, culminating in a mass of hideous ape-like faces almost resembling human flesh.

"I would love to know what was underneath this trashy graffiti," Ethan sighed. "Someone has gone to great lengths to keep secret what exists below."

Melantha looked up. Instantly assuming the role of an art critic, she considered the mural. "I like it as it is, Ethan. It gives off an arrogant, presumptuous vibe. It's confused and has a deliciously frustrating feel to it. The artist displays an independent strength that is very appealing and headstrong."

While she rambled on with her observations, Ethan discovered a beautiful chaise-longue. Set just beyond the sixth painting, it was upholstered in duck-egg blue, sumptuous velvet. It would have epitomised relaxation and rest, had it not been strewn with an array of odd items. A hefty can of weed killer moulded into the main pillow. Occupying the position where man should lay his weary head, it looked cumbersome and out of place. Other items scattered across the couch included dirty garden tools, a pile of sharp brambles and thistles, a bag of old coins, a cookery magazine on bread making, several books on horticulture, and a worn copy of Darwin's 'Origin of Species'.

Still clutching his bottle of wine, Ethan glanced out at the pink sunset. He'd got what he'd come for.

"Come on, Mel, let's head back to the car soon, we could just look in a couple more rooms."

He reached down for her hand and pulled her up. He knew she was no good for him but the sense of danger he encountered from being around her overruled his gut instinct. The adrenalin rush had become an addiction.

From the far end of the hall, a dim corridor led out into the west wing. The mystery of what might be found behind each door proved irresistible.

Most rooms were empty, yielding nothing more than vacant spaces and blank walls.

Growing bored, Melantha carelessly wrapped her fingers around a chunky brass handle. In doing so, one of her magenta nail extensions bent back on itself. She let out a yelp and angrily kicked at the door. Swinging wide before them, it revealed the sculptured marble fixtures of a white bathroom. In the middle stood a Victorian, double-ended, roll-top bath. Made from volcanic limestone, it gleamed in the setting sunlight; its silver ball and claw feet rested elegantly on the tiled floor.

Presenting itself as a strange aberration, a child's Noah's ark floated on top of the bath. Glimmers of light accentuated its form as the beautifully carved boat rested on the brim.

Ethan observed it from a distance, enjoying nostalgic memories of one of the first toys he had ever played with. Many happy hours had been spent marching his animals, two by two, up a wooden ramp.

Slowly approaching it, he flinched.

A dense soft-pink shape filled the bath water.

His deepest fear was thankfully alleviated upon realising that, crammed into the large space beneath the ark, was a mass of miniature, flesh-coloured, plastic dolls. They were so solidly packed in, that very little water was needed to keep the boat on the surface.

He stared at the scene long and hard.

Running his hand through the condensed sea of tiny moulded bodies, he discovered rubber creatures of every kind – dinosaurs, birds and mammals. The models represented every form of life. Swirling and lifting them through his fingers, he scooped up elephants, monkeys, lions and wolves. The little animals resembled a thick soup.

"Wow, that's weird," Melantha mumbled under her breath.

"Not really," Ethan deliberated. "We always think of Noah's ark as a cute little story for kids about rescued animals and rainbows but no one ever talks about the fact that every living creature on earth was obliterated."

"It's a stupid, kids' fable, Ethan," she retorted. "If it had really happened you'd expect to find masses of petrified dead things buried in seams of rock."

She marched off into an adjacent room, leaving him deep in thought.

A shrill cry jolted him from his reflections and caused him to rush after her. He discovered her sitting on the floor of a grotesque nursery. Her howl had been one of peculiar delight.

"I *love* this room," she kept repeating, strangely energised by its morbidity.

Knowing her, he could understand why. Its decorative style was very much home from home.

The soft furnishings of the nursery were dominated with the presence of black lace. It was draped in ornate swags over the window and hung as a hooded veil over an old-fashioned bassinet. The baby's cradle would have exuded romantic charm had it not been for this miserable fabric.

Ragged in pale grey, the walls displayed a painted border of wild plants. Hellebore, silphium, rue and pennyroyal had been skilfully applied as a repeated pattern that spanned the room.

Dark roses rested on a mahogany tall-boy surrounded by several tea-light holders. Old purple wax pooled in the bottom of them, dusty and grimy.

A porcelain model of a birthday cake lay on the floor, its single candle snapped in two.

Discarded in a waste bin, a teddy bear's furry legs dangled over the edge.

Ethan was repulsed by what he observed. Surely a room of this nature should be lavished with a welcoming, tender, respect for innocence. This special space would give a child their first impression of the world.

The only soft colour came from a delicate fleecy pillow within the cradle. As Melantha pulled it out from beneath a black sheet, she unearthed a flawless embroidered image of a tiny pre-born baby. Turning it over so Ethan couldn't see it she stuffed it back under the cover. Gently rocking the cradle from side to side she sang to herself in a low mutter, words that he could not distinguish,

"Dark, dark is the night and you cannot come through.

Your form will never reach fruition; your dreams will not come true.

For you the gateway has been barred, it shall not be undone.

The light of day you shall not see, your song will not be sung.

Moloch – he will cut you down before you grow too high.

Tiny gift of beauty, you must die."

The impending night sky eventually drew them out of the house. Going back the way they had come in, they stepped down into the basement cavern.

Melantha sped past the table and twelve chairs. Almost running up the staircase to the landing, she hovered nervously, agitated by Ethan's sauntering. He strolled casually through the cellar, eyeing the wine racks for another bottle.

Something stopped him dead in his tracks. As if frozen to the spot, he stared down at the gap from which he had stolen the first bottle. It had been replaced!

He span round viewing every facet of the circular chamber. Adrenalin pumping, he raced towards Melantha. Hitting the switch they rushed out, leaping up the staircase, through the corridor and into the first room where they had entered. Scrambling through the window with pounding hearts, they left the building and ran for the car.

They drove swiftly out of the grounds. The avenue wound its way past untidy formal gardens, wooded parks, hills and streams. Eventually exiting Beulah's ancient gateway, they sped off towards the village.

Ethan's phone rang. Melantha picked it up and raised her eyes to heaven – Adele!

He took the call.

After a worried exchange of words he tossed the phone down.

"I've got to get home right away," he said anxiously. "Imogene has been admitted to hospital with suspected meningitis."

Melantha said nothing.

Full of concern over his little girl's wellbeing, he pulled into a lay-by near the village.

Melantha slowly removed herself from the vehicle. She stood on the pavement in the twilight, nonchalantly unbuttoning his jacket. Flinging the borrowed garment onto the back seat, she pressed herself towards him. Loving the power she held over him, she mused, "Better check it for long auburn hair, Ethan. Oh... and you're going to have to figure out an explanation for the perfume. It's smothered in jasmine, rose and patchouli!"

Spinning the car into a fast u-turn, he tore off. Her heady scent would be difficult to mask. Raging at her hard indifference, he vowed he would never make personal contact with her again. Out of a recess in his mind, his mother's voice came, bringing instructions from when he was a teenager, "A beautiful woman who lacks discretion is like a gold ring in a pig's snout."

Chapter Six

WISDOM AND WINE

DENSE, HEAVY RAIN clouds started to build up as Ethan drove home. So did the tears in the back of his eyes. The seriousness of the situation and the time spent alone, gave him the space to contemplate what really mattered to him. His philandering with loose women was beginning to feel shallow and meaningless.

A growing conviction led to a heartfelt prayer,

"God, please save my little girl. I don't deserve your help and I've been really stupid but please don't let her die." He glanced down at the clock. It was 11:36pm.

As a sharp chill bit into his body, he activated the roof of the sports car to close. Pulling into the hospital grounds an hour later, he ran through the pelting rain into the reception area.

Having purposely left his jacket behind, his shirt stuck to his flesh.

A tired looking orderly advised him which way to go and he hastily walked up the polished corridor to the lift.

A pleasant nurse welcomed him onto the softly lit children's ward. She led him to a quiet side room where little Imogene lay sleeping.

Adele was slumped on a chair with her head resting on the bed. Semi-conscious, she stirred as Ethan entered the room and visibly relaxed as he placed his firm hand on her shoulder. She smiled up at him and spoke in an excited whisper.

"She's alright, Ethan! She's fine now. The fever suddenly left her. They're just going to keep her in overnight for observations. I was frantic earlier. Thanks for getting to us so quickly, I hope it didn't mess things up for you too much!"

He kissed the top of her head, immediately roused by its sweet fragrance. He didn't deserve this woman. Looking down at her, he marvelled at her trusting, kind nature.

Despising his divided heart, he vowed to change. It might be nigh on impossible but he would attempt to discipline his soul with the same vigour that he used on his body each day at the gym.

The following evening disturbed Adele. Everything she had ever longed for began to take effect before her very eyes. Although it was unheard of for Ethan to get involved with settling his children at bedtime, tonight he insisted upon it.

Grappling with a sense of redundancy, Adele was slightly affronted that the children didn't protest. Instead, they easily complied with their father's instructions and seemed to delight in his attention.

When all was quiet and settled, she wandered upstairs and peeped in on them.

Blissfully content, Daniel lay snuggled into a pile of brightly coloured cushions under his cabin bed. Having played an exciting game with his dad, he had completely crashed out. On crossing the hall, she found Imogene tucked up in her duvet, fast asleep beside her favourite cuddly rabbit.

After showering in their en suite, Ethan towelled himself down and started to get dressed. Adele glanced into the bedroom to find him standing at the towering French windows as if mesmerised by something. Wearing a pair of cream chinos, his upper body was bare. The uprightness of his strong muscular form reflected his resolute mind. He stared into the distance, pensively, caught up in some deep thought process. Within his heart he heard the call of wisdom.

The beautiful sunlit evening served to fortify the urgency.

He must break through all that was false and compromising.

Feeling a yearning to wash off his guilt, he viewed the green fields rolling out ahead of him. Maybe it *was* possible to find freedom? How great would it be to receive an unblemished start?

Coming up behind him, Adele slipped her arms around his waist. She pressed her head onto his shoulder and kissed the hollow of his back. A pleasant heat swept across his body but he stood motionless. The conflict within him was almost unbearable.

"I'll go and fix supper," she whispered, aware that he needed to be alone for a moment.

The thought of dinner reminded him of the rare acquisition lying on the back seat of his car. Pulling on a loose shirt and a pair of casual shoes, he went down to the garage.

Upon discovering the wine shrouded in the folds of his jacket, Melantha's bitter words drained his cheer. He stuffed the garment into a plastic bag and flung it into the bin. His wardrobe was extensive. Adele probably wouldn't notice it was missing. Even if she did, he could say he'd left it somewhere in the haste of getting to the hospital.

As he placed the prized bottle on the table, he noticed Adele had already uncorked some Chablis to go with the braised chicken.

"We'll drink this little beauty after dinner," he said, showing her its handsome label.

Their meal was consumed in quiet reflection. Normally she would ask him questions about his trip but she felt constrained not to pry. There was something sincere and earnest in his stance that she wanted to respect.

Later, as he led her to the sofa, it wasn't just the cosiness of their living room that made it inviting. It was something in his demeanour. Holding her gently in his strong arms, he twisted a strand of her hair through his fingers. As it curled around his wedding ring, he pulled her close.

A large, gel fire-bowl cast its golden glow, as soft music quietened their stressed minds. Pouring his vintage find, he passed her a tall-stemmed glass. Soon, they both tasted a richness of earth and place that spoke of ancient origins. Deep old world elegance, mingled with new world spice. A fine aroma filled the air, as hope permeated their hearts. Adele looked up at him with moist eyes. She had never felt secure in their marriage, until now.

Chapter Seven

A HOSTILE INTRUSION

A LICE JIGGLED HER pendant nervously, rolling the amethyst flower between her fingers. This gift from Melantha for her eighteenth birthday had not left her neck since it had been ceremoniously placed there.

"It will bring you good luck," Melantha had pronounced as she fastened the clasp.

From that day, Alice had felt a tight knotted sensation in her throat. Too fearful to remove the charm, she wore it religiously – the pretty floral emblem an object of bondage.

As she descended through a lightly wooded area, Beulah, in all its sunlit glory, beckoned her. Although she had a sense of foreboding, Alice felt compelled to follow in Melantha's footsteps, as if on a pilgrimage.

Drawing close to the great house, beads of perspiration formed on her face and neck. Although easily dismissible as an effect from the warmth of the day, Alice's racing heart knew better.

With trembling hands she lifted the small window. It was exactly as Melantha and Ethan had left it, slightly ajar.

As if opening a gateway to another domain, the deed of clambering into Beulah activated a mystical portal inside of her.

The physical reality of the brick and mortar surroundings posed little threat. Far more oppressive than the fear of what the house might contain was the invasive materialisation of something that had been locked up within her.

A hostile intrusion gate-crashed her mind as she edged her way along the corridor and down the rickety stairs. Murky corners of her imagination began to be unleashed.

Her trespassing was rousing inner squatters.

By the time she reached the cellar doors, a hauntingly seductive song was playing in her head. It made her feel suicidal; worse, it suggested it was an attractive option.

The soft, dark lullaby conjured up images of an escorted journey to oblivion. Thirteen hooded figures lined the path. Each held a long, fire-tipped torch that broke up the black sky. A powerful, destructive force drowned out sense and reason. Annihilation presented itself as a desirable end.

One figure stepped forward whispering intimate arcane words.

Alice instantly recognised him as her spirit guide, Darcus.

Ever-present, since that dreaded night in the Three Castles, a voice in her head whispered that if she leapt from the landing he would sweep her up in his arms. The thoughts would have overpowered her, had it not been for a strange intervention.

As she stared down into the golden cavern below, a glistening light illuminated the twelve coloured stones built into the table. Glowing and sparkling, the strength of their presence weakened the control of the ghoulish figures. As the light brightened, the fiends started to fade away, their form turning transparent and vaporous.

Enjoying temporary relief from Darcus' familiar tongue, Alice moved swiftly past the ancient furniture and mounted the bell tower staircase. Mid-way up, she remembered Melantha's instructions about how to gain access to the grand hall. With great anticipation she turned the handle of the small arched door.

It was locked.

Bitterly disappointed, she sat down on the stone stairs. The frustration of the closed door gave vent to a whole host of grievances. There had been so many setbacks and obstructions in her life. Resentment had grown within her heart like a gnarled thorn bush.

Sitting there, alone and cold, reminded her of a night fourteen years ago.

Woken by the sound of her parents arguing, she had slipped out of bed and moved silently to the staircase. There, picking at the dirty carpet, she nervously listened to the screaming and swearing that had become commonplace.

It was worse that night.

Her mum and dad had burst from the living room into the hallway yelling and shouting. Alice's little hands were too tiny to fully cover her ears. The sight of these people that she loved grappling with each other terrified her. In rage, Dad opened the front door and staggered out, cursing. Mum slammed it shut and Alice never saw him again.

Being offered no explanation, nor hope of reconciliation, Alice just had to accept his absence and absorb her mother's unhappiness and pain. As the months and years passed, rumours abounded that he lived in the neighbouring village and had another family. This only added to Alice's torment and deep feelings of rejection. The appearing of strange men in her home drove her into isolation. Her mother, blind to Alice's inmost needs, provided a roof over her head, clothes and food, but abandoned her emotionally. Although there was the outer appearance of a relationship, it was very superficial. Neither one of them ever showed each other what was going on beneath the surface.

As she sat there in the bell tower, she undid a piece of jewellery attached to her top. Lacerating her skin with the sharp pin from the brooch, she cut into her flesh and appeased the numbness she felt inside.

The self-hatred had grown with the rejection.

By punishing herself, she could at least make sense of the disregard people had for her. No one ever wanted to know her true feelings.

Eventually refastening the bloodied pin, she returned to the basement. Lifting a bottle of wine from the racks, she hastened back through the house to the small window and scrambled out.

Greeted by a sundrenched afternoon, she made her way around to the front of the property and headed off to her caravan.

All the time, someone had been watching her.

After a long trail back, the sight of Vanda in the meadow lifted Alice's mood. The horse's relaxed temperament made her a trusted companion. Patting Vanda's strong neck and shoulders, Alice eyed her compact frame and short, robust legs. Fetching an apple, hoof pick and stiff brush, she set about grooming her. This strong and capable cob was easy to care for. Alice brushed her coat with vigour until it shone and picked out her hooves to remove the packed-in dirt. Getting a bowl of warm water, she gently rinsed Vanda's legs.

As early evening fell, she mixed together a three bean salad and made a stack of warm chapattis. The House of Beulah wine took time and strength to open, but it was worth labouring over. It was so rich, she only had one glass. Its mellow flavour accompanied the sight of the sunset perfectly.

She rested on the caravan step, daring to absorb this moment of peace.

As her eyes grew heavy, she reached to twiddle with her necklace.

It wasn't there.

Somewhere on her travels it had worked loose. Feeling flustered, yet determined to at least attempt to find it, she planned to return to Beulah the following day.

Chapter Eight

THE UNUSUAL FIND

EMERGING FROM THE caravan at first light, Alice almost slipped on a puddle of dew that had formed on the wooden steps. The chill in the air sent her back inside for her shawl. Pulling the black crocheted poncho over her head, she set off through the soggy meadow and picked up the main trail to the house.

With soaking sandals and wet feet she ambled along the drive. The country walk offered many visual delights – banks of flowers, butterflies, toadstools and darting birds.

Gradually, the growing warmth of the sun dried her off.

She left the road and strolled around to the wooded area that led down to Beulah. If her necklace had fallen there, the dense grassy slopes would have easily swallowed it up. Her only hope of finding it would be if it had unfastened indoors.

Approaching the front of the house, she made her way through a maze of tangled bushes and overgrown shrubs. She was just about to step out onto the gravel when something arrested her. A sudden movement up ahead stopped her in her tracks. Startled, she quickly bobbed down.

As she peered through the foliage, she glimpsed somebody bending over with their back towards her. She crouched low and silently observed them hard at work.

The lion statue that had once been beheaded now stood fully re-instated. From Melantha's description, Alice wondered if someone had repaired it or whether a new one had been fashioned. The marble appeared clean, polished and restored.

As the person lifted themselves up, Alice could clearly make out the form of a young man. He turned and paced towards a pile of tools that lay just a few metres from the bush in which she was hiding. From her vantage point, she studied his handsome features.

She guessed he was in his early to mid-twenties. His soft-brown hair was cut in a choppy relaxed style. It hung below his collar in jagged layers. Some lightened strands suggested he spent plenty of time outdoors. His face was lean with a good angular bone structure.

He wore a pair of blue vintage-denim jeans. They were slim fit and faded. A charcoal and burgundy checked shirt was fully unbuttoned, revealing his highly toned torso. Sweat glistened on his tanned chest.

Taking a break, he threw himself down on the ground, and glugged back most of a large bottle of water, pouring the remainder over the top of his head. With rugged hands he massaged his face. In doing so, his sleeves fell back revealing several tattoos. After a few moments he arose and headed over to the lions again.

Alice felt frustrated and annoyed. It would be difficult to get into the house with him around. There might even be other labourers carrying out repairs elsewhere.

She slunk reluctantly back to her base, consoled only by the fact that she could get some lunch.

All that remained of the day was spent squashing her toxic bouquet into an old wooden flower press. They would make an attractive birthday card for Melantha.

Chapter Nine

DANCING WITH DARCUS

THAT SAME EVENING, Alice perched on the top step of the caravan holding a wooden flute. The hardy instrument was encircled with several bands of silver.

Light flickered from glass lanterns, helping the moon to diminish the darkness. It was a breezy night and often its bright face was completely covered by banks of cloud.

Dressed in a rich, red gypsy skirt, Alice played a soft melody into the midnight air.

The music drew Darcus to the forefront of her mind. This phantasm, so easily conjured up, materialised in front of her.

Breaking through the pitch-blackness, a faint cloaked figure came near and reached for her hand. He brought a strange comfort that numbed and seduced. Leading her out into the field, his indistinct presence enveloped her.

There they danced.

From somewhere unearthly, pounding, hypnotic drum beats drenched the atmosphere. Soporific rhythms caused Alice to plunge into a stupor.

The vivid flowing fabric of her skirt mingled with his silky robe.

Darcus was overwhelming her.

Giddy and swirling she raced, as if in a misty whirlpool, spiralling down and down until she thought her mind would spin out completely.

The wild, free feeling soon gave way to one of enslavement. Her escort's companionship didn't come without a cost.

His embrace gradually tightened around her soul – first restricting, then binding, until such heaviness fell upon her, she could hardly breathe.

Pressing up close to her ear, he whispered, "You are mine, Alice – all mine!"

An appetite welled up inside her that craved to belong to someone. She was so hungry to be desired that she didn't question the consequence of his attention. Although sensing a malicious bondage, her emptiness yielded to his pursuit.

He wanted her and that was all that mattered.

"Yes, Darcus," she replied wholeheartedly. "I am yours."

As the words left her lips, the strength of his presence immediately subsided and he disappeared.

His abrupt departure abandoned her to mundane reality. The anticlimax left her deflated and lonely.

Having collapsed in the cold grass, she staggered off to bed. The sheets in the bunk felt damp and uninviting as she gathered them around her body. Scrunched up, with her teeth chattering, she longed for sleep to take her fretfulness. Eventually, she passed into an erratic slumber.

Shaken from her dreams by a thud, Alice stirred.

Maybe a bird had landed on the roof? Glancing at her watch, she was surprised to see it was already late morning. She pushed open the wooden door, stepped outside and gazed around the meadow.

Nothing seemed unusual.

As she turned to go in, she caught sight of something. A cream embossed envelope lay on the top step in a small wicker basket. Startled, she grasped it, nervously looking in every direction, before hurrying back inside.

She clambered onto the bunk and parted the curtains. As the light burst through the window, she lifted the paper flap and examined the note.

A simple scrawl read:

Returning something that belongs to you. Destiny lies in people, not objects. I'm down by the brook if you want a chat.

Reaching deeper into the paper pocket she drew out her amethyst flower pendant.

Chapter Ten

KES

D RESSED IN AN indigo T-shirt and jeans, he sat on a rock at the edge of the brook. Casting pebbles, he gazed down into the water. Alice cautiously approached from behind.

Sensing her nearness, he swung towards her with a radiant grin. She couldn't help coyly smiling back. His countenance was so open and friendly.

Coming closer, she instantly recognised him as the labourer from the day before.

He looked pleased as he studied her. With her long hair scraped into a pony tail, she still had on the outfit from the night before. Having just tumbled out of bed, the scarlet gypsy skirt was badly creased. Feeling unattractive and dishevelled, she picked at a ribbon that flowed from her blouse.

"Hey, Mr Lion-Fixer," she said with a false bravado – she wanted to quickly gain the upper hand by letting him know she knew something about him – "I'm Alice."

He didn't seem surprised by the way she addressed him. He just laughed.

"Alice, eh? Then I'm hanging out with nobility, am I?"

Impressed that he knew the meaning of her name, she sat down on the bank and immersed her feet in the cool water. Tiny minnows flashed beneath her toes.

"How did you know the necklace belonged to me?" she questioned.

His eyes met hers. He stared at her intently. "I was sitting a few steps up from you in the bell tower."

She shuddered at the thought of a stranger having been in such close proximity without her knowing. It was during that time on the step when she had deliberately cut herself. He must have watched her do it! Her shame gave way to anger.

"Look, I don't know who you are or what your game is, but the thought of you doing that freaks me out!"

Although fully aware that she'd been spying on him through the bushes, he chose not to retaliate.

"Well, I promise I won't do it again," he generously offered. "I'm Kes and I'm living in the gamekeeper's cottage while I work on Mr Brunswick's house and estate."

He gestured to a wooded area, beyond the field towards the property.

"It's just off the main track, about fifteen minutes away."

Aware of her trespassing, she wondered what he thought of her hiding out on the grounds.

As if reading her thoughts, he volunteered, "Nice little secluded spot you've found here."

Determined not to respond, Alice refused to open the subject up. With so much rejection in her life, she was always ready to flee. Any challenge would make her swiftly pack up and move on.

They sat for a while in silence, each nursing their own thoughts.

Eventually, jumping down from the rock, he said brightly, "Well Alice, I have lots to be getting on with at the big house today, but how about I cook you some supper tonight at my place?"

The thought of a substantial meal made her tummy rumble. She looked up at him, immediately struck by his soft grey eyes.

"Yeah, I'll come along, but I don't eat masses and I'm a vegetarian."

He walked confidently towards her.

"Okay, courgette special it is then. I'll put away the pheasants. Do you know the huge oak tree just off the main path to Beulah?"

She nodded. It was outstanding – a glorious natural landmark.

"Meet you there at seven," he called as he strolled off through the field. "And wear that skirt, I think it's cute."

She blushed, shocked by his attention to detail and pleasantly troubled that something about her was attractive to him.

⧄

Alice had erected a makeshift tent in the field. Housing an old enamel tin bath, it made for a suitable bathing area. Eight wooden poles had been banged into the ground and were surrounded with candy-striped fabric. Inside, she had placed a collection of sweet-smelling toiletries on an upturned crate. A large water pitcher stood in one corner and a small scuffed sign hung at the entrance. It read *Salle de Bain.*

The encounter with Kes had thrown her into a flurry of activity. The release of nervous energy made her try too hard at everything.

In order to calm her excitement about what the evening might hold, she attempted to make daisy chains.

It proved futile.

When her hands shook too much, she cast the flowers down and picked up her knitting. Even this turned out to be difficult; her usual perfect stitches gave way to clumsy holes.

She endeavoured to paint her toe nails. Soon blobs of nail varnish smudged the caravan steps where she'd overloaded the brush.

Later she went off to soak in a bath of bubbles, having mixed a few buckets of water fetched from the brook with some taken from the wood-burner kettle. As she stepped into the scented water, white foam cascaded onto the grass. She tried to lie back and relax for a few minutes, but found it impossible to be inactive. Soon, a trickle of crimson blood flowed down her calf – evidence of heavy-handed shaving.

Tousling her freshly washed hair in the sun's warmth, she was surprised at how slowly the time dragged. Her mind wandered. She had all sorts of questions about *him*. Was she wise to go to a complete stranger's home? If he spent his days labouring hard on the big house, would his place be scruffy and uncared for? She reasoned that his cottage was probably dilapidated and drab. With her thoughts swinging between adventure and trepidation, she waited for the impending event.

6:15 sounded the alarm for final preparations. She made up her face, brushed her hair and smoothed body lotion onto her limbs. Stretching the red skirt over her slim hips, she finished off her outfit with a strappy black top.

The depleted bottle of Beulah wine would be her gift for the host. Alice scraped and peeled back the label – she didn't want Kes to know she had pinched it.

In great anticipation, she stepped into the meadow and almost skipped towards the oak tree.

The sight of a blue camper van stationed at their meeting place was not what she had expected. Slumped on the driver's side with his eyes closed, Kes looked exhausted. As she tapped on the window he stirred. Breaking into a wide smile, he reached over to the passenger's door and welcomed her in.

"Hey, little lady, jump up. I thought I'd pick you up in style."

Within a few minutes, they were pulling into a clearing outside his home. The detached, single storey cottage stood in a woodland garden.

He led her through a gate and up a short path; they dodged a pile of footwear strewn across the porch.

"Welcome to my crib," he laughed.

Alice was shocked. She had expected the interior to be a certain way and was surprised to step into a comfortable modern space. Nothing was as she had imagined. Instead of it being old, dark and dingy, it had a light Nordic look about it.

Whitewashed walls encompassed the open plan living area.

Set around a fireplace, a modular floor sofa surrounded a low wooden table.

"Seating and dining all-in-one," he said, motioning for her to sit down.

A nourishing, wholesome smell wafted from the oven. It filled the entire room with a pleasurable greeting.

"You relax here, Alice, I'll sort the food."

She placed the wine on the table and settled herself down on the soft cushions.

Gratefully acknowledging her gift, he brought over two glasses.

He seemed very well organised and in control. Plonking down a large bowl of colourful food, he returned to fetch a hot, sizzling dish from the oven.

The rustic table was soon laden with a delicious spread.

Golden cheese bubbled on top of a pile of chopped courgettes. The accompanying dishes were a tub of natural yogurt and a mound of couscous packed with olives, chick peas, cucumber and fresh mint.

Alice, having taken a little portion of everything, was shocked at how much he piled onto his plate.

He noticed her staring. "Haven't been around a man for a while, then?" he questioned.

Pushing her fork to and fro, she put a tiny scoop of couscous into her mouth.

Flashbacks of mountains of fatty sausages, chips and beans brought up awful memories of living with Jimmy and Mum. Jimmy had only ever bought cheap food and nearly all his culinary efforts dripped with lard.

Disregarding any protocol, she stretched for the wine and hastily topped up her glass; having filled it to the brim she gulped it back. The bottle now stood empty.

Kes quietly watched. Her distress was easy to read and he knew she was attempting to calm tempestuous seas.

As she continued to play casually with her food, he finished a second helping.

Reaching for his wine, he examined it. Like a connoisseur, gently swirling the stem, he took a measured sip, allowing it to pass slowly through his mouth.

"Wow, this is great stuff. Where did you get it from?"

She eyed him sullenly, wondering if he knew she had stolen it from the cellar.

"I took it from Beulah," she snapped defiantly.

He picked up his guitar and started to gently strum. With kindness twinkling through his eyes he focussed his gaze towards her. "The truth will set you free, Alice; the truth will set you free."

Meditating on his words, she rested back on the sofa and let the music wash over her. Evil hallucinations often visited her at night but somehow his playing held them at bay. Pulling a throw over her dainty frame she snuggled into its tactile softness.

Kes noticed she was vulnerable to the evening chill. He popped a few logs into the grate and lit a small fire. As the flames leapt up, tiny sparks of peace began to break into her hopelessness.

This rare atmosphere of wellbeing was alien to her but delightful. Visibly loosening up, she slipped off her sandals, fanned out her skirt and lay back. Her eyes grew heavy as she concentrated on his skilled fingers gliding across the strings. The room had become so cosy that she started to nod off.

After about an hour, she awoke to his voice.

"Someone needs tucking up in bed," he volunteered, gently rousing her. "Come on, Alice, time I took you home."

She couldn't remember leaving the cottage. It had all felt like a dream. What she could recall was the sensation of his warm hoodie covering her shoulders as he guided her back to the caravan.

After that, Kes disappeared for a few days. During his absence, she thought deeply about the strange estate of Beulah. More importantly, she missed him.

He visited her one afternoon.

As she lugged a heavy pail of water to her bathing shack, she found him standing there.

"Go up and use my place whenever you want," he kindly offered, pressing a spare key into her hand. "Feel free to use my shower and help yourself to anything out of the fridge. I'm gone by the crack of dawn."

From then on, she often dropped by. It made her life much easier.

❧

Chapter Eleven

BODY TALK

KES PULLED HIS van to an abrupt halt, dragged his fingers through his hair and leapt out. It had been a long, strenuous day. Singing as he walked up the path, he flung open his cottage door.

Wham! He was instantly hit with a wall of soft feminine perfume. Rose oil and exotic fruits mingled in the hot steamy air.

Alice had been there.

Feeling strongly stirred, he peeled off his work gear and threw himself under the shower. With renewed vitality, he towelled down, pulled on a fresh set of clothes and went to the kitchen. Reaching for a bread knife, he chopped the top off a round loaf, scooped out the middle, moulded it into a ball, and stuffed it in his mouth. Into the hole, he hastily layered slices of cheese, sun-dried tomatoes and roasted peppers. His giant sandwich was soon filled to the brim. Roughly slicing it up, he wrapped it in foil and slung it into a large canvas bag. After shoving in a few other items, he rushed out of the house, jumped in his van and headed down to the glade.

Alice was folding laundry into a wicker basket as she sat in the meadow on a throw. Richly textured, she had made it herself, adding a long fringe all around the edge. The earthy tones mirrored her lightly tanned skin.

Kes emerged from the cover of the trees and approached her. Conscious of movement, she glanced up. As he walked towards her with the holdall in hand, she couldn't help noticing how his strong thighs filled out the top of his jeans. Her heart pounded as he dropped down beside her.

"I've brought supper," he said brightly, rummaging in his bag. "Oh... and I've also got our evening's entertainment."

He pulled out a chess set and unfolded the board.

Alice didn't look very enthusiastic. Being a fledgling player, the thought of exposing herself to embarrassment placed her in an awkward situation. She frowned at the likelihood of defeat and attempted to excuse herself from participating.

"I'm rubbish at this. I've only ever played a few times against my mum," she admitted.

Kes was so keen and energised, he easily disarmed her protests.

"Ah, give it a try, Alice, it'll be fun. Your first time with a guy, I'll go easy on you."

Their eyes engaged. He hadn't purposed an innuendo. Alice struggled to comprehend his manner towards her. He displayed tender actions that were almost brotherly, yet his behaviour seemed to probe and search for something that no one else had ever gone looking for. Although there was benevolence in the way he related to her, she longed to know how he viewed her as a woman.

The heavily weighted pieces were soon set up across the board. Intricately carved out of ebony and boxwood, they were quickly aligned ready for combat. The kings and queens stood majestic and lustrous.

Alice hated losing important pieces. A few pawns would be fine but she loathed getting anything else confiscated.

"Choose your colour," Kes urged, tearing the sandwich into pieces. "Why not take white, and then you start with an advantage?" He had already angled the board so that the pale pieces lay at her fingertips.

Assuming failure, she reasoned she would need plenty of help, but not from Kes.

No, she would evoke some hidden power to win this one. Tap into something that had stealth and genius.

"I'll take black," she replied insolently. A calculating, guileful determination swept across her face as she carefully turned the board.

Kes' expression became solemn. "Okay," he answered. "Let's see what the game draws out."

It all started amicably. Bites of bread, followed by the simple pushing forward of pawns. Having attempted to advance her least valuable pieces, Alice watched as several of them were lifted out of the game.

It didn't take long for her to surrender a knight and two bishops.

Her loss was his glory.

Kes was a brilliant player, not only making great tactical moves but demonstrating strategic insight. Swiftly taking advantage of her weakness, he easily gained control of the four central squares.

Alice felt the pressure building as move-by-move he overcame her defences. Coordinating his rooks with skilful precision, he started to intimidate her major pieces. It all became too much when his knight took her queen.

Kes placed it with pride alongside his bounty of ebony characters.

With her king under serious threat and her downfall looming, some drastic action was needed.

She scanned each position, appearing to be evaluating the dilemma. After closing her eyes for several moments, her lips twitched as if forming words. Summoning up a force within her spirit, she stared down at the board. Immediately an intelligent counterattack started to manifest. Something powerfully adept was at work, attempting to change the outcome in her favour. Suddenly it overstepped the mark and came out of obscurity into the forefront of the game. Her rook slowly slid across the board without her touching it.

Kes didn't flinch.

Calmly looking up at her with strength in his eyes, a soft smile broke across his handsome face.

"Oh, Darcus is playing is he? Isn't that cheating?"

Her eyes blackened with an intense, unearthly darkness.

Snarled words spat from her pretty mouth. "How do you know about him?" she demanded.

"Someone told me," he coaxed. "Let's call it discernment."

His genuine lack of fear seemed to defuse the situation. Confidently resuming the game, he thrust his bishop forward. In doing so, their hands unintentionally met. Folding his fingers into hers, he gave them a brief squeeze. His desire was not to belittle her.

"Check," he called softly.

Traces of tears formed in her eyes and a tiny drop of blood spread across her bitten lip.

"There's so much tension locked up inside of you, Alice."

He stretched out his hand and gently removed the blood from her face, wiping it across his shirt. The smear rested just above his heart; its red stain stood out against the white cotton.

Alice knew that within a couple of moves the game would be over. She resigned herself to the fact that he had won. In a symbolic gesture, she lay down her king and conceded.

She stared over at all her captured pieces.

Something felt good about seeing them all gathered at his end of the board. She was pleased that they were held in his possession. They cried out that he was the victor.

Considering her defeat, she was surprised at not experiencing the usual gloom of humiliation. On the contrary, she actually felt glad. Secretly, she was ecstatic that he had won.

As he packed the chess set back into his bag, she wondered if he might be leaving. Perhaps everything had become too alarming.

He didn't appear to be disturbed. Instead, lounging out across the blanket, he asked if she had any wine in her caravan.

"Shall we go and settle down for the evening by your fire?" he suggested.

They collected up all their things and walked across the field towards her home.

Kes placed tinder and kindling wood into the centre of the fire ring, while Alice made a couple of trips back and forth from the van.

It wasn't long before she'd set out a bottle of Jimmy's homebrew, her stash of marijuana and a couple of glasses. As the firewood began to crackle, she poured out the drinks.

Kes took up his glass. He spluttered and choked back the pungent elderflower liquor.

"Man, that's a bit rough," he laughed.

"Yeah, the bloke who concocted it was harsh, too," she retorted.

He reached into his bag and pulled out a large pack of marshmallows.

"Well," he said, tossing a spongy sweet into the air and catching it in his mouth, "we could play 'chubby bunny' and stuff our faces with these things *or* we could get down to something far more intimate and revealing." He paused and added slowly, "You know, let our bodies do the talking."

Her deep feelings towards him were roused. The past few days had been really hard for her to understand. She felt he viewed her more like a little sister than a potential lover.

She was aware that her flimsy gypsy top had fallen loose from her shoulder, and that the exposure of her skin was provocative and inviting. Her eyes made it clear to him which of his propositions she most desired.

Kes leant into her. Running his hand across the soft fabric of her blouse, he lifted her sleeve back over her bare flesh so as to cover her.

"Alice, we haven't had all this stuff written across our bodies for no reason. We need to get to know one another. Let's read each other's tattoos."

At first she was perplexed. She had always prided herself in being able to outwit people but Kes baffled her. Having completely misunderstood his suggestion for their bodies to communicate, she needed time to adjust.

Eventually she sat up and agreed to take part in the second game of the evening. "Right, Kes, you get to go first. See if you can translate this one."

She swept her long black hair away from her slender neck, revealing a Gothic styled skull with a dagger flung through it. The image looked angry and intimidating – a complete contrast to the beauty and softness of her back.

As his eyes ran over it, he volunteered, "There's someone you hate and you wish they were dead."

Astonished at his accuracy, she dropped her hair back over her shoulders and drew up her ankle. He glanced down at the freshly etched birth sign.

"You want your life to be significant – to know you're unique and born with purpose and destiny."

As tears pricked her eyes, she reached for his hand. Pushing his forearm upwards, she read out the beautifully inscribed sentence that ran its entire length. It had fascinated her for days. "Okay, Kes, so what does *Trevanna Bay ain't ever going back* mean? Why 'ain't you ever going back'? Is the place that awful?"

A serious expression came over his face. His countenance was firm and resolute. "Trevanna Bay is very beautiful. I'd return to the place, but I ain't ever going back to the lifestyle."

The mellow fragrance of her spliff filled the air around them, transporting his mind back to his days as an art student.

Chapter Twelve

LIVING THE DREAM

3 years earlier...

K ES STORMED THROUGH the doors of the studio.
"Taran, we got it, mate! We can move into my old
man's house."

Putting down his camera, Taran turned around in delight.

It had been hard for Kes to persuade his father to allow
him and his friends to rent his property. Desiring to use
it for their second year at art college, Kes had eventually
convinced him it was a good idea. "But Dad, with you

living overseas it would make good sense. I can keep an eye on it for you."

Seldom used, the lovely modern beach house was fully equipped and ready to receive occupants.

Situated on the north shore, the three storey building stood in an ideal location for both surfing and college.

Kes pulled out his phone. "I'll call Blake and the three of us can drive over."

Within the hour they were sitting in a beautiful open plan living space, drinking black coffee and gazing out over Trevanna Bay.

Taran hovered around a large bi-fold door. He unlocked it and stepped out onto an expansive lawn that led down to a beach path. He called to the others.

"Hey, guys, surfing is going to be so easy. It's only a short walk to the ocean."

He turned and went back inside with a big smile on his face.

As they explored the rest of the house, they fought each other over the bedrooms. Kes won the largest with the best view. Taran and Blake quickly conceded to him claiming it. Without him they wouldn't have stood a chance of living in a property such as this. While they went off to choose rooms for themselves, Kes opened the enormous glass doors that accessed a long balcony. He could imagine himself sitting out here, watching the golden sunset fill the sky. It was perfect. With a cool drink in hand, he'd be able to completely unwind and gaze upon the ever changing sea.

They piled downstairs and checked out the other facilities. There were great whoops of delight at what they discovered.

Blake stared inside a massive fridge. "Whoa! This is gonna stock a whole load of beer," he laughed.

Everything about the beach house was in complete contrast to all that they had known in bedsit land. They were so accustomed to cramped living conditions – cold, sparse and basic. The guys had been used to having one tiny room each with a kitchen, bathroom and toilet to share with hordes of other people.

"No more grotty, nightmare kitchens!" shouted Kes. As an avid watcher of cookery shows, he considered himself quite an up-and-coming chef.

Compared to the grim, ill-equipped place they were leaving, this was paradise. Now, they were surrounded by high quality appliances, including a range cooker, dishwasher, coffee machine and a fabulous barbeque.

Blake was shocked at having landed in such opulence. He looked astonished. "Wow, your old man must be loaded, Kes. We're gonna live like kings! Let's scout out the rest of the place."

A ground floor shower was perfectly situated for people coming back from the beach. The rear door led through a utility space and straight into a wet room. Several wetsuits were already hanging on the rails. A couple of surf boards lay up against the wall awaiting some action. Taran could hardly bear to walk past them. If he had his way, he'd be spending more time on the waves than indoors.

They followed a passage down to the basement. Blake pushed the door. It opened into a well equipped weights room. For young guys interested in developing their physiques, it was stocked up with all the basic necessities.

"Ooh, why d'you think your dad painted it bright red?" Taran mused, feeling the bounce on the thick, expensive, rubber flooring. "It's a bit loud, isn't it?"

"Knowing him, he just wanted to use an aggressive colour," Kes shot back. "When it comes to his fitness and strength, he's always been quite in your face. It's savage, but at least it'll wake us up in the mornings." Taran noticed anger in his expression. He looked back at the paintwork.

The space seemed even more dynamic with a wall decal, which broadcast *Fortune Favours the Strong* in bold black lettering.

Kes read it with irritation. "That's typical of Dad," he thought to himself, sullenly.

Blake ran his hand over the power rack and tried out the adjustable bench. He loved using Olympic bars and weight plates. This was going to make work outs so convenient.

They left the gym and went back up to the main living room.

On the whole, Kes' dad had impeccable taste. Everything had been finished to a very high standard. Stylish, but also functional, the entire place spoke of easy living.

A large flat screen television would accommodate great movie nights and the living area was spacious enough to hold lots of house guests for partying. The lack of immediate neighbours made it all the more excellent.

Having discovered that a huge L shaped leather settee was blissfully comfortable, Taran and Blake lounged out, mesmerised by the swell of the ocean. From here they would be able to check the surf and hit the waves within five minutes.

Kes clicked on the end of a ballpoint pen. "I just need you guys to sign the paperwork and then we can all start to move our gear in. It should be ready to go by the end of the month." Taran and Blake responded swiftly. Never had Kes witnessed his mates so keenly apply themselves to admin.

Chapter Thirteen

MOVING IN

IT DIDN'T TAKE long for the beach house to become animated. With high spirits the guys brought in all their personal possessions. Soon, treasured guitars, artwork, laptops, surf gear and a whole host of individual belongings turned the place into a home.

Kes settled into his bedroom. It was huge and had its own en suite. The white walls were perfect for displaying his large acrylic paintings. Having specialised in modern iconic images, he set about hanging the bold illustrations. His great interpretation of pop art created nostalgic journeys into past decades. The female form was a key component in several of his pictures. More recent work blended text with bright, abstract shapes.

Straddling a storage chest, he picked up his guitar and began to strum. As its warm, full tone filled the air, he broke into song. He always felt carefree when playing; getting totally caught up in the moment, he let the music carry him away.

In an adjacent room, Blake smiled to himself as he unpacked his clothes into the closet. It was lovely listening to his mate improvise. He looked in on Kes and stepped out onto the balcony. The view was breathtaking. Vibrant layers of red and mauve filled the sky. Everything felt superb. As he turned to leave, he encountered Kes' latest painting hanging in pride of position over the king size bed. The lettering across it read *Live it wild and Live it fast.*

"That's exactly what we're gonna do, mate!" he laughed, heading across the hall.

Once back in his room, Blake gathered together a pile of framed photographs. After studying them carefully, he worked out the order in which to arrange them across his walls. His college tutor considered the images to be exemplary. He had praised Blake for having developed such great skill in seascapes. The pieces he had composed drew the viewer's eye into the shot. His knack of finding patterns and structure in the foreground had brought him many compliments.

He couldn't wait to get out on the cliffs that surrounded the bay. The large rock formations and jagged faces would be perfect for advancing his art. His project for the summer holidays would involve shooting the same beach at different tides and experimenting with wet sand reflections.

Taran shouted up to them from downstairs, "Help me unload the beer, guys."

Having arrived back from an evening run to the supermarket, his van was chock-a-block with provisions. As they brought in crates of booze and several full carrier bags, they pulled out 'man-food'. Along with lots of other stuff, they unpacked great quantities of eggs, bread, cheese, burgers, and hot pepper sauce. They were happy with Taran's selection.

"At least this will start us off," he said, breaking into a satisfied smile and opening a beer.

Kes quickly set about cooking. He threw some burgers onto the griddle, and soon produced giant double-deckers with cheese dripping out of the buns. He'd wrapped the beef in bacon and pressed a sautéed mushroom and onion mix into the centre.

At the push of a button, an ice maker on the front of the fridge chucked out cubes for their drinks.

Blake tossed a mixed salad into three bowls and soon they were all sat around the breakfast bar, enjoying the hearty supper.

After the meal, Kes led the guys with the cleaning up. They were all willing to oblige, wanting to get everything off to a good start.

As Taran loaded up the dishwasher, his thoughts drifted back to the communal kitchen of his previous home. It was not uncommon to be surrounded by an accumulation of filthy dishes – sometimes they would pile up on the work surface for days. But here, apart from the char-grilled smell that hung in the air, nobody would have known the kitchen had been used.

Taran and Kes went back upstairs. Blake followed, scanning a long list of instructions on how the place needed to operate.

"Your dad insists we all keep mattress protectors on our beds," Blake called out laughing. "Can't have any spills."

"Well, make sure you get yours on quickly, Blakey." Kes shouted back.

Blake walked off to his room and lay down for a rest. Opening up his laptop, he viewed some of his favourite sites. Eventually, stretching out across the bed, he reached for his phone. His contact list was packed with the numbers of several girls from college that he'd been flirting with. Feeling completely stoked, he messaged some of them. Within a few minutes, he flicked through a whole host of replies. He smiled to himself and spoke out loud, "I've hit the honey trail! This is gonna be a good summer." His humorous banter and attractive looks made him a bit of a magnet. He couldn't wait for the next few months to unfurl.

Taran's room soon came together. He liked to keep everything in good order. Most of his gear related to surfing and was already laid out in the utility space downstairs. He folded a stack of T-shirts into a cupboard and started to make his bed. The linen felt fresh and unused. As he pulled the cover over the king size duvet, he marvelled at the quality of everything around him. The mattresses throughout the whole house were exceptionally comfortable. Each had a deep memory foam layer on top. All the bedding they needed was provided and a huge cupboard yielded an abundance of brand new towels.

With the hot water system up and running, Kes went off for a long soak. He poured in eucalyptus oil and dropped his weary body into the sunken bath. Relaxing in the warmth, his tired, aching muscles soon de-stressed. He leant back, closed his eyes and reflected on the quick turnaround of events. Emerging an hour later, he got into bed leaving the blinds wide open.

The only light left on was the moon. It hung against the inky sky, full and bright.

Taran sat up until midnight watching a surfing movie. He arose, switched off the television and stood in the dark, looking out over the bay. This sudden change of circumstance was hard to take in. He exhaled a deep, contented sigh and laid his forehead against the glass. The white water, on the crest of the waves, lit up in the moonlight. Tomorrow morning, if conditions were favourable, he'd be on dawn patrol.

He awoke early to the beautiful sight of consistent waves sweeping onto the beach. The moderate offshore wind had created clean lines and perfect barrels. Hurrying down to the kitchen, he made himself a banana and honey sandwich and went to get into his wetsuit. Picking up his pre-waxed short board, he was gone.

From the bottom of the garden he followed the track down to the sea. The constant rhythm of the waves was music to his ears. As he hastened along, he thought how perfect the dawn twilight would be for Blake's photography.

Surfing could easily have become the central focus of Taran's life. It wasn't just a recreational activity for him. Even his work at art college was predominantly composed of water sport images. Using a high-grade camera with waterproof housing, his style had quickly progressed. He had achieved amazing results because he'd been prepared to take the risks. Out in the ocean, with powerful waves, riders and boards pushing towards him, the possibility of getting run over had been very real. He had broken bones in the pursuit of a great shot, yet photography didn't even come close to his love of the sport. Already trained as a surf instructor, he hoped to spend the summer months doing what he enjoyed most.

Three hours later, totally psyched, he returned to the house. It had been exhilarating out there. The long range swell had brought in some great waves. He peeled off his wetsuit, rinsed it through and let it hang over a specially crafted drip trough. After taking a shower, he dressed in a T-shirt and board shorts, rubbed his shaggy hair with a towel and stepped briskly to the kitchen. Dry frying four eggs, he piled them onto a mound of baked beans and took the plate out to the garden. A long hardwood table stood on a decked patio. Eight folded chairs leant in columns against the wall. As he sat in the morning sunshine, he deliberated about his immediate future. In time, he would check out if there were any jobs going at the local surf school. *Life was good.*

Kes and Blake were delighted to join Taran in spending
most of the daylight hours in the ocean. They gladly put
off searching for work for a few weeks. The weather was
consistently hot, lending itself to al fresco living. It all felt
like one big vacation. Unrestricted and free of routines, they
seldom even glanced at a clock. Sunrise and sunset were the
only markers. With no fixed meal times, they just ate when
they were hungry. It suited their personalities to live so
casually. Even looking for a job could be self-directed, and
not a pressured necessity.

Kes had made a deal with his father that the three of them
would help maintain the property. Their rent was therefore
minimal. Although his dad had known this was a bit of
a joke, he felt guilty for abandoning his son after a long
and difficult divorce. During a moment of weakness, his
remorse had overtaken his better judgement and made him
give in to Kes' suggestion. Afterwards, he consoled himself
that at least he was helping to put a roof over his head while
he studied.

Hanging out with Taran was like being in permanent surf
school. With his great knowledge on techniques and water
safety, he naturally shared invaluable information.

Blake, the least experienced surfer, was a fantastic pool
swimmer but Taran had to educate him on the ocean's
hidden dangers. He knew Blake was prone to life's excesses
and felt the need to warn him not to be frivolous.

"Watch what you put into your body before you go
surfing. You gotta be careful man, respect the sea. Being

out in that ocean is a whole lot different to swimming in still water. You gotta be aware of undertows, rip tides and how to navigate the big waves."

As they chilled out together in the evenings, he would tell stories of occasions when he had wiped out and been tossed around in the water as if he was in a washing machine.

The days were happy and relaxed. They all enjoyed each other's company and felt privileged to be in such a fortunate position. Frequent workouts in the weights room, along with constant water sport, sculpted their tanned bodies. With a regular dose of sunshine and good nutritious food, they looked healthy and fit. In the evenings they would bring down their guitars, watch movies or play on the games console.

Kes set up a creative space in one of the unused bedrooms. There, he would often take himself off to paint canvases. Sometimes he would stay up through the early hours and wouldn't hit the sack until three or four in the morning.

Taran and Blake swapped ideas about photography. They both admired each other's work and hoped one day to put on an exhibition together.

On returning from the beach one evening, Kes showered, pulled on his board shorts and walked shirtless into the kitchen.

Music was blasting out and four girls were sitting on the settee. Blake lounged in their midst with a big smile on his face.

Kes nodded over, recognising a couple of the girls from college.

As he proceeded to fix some supper, he lifted a pile of handbags off the kitchen work surface and plonked them onto the dining table. He didn't hide his irritation as he slammed a potato into the microwave, opened a can of tuna and mashed it down.

Something didn't seem right to him.

The usual peaceful atmosphere had been disrupted. Feeling uncomfortable, he leant up against the counter and looked over at them all. Fortunately, the room was so large that at least he had his own space.

Blake shot him a smirk, opened a bottle of cheap vodka and lit up a joint.

Kes knew that mixing weed and alcohol didn't always end favourably. Getting high and plastered could leave you spinning.

He pulled the ring on a cider, drew up a stool and ate his meal.

There was a strong vibe in the air and he could feel some of the girls staring over at him. Apart from his red board shorts, the only other thing on his body was a hemp and leather bracelet. He was aware that he looked cool and laid-back.

For some reason he didn't want to socialise. He felt ambushed and offended. He'd been enjoying life with the guys and suddenly he felt pressure.

One of the girls wandered up and slouched across the bar. She was what Taran called an 'under and over chick'. Underdressed and overdone. The shoes she had on were so high and spiky they looked like dangerous weapons.

There was no doubt she was attractive but she was also overpowering and intimidating. To Kes, she was sexy but not beautiful.

Ignoring her, he scraped off the remains of his food and rinsed his plate. Glugging back the last drop of cider, he tossed the can into the bin and left the room. As he took himself off to bed, he hoped they would all go home soon.

When he woke up the next morning, his initial sense of wellbeing was stolen by memories of the night before. Jumping out of bed, he made his way downstairs to check out the lie of the land. He was glad to see the handbags had disappeared and the only evidence of the girls having been there was a coffee table littered with empty alcopops and a few scratches on the wooden floor.

As soon as Taran came in from the beach and Blake finally surfaced, Kes called them together for a conflab.

"Listen guys, I don't mind girls coming over and I don't care if they stay overnight, but let me get one thing straight. I don't ever want any of them moving in with us." Aware of the fact they had two spare bedrooms, he wanted it to stay the way it was – just the three of them.

"Cool by me," said Taran.

"Mate, what was up with you last night?" questioned Blake.

Kes avoided answering him and turned on the game console.

"Oh, and another thing," he stressed, "if they come over in those crazy heels, tell them to leave them at the front door."

⌘

Chapter Fourteen

DEVELOPMENTS

TARAN PACED THE living room like a caged lion. A prevailing south-westerly had churned up the ocean into a mass of white, messy water. Pumped with energy, he had no outlet – he needed some activity quickly. Stretching his limbs like he was preparing for a football match, he headed down to the weights room.

At the kitchen counter, Blake sat on his laptop sending emails. He was in conversation with a national company who had shown interest in buying his images. Planning was already well underway for the production of their following year's calendar. Blake's artwork was on their shortlist.

Taran came back up from the gym and stood staring out to sea. Still agitated, he asked if anyone wanted to join him in search of the perfect wave.

"Let's drive down the coast and check out a better spot. I reckon it could be fine at Jachin Point." The beach he was referring to was well known for its powerful, hollow waves but it also featured a high headland which protected it from sweeping winds. On a good day you could score long barrels.

Kes dropped his controller. "Yeah, I'll come with you." Happy at the thought of some vigorous action, he went to get his gear together.

Taran instantly became less fraught. With the stress visibly melting off him, he went to the fridge and made himself a smoothie.

Chopping a ripe pear and some kiwis, he threw them into a blender with some big handfuls of spinach. As he added a dash of organic apple juice, it whirled into a bubbly liquid. He poured the thick, bright green fluid into a pint glass and glugged it back.

Blake walked over, laughing at him. "You never cease to amaze me, sucking in that pondweed sludge!"

"Better for you than the type of weed you're into, Blake," he replied. "Your body is a temple, man; it just houses and contains the real you. It's your earth suit and while you live down here you gotta treat it good."

"You're funny," retorted Blake, genuinely loving his friend. "I don't know what you're on, Tar, to come out with the stuff you do, but I think I'll stick to my own weed, thanks." He ruffled Taran's hair in an affectionate gesture and opened a beer. "Have fun surfing with Kes, I'm staying put."

Several hours later, the sound of the van screeching to a halt signalled their return. Along with their surfboards, they carried a heroic demeanour as they strode through the hall. They'd come back elated, like conquerors arriving home from battle. Although it had been rough, the powerful waves had held their shape.

After showering, they walked into the living room, fresh and calm. At last Taran's strength was spent and he could manage to sit still.

Kes checked his phone and brought up a message. "Oh that's class!" he shouted, as the voice finished. "You know that guy who owns *Jett's Seafood Bar*? Well, he saw my paintings at our end of year show, and he's interested in buying some for the restaurant."

Kes remembered the conversation that had taken place during the exhibition. They had connected well and discussed his art in some detail. He wandered into the garden, called Jett Ramos and arranged to have lunch with him.

ॐ

Chapter Fifteen

JETT'S PLACE

KES SELECTED a few canvases from his bedroom wall and prepared for the meeting with Jett.

He knew the restaurant was a laid-back kind of place, so he dressed casually. It felt strange to pull his jeans on – he was used to living in his board shorts. His black fitted T-shirt was plain and understated, perfect for presenting the bright details of his illustrations. Slapping on a gorgeous pepper and patchouli aftershave, he glanced in the mirror at his rugged face.

Deeply tanned, his complexion set off his blue-grey eyes. They sparkled with the vibrancy of fresh outdoor living. When he broke into a smile, the whiteness of his teeth stood out all the more from the regular flushing of sea salt and the windburn on his skin.

As he put on his watch, he experienced a pang of repulsion. Not wanting to get back into the rat race, he had to tell himself this was just a 'meal for a deal' and then he could split with no ties. His free spirit hated convention. Wrapping the black nylon strap around his wrist, he snapped the clasp shut. It was 11:20 am and Jett was expecting him at mid-day.

The drive into town was strange. After spending so much time away from the masses, thick traffic and hordes of people felt alien to him. Pulling into a space in the restaurant car park, he unpacked his pictures and carried them in.

Jett was seated at the bar waiting for him. Jumping up, he shook Kes' hand and gestured towards a quiet corner. Being an astute entrepreneur, he was instantly impressed that Kes had walked in five minutes early.

"I have good staff, great food and an excellent atmosphere. I think your artwork will add the finishing touch!"

He fetched Kes a drink from the bar and sat down to talk over the ideas he had to enhance the decor.

After a while, he signalled for a waitress to bring over the menus. Kes was so engrossed with showing the paintings that he didn't notice the person who came over. As Jett motioned for him to choose his food, he looked up into the face of the prettiest girl he had seen in a long time. For a moment he completely lost his train of thought and got tongue tied. Jett observed the instant attraction and laughed as she walked away to put their order in.

"She's a beauty our Ruby, isn't she, Kes?"

Stunned and distracted, Kes sat longing for the moment that she would come close again. He hoped the chefs were efficient.

"Hungry, aren't you?" Jett teased.

The kitchen doors swung open and Ruby walked towards them carrying two full plates. When she stretched politely around him, he noticed her delicate wrist was wrapped in a hemp bracelet. "Snap," he said, raising his braid to show her. Putting his meal on the table, she smiled down at him. As she turned to walk away he noticed her lovely blonde ponytail. It reached a long way down her back.

"Quite smitten, aren't you?" Jett laughed. "You ought to get in there, she's not dating anyone. She's only recently arrived in town to work the season. Come to think of it, are you looking for work? I could do with a guy like you around the place, manning the bar at the weekends. What do you think, Kes? You'd fit in well with my staff."

Kes hadn't been that bothered about work, but he knew he would have to get something eventually. The sudden proposal seemed irresistible. He was shocked to hear the words come out of his own lips. "Yeah, thanks, definitely. When d'you want me to start?"

As he drove home, he wasn't excited about the fact he had just sold £900 worth of artwork.

Fully revved up, he couldn't get *her* out of his head.

On Friday, he would get to study her all night, and *that* was going to be a very pleasant experience. His friends noticed a spring in his step as he came into the house.

"You struck a deal, mate, didn't you? I can tell by the buzz all over you right now."

"Yeah Blake, I struck gold, but not in the way you're thinking."

Chapter Sixteen

RUBY

FOR KES, FRIDAY night couldn't come quickly enough. Jett had sent him a text asking him to come in two hours before opening. He needed to show him around the bar and get him conversant with the way he liked things done.

Just as he was about to leave the house, Blake popped his head around the bedroom door. His eyes looked wild and excited. He spoke speedily.

"Kes, we've got some friends in tonight. Just warning you, 'cause when you get in buddy, we'll be *partying!*"

"Yeah great, no worries, I'll look forward to joining you." He found it hard to concentrate on what Blake was saying.

His mind was way too distracted. As he closed the front door behind him, his thoughts were only on *her*.

He jumped into his van, put his foot down and sped into town. The sooner he got there the better.

The restaurant looked quaint from the outside. This historic building had once operated as a chandlery. Its minimal interior design and natural furnishings made way for a modern cuisine. A Mediterranean menu had been fused with the occasional Asian influence. The specials board reflected an eclectic offering of the best seasonal, local produce. The air was full of subtle, spicy aromas.

Well-accustomed to being around all types of booze, Kes familiarised himself with the layout of the bar. Serving cool international beers, alongside an extensive range of wines, different countries and regions were well represented. Jett told him to keep track of the inventory and to order more of the most popular brands and types. He also showed him how to prepare the garnishes for the drinks.

"I hope you're good with people, Kes, because a bartender is also a therapist." He winked. "I'm off for the evening, it's my wife's birthday, and I'll be shot if I'm not home soon."

A memory tried to surface of Kes' dad taking his mum out for one of her birthdays, but he quickly forced it down.

"I might have to wing the therapist bit," he grinned.

Jett scanned over the entire area. The lights were on, the music was at the correct volume and the tables were beautifully laid.

"Your paintings have been mounted in the upper gallery. We've had some good feedback already. You'll be famous one day and those will make me a small fortune! Have a good evening."

He left as Ruby arrived.

Kes was relieved. Jett wouldn't be constantly watching any interaction between them. He didn't need his help to connect with this girl. He could do it all by himself.

The restaurant heaved that night. There were five people serving – Ruby, two other girls and two guys. Watching her from the cover of the bar, he could see she was good at her job. Amongst a whole host of other tasks, she hovered to anticipate customers' requests, carefully checked the status of the food orders, and offered additional condiments just at the right moment. It was obviously mentally and physically demanding work. The contributions she brought to the communal tip jar made it soar. As Ruby put customers at ease with her infectious smile, Kes noticed how the men slipped her approving glances. Her slim yet shapely form glided smoothly between the tables. The soft lighting put a glow on her pretty face.

His eyes climbed her every time she had to mount the spiral iron steps; her slender legs were accentuated by her fitted, above-the-knee skirt.

He gave her his full attention whenever she approached for drinks; he loved the fact that she had to stand so close to him. There were several moments when she stepped behind the bar into the confined space beside him. Whenever her body brushed past his, he got all charged up. Not giving anything away, his cool persona masked the fire that raged inside of him. Catching a breath of her scent, he felt his blood pumping. He was going to have to move in quickly and hitch this up.

What he didn't know was that she was completely besotted with him. When he'd walked in to see Jett about his paintings, her heart had raced. While Jett had been talking to him, she had positioned herself so she could privately check him out. She loved what she saw. As Jett called her over, a surge had rushed through her body.

Since that day, she had relived the moment he called 'snap', hoping that his attention to such a minute detail was a signal of attraction. On hearing that he had been hired to run the bar, she was overjoyed, even swapping shifts with another girl.

"Are you sure you want to do Friday night? You usually hate doing the weekends!" her colleague had remarked.

All night she had relished taking her customers' drinks orders to the bar. Far more persuasive than usual, she had encouraged refills. She could hardly contain what she felt on being up close to him.

The sleeves of his casual white shirt were rolled slightly, displaying his lean tanned arms. As she stood, dutifully watching the diners, she imagined those strong arms wrapped around her. The thought was more delicious than the chocolate parfaits that were storming out of the kitchen.

When the last customers finally left, one of the waiters locked the front door and turned the sign to 'closed'. The chefs cleaned the kitchen while the rest of the staff cleared the remaining dishes, swept the wooden floors and re-dressed the tables.

Kes stood polishing glasses as Ruby collected her handbag.

She called 'good-night' to everyone and started to walk out.

Just as he thought she was slipping away, she turned. A sweet smile broke across her face as she came back to the bar. Quite out of the blue, she volunteered a compliment about his paintings, "Kes, I just wanted to say, your artwork is amazing. A few of the customers passed comments about that big one at the top of the stairs. You're a great artist. I really like your style."

A reply flashed through his head, "I've got a whole gallery you could visit in my bedroom," but he restrained himself. Instead he casually offered a "Thanks," put down the cloth and picked up his keys.

As he stepped out from behind the bar, they ended up making their way to the side exit together. Manoeuvring through a tight space, there was definitely an electricity building between them. He opened the door onto the car park and strolled up to his van. He felt a rush of adrenalin as he got in and called back to her, "Ruby, there's a party going on at my place tonight, d'you wanna come?"

Elated, she walked over to the driver's window. "I'd love to, but could you drop me at my flat first so I can change out of this uniform? It's only a couple of minutes away."

"Sure. Jump in." He was shocked at how he managed to sound so chilled.

Waiting outside her apartment, he tapped his fingers impatiently on the steering wheel. He couldn't have been more delighted at how things were progressing; his eyes were stuck to her front door.

As she stepped out onto the pavement, he wasn't disappointed. She'd let down her long blonde hair, and it cascaded over her shoulders.

Wearing a pair of pale blue jeans, a white vest top and a huge smile, she climbed into the passenger seat. Her delicate perfume filled the van with a sparkling floral scent.

He felt high as he drove home with Ruby beside him. When they stopped at traffic lights, he got to glance at little details about her. He noticed she was wearing flip-flops. They were glitzy and glamorous, but well suited to the environment he was taking her into. She was definitely his kind of girl, unlike Blake's who always looked like they were about to go on stage.

Drawing closer to Trevanna Bay, he felt proud about showing her the beach house. It had kudos.

She was so excited about being with him; she wouldn't have cared if he'd lived in the scruffiest of bedsits in a tiny box room.

Nevertheless, turning into the driveway, she gasped, "Wow, is this really where you live?"

"Afraid so. Jump out and come and meet my crazy friends."

The open plan living area pulsated with psychedelic funk music. The atmosphere was dense with a heavy sensuality. Twenty or so people were well spread out. Bawdy and unrestrained, they lounged, danced, drank, smooched, and smoked pot.

As Kes walked in with Ruby, he found himself wanting to guard her. Fiercely desiring to keep her all to himself, he couldn't let her loose in that jungle. The guys would have swooped in like vultures. Inviting her to the party had been his covert way of dating her, but now, he longed to get her alone.

It would be too forward to suggest going up to his bedroom.

He had to play this tactfully. Pouring her a large white wine he seated her at the breakfast bar and stood close.

Blake spotted them from across the room and made his way over. His shirt was unbuttoned and he looked wasted.

Stumbling up from behind, he leant his chin on Kes' shoulder. Clumsily whispering into his ear, his lips brushed Kes' lobe. "Hot chick!"

As Blake continued murmuring something obscene, Kes kicked his foot back to push him off. He knew what his mouth was capable of and didn't trust what might come out next.

Completely possessive of Ruby, he wouldn't allow Blake to screw things up for him.

He glanced around for Taran who was nowhere to be seen. "Where's Tar, Blake?"

"I dunno, down on the beach I think."

Turning to Ruby he suggested a stroll. When she responded positively, he led her swiftly outside.

Guiding her through the garden in the dark, Kes picked up the narrow path that led down to the sand. Using his phone torch he lit the way, turning to help her as they went. In doing so there were several occasions where he reached out his hand to steady her. It provided such a natural way for them to touch. They both felt a rise in their pulses.

The heat of the day had long passed. A little way up the beach a group of people sat around a bonfire.

Taran looked up as they approached. "Hey, mate, come on over, have a beer. Sorry we haven't got any food left but there's plenty up at the house. Blake's ordered in loads of stuff. Have you been up there?"

"We stuck our faces in for a few minutes. It's heaving."

Kes stood aside so he could introduce Ruby. "Taran, this is Ruby, she works at Jett's."

Taran smiled at her, immediately understanding why Kes was with her. She was very much his type – simple, not overdone and very pretty.

"Hi, Ruby, how's it going? Come and join us!"

Kes felt secure with Taran. Ruby would be out of harm's way in his company. Unlike Blake, he had good character. He always behaved honourably. Kes secretly admired him and listened carefully to what he had to say.

Although Taran was not a risk, he was incredibly good looking. The girls at college often discussed who they thought was the hottest out of the two of them and usually concluded they were both equally attractive but in different ways.

Kes still wanted to be shrewd with Ruby though. She was a rare find.

He needn't have worried. Ruby's desire was totally for him.

The guys and girls sitting around the fire were mostly lifeguards and surf instructors who had come to Trevanna Bay to work the season. Mellow and easygoing, they were enjoying the freedom the beach offered. One of them had brought down his guitar and was playing a soothing melody that echoed the rhythm of the waves.

Ruby tested out Kes' intentions towards her by sitting as close to him as she dared. Although she'd been exhausted after work, there was no way she would have turned down his invitation. As the warmth from the fire lifted the chill from her body, she rested back on the sand and enjoyed this cosy and romantic end to the day.

Kes relaxed with a couple of beers and gradually drew his body closer to hers; before long neither one of them could have been in any doubt of their feelings towards each other. Ruby subtly used every movement to edge her way into his personal space. The tension between them continued to build when, reaching for his drink, his hand gently swept her leg. Her body language signalled her approval. As she twirled a strand of her hair through her fingers, their eyes met in the firelight. They expressed a communication that words were unable to say. Both of them sensed something was imminent.

Assured of her compliance, he knew he could come on stronger. Rising to his feet, he proposed they head back to the house. Almost sedate, she picked herself up from the sand, dizzy with happiness.

Leaning into him as they walked back up the beach, she felt both sleepy and captivated. Slipping his arm around her shoulder, he pulled her into his side. As they reached the dunes, the dam that had held back their passion burst. Holding her face in his hands he kissed her. The gentleness gave way to fervour.

Roused by the morning light streaming through the window, Kes opened his eyes and met Ruby's gaze. She had been awake for a while just staring at him. Under the warmth of the cover, he reached out and pulled her to him, letting out a satisfied groan.

The garments strewn across his bedroom floor told a story; some of them had fallen onto an empty pizza carton.

Closing his eyes again, he went back to sleep.

Tears trickled down her face making her lips taste salty. It had been her first time with a guy. She had completely given herself to him.

Staring down at the messy floor, with her clothes lying alongside the discarded takeaway packaging, a painful thought entered her mind. Had she meant anything more to him, than a late night snack to satisfy his appetite?

Lust wasn't the same as love, but it was easier.

Kes slept while Ruby lay in bed thinking.

Memories surfaced of her early years, when she had first learnt about the differences between a man and a woman. Back then it had seemed embarrassing and worrisome.

Growing up, she'd dreamt of the day she would meet someone special and give to them the deepest treasure she possessed – herself.

In the early hours, that precious moment had unfurled. When she'd surrendered her body to him, she'd released her soul.

After about half an hour, she sat up and looked out to sea. Knowing that her heart had been opened to him, there was a lot at stake. Sanity rested on soundness of judgements.

Did he have it in him to be able to love and cherish her?

Yes, she'd been flighty, but she still hoped she'd found the right guy.

Slipping out of the cover, she went to his en suite and showered. She put a squirt of his toothpaste onto her finger and wiped her teeth with the fresh minty gel. Anticipating the warmth of his arms, she hoped for some prized time with him before he took her home for the lunchtime shift. Trying hard to be as quiet as possible, so as not to disturb him, she carefully closed the shower screen and went back to the bed.

He had gone.

Pulling on her crumpled jeans and top, she went down into the kitchen.

Blake was playing on the console. He didn't even turn around to speak. Walking over to him, she asked if he'd seen Kes. Without looking up at her, he mumbled, "He's gone surfing with Taran; he knows you're working this lunchtime and asked me to tell you to get the bus. Leave your number. He'll ring you."

The timetable for the country bus route was sporadic. An old lady at the bus stop told her it could be a bit hit-or-miss. Her anxiety over Kes' behaviour was intensified with the fear of being late for work. She had to go back to her flat and change first. When eventually the bus arrived, she was fretful and angry. Resting her head on the window as she travelled home, she felt dreadful.

Last night had been so amazing, she didn't regret it, but she was alarmed that he had treated her so casually.

Fear stabbed her mind as she struggled to read the situation. Why hadn't he been waiting for her when she came out of the shower? How could he have gone off without saying good-bye? Didn't he want to take her home? He had been so into her the night before. Was surfing more important to him than her?

There were so many painful questions.

She attempted to ignore her doubts and concerns by determining he was a prize worth sacrificing herself for. The memory of how good it had felt in his arms overruled common sense. She could still feel the intoxicating warmth of his body. There was such a yearning inside her to belong to someone; she wanted Kes to be that person.

Intent on doing all she could to keep him, she would happily put up with his selfishness. It was a price she was willing to pay.

If she was to continue with this relationship, logic would have to be buried and wisdom take a back seat. Already, her mind could feel the cost.

Dating him would be dangerous.

At work, she was unusually clumsy and distracted. Jett could see she wasn't herself. "What's up, Ruby love?" he enquired. "Have a late night?"

"Yeah, Kes invited me to a party back at his beach house."

Jett's eyes widened. "Say no more. I knew he was pumped over you. He was all cranked up when he came in with the artwork. He's a quick mover isn't he? Make sure he treats you as you deserve. He's fortunate to find a girl like you. Nice out on the coast at Trevanna Bay, isn't it?"

Ruby didn't answer any of his comments. She was so full of apprehension. She couldn't possibly tell him all that had gone on.

Jett was in many ways a father figure to her. She wanted to cry. Let him know how scared she was. Beg him to tell Kes that she was worth caring for. Instead she just smiled politely.

The second she got out of work she grabbed her phone. Kes had called.

Her heart leapt with joy.

Eagerly playing back the message, she heard his voice.

"Hi Ruby, I was so burning after last night, I had to throw myself in the sea!"

She burst out laughing, releasing the hours of bottled up tension. Everything felt perfect again and she couldn't wait to see him.

"I'll be in work tonight. I'll bring you back afterwards and we can take up where we left off."

As he managed the bar that evening, their eyes kept meeting in a knowing way; she walked tall, delighted that his gaze was continually all over her.

She kept smiling at him, languishing in the fact that she was *'the girl he was seeing'*.

Soon she'd be back in his arms again.

From then on their relationship intensified. Night flowed into night and they saw each other constantly.

She adored him. He enjoyed her.

෨

Ruby quickly learned that in order to relate to Kes, she had to be content with superficiality. In many ways, he was emotionally unavailable. This meant that she had to keep a tight lid on her feelings and suppress the issues she longed to discuss.

He controlled everything by living in a casual, lightweight manner, avoiding any sentimental pressure. Secretly, she knew that if she'd ever dared to raise her deeper questions and needs, he wouldn't have had any answers to them.

Her fulfilment in being with him had to come purely from their physical relationship and very little else.

He would never allow her to see any vulnerability and was very wary of demonstrating affection other than sexually.

The family that he had grown up in had shaped him that way. What he'd observed of his parents' relationship had not given him any hope for longevity with a partner. He hadn't seen much happiness or friendship in their marriage. In fact, it had been the opposite. They always seemed to be at war with each other and were miserable and angry most of the time. As far as he could see, his dad had been hard working and his mum had been hard work.

He'd watched the frustration as Dad had tried to please Mum but her needs never seemed to be satisfied. What Kes hadn't understood, was that her constant demand for his dad's attention had been her attempt to reach his heart. She'd made an idol out of him and seemed completely unfulfilled. Eventually, Dad had an affair, and what was already broken, fell apart.

All Kes knew to be safe ground was the outward pleasure found on the surface of a woman. Anything else was dangerous; to go mining for something additional could prove lethal and would probably end up with the roof caving in on his head.

Ruby gave up trying to unearth what she couldn't access, settling for the little of him that was obtainable. She grew to love his quick humour and his passionate ways.

But she never knew his heart. How could she fathom it, when he had never been there himself?

Chapter Seventeen

EVERYTHING CHANGES

BACK AT THE beach house, subtle changes were beginning to take place in everyone's lives. The only thing they really shared in common was the roof over their heads. The directions they were going in were becoming noticeably more separate.

It had been indistinct at first, but slowly they began to grow apart as they got active in different circles.

Taran took up work at the local surf school and spent lots of time teaching.

Blake got a job at the Trevanna Bay Hotel and continued to party hard in his spare time. If he wasn't hosting something at the house he would be out at someone else's place. It was common knowledge that he was regularly doing drugs.

Kes continued at the restaurant and spent lots of time with Ruby, either in his room or occasionally at her flat.

Bored with his job at Jett's, he became unsettled. It had served its purpose. He'd got Ruby. Now, growing restless, his creative gifting needed to be stretched. With his second year of college looming, he felt greedy over his time, not wanting to waste a moment unnecessarily to anything humdrum.

It wasn't long before an opportunity presented itself.

Strolling into the restaurant one Friday evening, he caught Jett very agitated. He'd just got off the phone from a call with his events manager and had something he needed to fix quickly.

"Don't know any DJs who could do a slot for me tomorrow night do you, Kes? The one Erin has booked has let her down."

Amongst his other acquisitions, Jett owned one of the best nightclubs around. Telling Kes his woes brought a swift solution.

"Jett, *I'm* your man. I've got my own style of mixing and I know how to combine great world music with dance rhythms. Give me a try. I'd love to do it."

"Yeah, but I've still got this bar to run," Jett protested.

Kes was already a step ahead of him.

"Dominic is only doing part-time waiting. He was telling me the other night how he needs extra hours. I could show him the ropes and he could easily cover it for you."

Jett admired Kes' resourcefulness, and agreed to test him out. Calling Erin, he told her he'd found a solution. When he got off the phone he looked less tense.

"Right, that's all sorted then. Give it your best shot and we'll see how you do. Here's Erin's number. She manages the place for me. Give her a ring and pop over to the club before tomorrow night to introduce yourself."

Almost instantly, Kes made *Attic* the coolest place to hang out for miles. Using electronic sounds fused with uplifting trance, he mixed in jazz undertones. Innovative and original, he was excellent at crafting together a number of scenes and styles. People flocked to the club when he was DJing.

Success brought admiration. The dance floor was a stage for parading girls and he was always the centre of attention. Everyone knew he was dating Ruby. Her beauty was hard to compete with, but his weakness lay in his inability to build beyond the external.

The foundations of his relationship with Ruby weren't strong.

Not being able to connect his passion to any rooted values, he was susceptible to skin-deep, fleeting temptation.

Ruby knew her position with him was exposed. Even though he appeared to be attached to her, there was nothing other than the physical dimension that held them together. Although he was totally gratified with her attractiveness, it was also a commodity carried by many other women. In the scene where he had immersed himself, there were loads of other girls constantly around him.

In truth, Ruby was terrified of losing him.

There was nothing more beautiful to her, than to lie with him under the sheets. There, beneath his body, in the dark, she would want to hold him forever. The torment for her was that in some respects, she could be anyone.

Desiring to be special to him, she hoped one day he would give her a sign of committment that singled her out as *his* woman – something that could seal her inmost heart with a promise.

Chapter Eighteen

BOYS WILL BE BOYS

K ES POURED HIMSELF an orange juice and sat at the breakfast bar reading a surf magazine. Taran had just left. He had a regular morning session down on the beach with a youth group. As usual, Blake was hung over and hadn't yet surfaced from his room.

A repeated, urgent pressing of the doorbell broke the silence and tore Kes away from his article. Begrudgingly, he whisked off through the passageway.

Flinging open the door, he was both surprised and annoyed to see Danielle Davis standing there.

The local glamour model was very well known by *lots* of guys in the area. Kes had frequently seen her in Attic.

Dressed in very little, she smiled confidently at him, flashing her long eyelashes.

"Oh, hi Kes, I didn't know you lived here. I was calling around for Blake. We're going together. Is he in?"

Eyeing her over, he could see that Blake's seasoned behaviour of 'any girl, any time, any place' was in full swing. Moving aside, he gestured for her to come in.

She'd just managed to step over the threshold when he imposed his footwear rule. "Sorry babe, you're entering a 'no-shoe zone'."

She frowned and reluctantly separated herself from her platforms, immediately shrinking five inches. Kes thought it was amusing. He looked her up and down as she sauntered through the hall in her hot pants and tiny top.

As an illustrator, he analysed her like a painting. He concluded that the ultra high-shine red coating on her toenails looked poisonous and her long sharp finger nails seemed capable of stabbing someone. That said, he figured she had her uses.

Still feeling guarded about who came around, he placed her in the front room and shot upstairs to inform Blake of her arrival.

Pushing the door, he discovered him sitting on his bed, laptop open, looking at his favourite porn site. His eyes were locked on the screen – they appeared black and dead like a predatory great white.

"There's a real live one of those waiting for you downstairs, Blake. How'd you get off with Danielle? Careful you don't catch something. She's toxic totty, mate, she gets passed around you know. She's always in the club with a different bloke."

Blake snapped his laptop shut, pulled on a T-shirt and made for the door.

"While you're here, Kes, I just want to talk to you about Ruby."

Kes tensed up, wondering what was coming.

"I thought you said girls couldn't move in. Are you breaking your own rules or is it that there's one rule for you and one for me? She practically lives here now!"

Kes smiled at him. "Yeah, but Ruby's different, she'll never take up a spare bedroom, she's my personal stash."

Taran didn't like the way either of them treated girls. Having two sisters, he hated the way men could devour without conscience. He was a safe pair of hands when the ladies were around. Always respectful and sincere, it wasn't that he didn't desire a relationship. It was just that he held out for certain principles. Getting into bed with a woman was a conclusion not a starting point.

He could always see past the external to the person inside and knew that just because a girl looked stunning on the outside didn't mean that she was good relationship material. For guys who just went for the outer packaging, the sexy dresses and lingerie were the wrappers to peel off to get to the goodies underneath. But Taran believed you could go deeper than that. He'd been around too many horror stories with guys who got hooked up with someone based on lust. Once they were 'caught', they got 'taught', and discovered that the real woman beneath was broken and difficult. The content wasn't always the same quality as the advertisement.

He wanted someone who didn't have all the baggage, and if she did, would at least be willing to own it as her own behaviour and deal with it. He'd watched many situations where two damaged people tried to build together only to end up in more pain.

A few days after Blake had started seeing Danielle, Taran came back from taking a surf lesson, to discover her sobbing her heart out on the doorstep. Slumped in a heap, with red eyes, she looked wild and angry.

Knowing Blake was always dating several girls at the same time, he guessed immediately what it was about. Fully aware of Danielle's lifestyle, he also knew Blake's disregard for her only served to highlight a whole heap of issues that ran through the core of her soul.

It was a repeated cycle – she would attract a man, get used and then be chucked away.

No serious guy wanted her as their regular girlfriend – there was too much stigma attached. You'd be seen as a laughing stock with poor judgement to date her for very long. If you dated her at all, everyone knew why.

Having spent all her energy and lots of money moulding herself into an object, she had become an image worshipped for sex rather than a person whose sexuality was just part of their identity. In gaining fame and notoriety, she had forfeited the lonely child within.

Taran could see past her raunchy appearance.

Reaching down for her hand, he drew her up from the floor. Two black lines of mascara trickled down her cheeks and her lipstick was badly smudged.

"Come on, Princess, let's get you a coffee."

Taking her down to the side entrance, they both walked in through the shower area.

"You go on through to the kitchen. Make yourself a drink or something. I'll get out of this wetsuit and be with you shortly."

As he began to shower, Danielle made her way through the hall. Instead of going into the living area, she raced up to Blake's room to see if he was hiding out. He wasn't there.

Still crying, she went back to the kitchen and waited for Taran. Before long he came in.

Wearing his usual beach house uniform of board shorts and T-shirt, he towelled over his damp, wavy hair.

A spicy, leathery fragrance hung all over him as he poured her a coffee. Grabbing a large pack of chocolate biscuits, he took it all across and sank down beside her on the settee.

"Come here," he said, reaching out his arm and embracing her.

Tucking her feet up, she drew near to him and cuddled into his chest. It felt solid and strong beneath his freshly laundered clothes.

Placing one of his hands on the top of her head, he tenderly stroked the crown and gave it a big, hard kiss. He spoke to her in a firm brotherly tone.

"Danielle, a heck of a lot of this you've brought on yourself, babe. You've set yourself up as an X-rated girl." He tipped her chin so she was looking into his eyes. "That's my code for girls like you – extra hot, extensions and extra parts!"

She giggled through her tears, like a little girl lost and in need of a dad.

Still holding her close, he gently told her off.

"Of course guys are gonna want you for one thing. See how you present it! They think it's all on sale in the shop window. You're more than that, honey. You're more than just your sex value. I've seen what it's like when you're down on the beach in your bikini – the guys can't take their eyes off you. I mean, how does that make you feel?"

It was the first time anyone had ever spoken to her about her feelings. She couldn't find an answer for a while. He remained silent, knowing she was wrestling with his question.

Lying against him, she could feel the steady beat of his heart; it was safe and reassuring. She dared to be vulnerable with him.

"I love the attention, Taran."

"Yeah, but once you get it, what happens then?"

"I dunno, I get asked out."

"And?"

"I go with a guy and it all ends up rubbish."

"Well, think it through, Danielle – why put it all on display like you're a commodity if you don't want the consequences? It's not just 'cause of Blake that you're unhappy, your life is chaotic; you go from one crisis to the next. There's only so much the human soul can absorb before it switches to overload. Don't sell yourself so cheaply down in life's bargain basement. You're worth more than that."

He paused. He knew his manner was serious, but her future happiness depended on the choices she was making. "I'm not gonna go easy on you either; you also manipulate, control and dominate guys. You gotta look at that if you want a successful relationship one day."

She didn't move. Snuggling up to him and listening to his pep talk was the loveliest thing she had done in ages. It was bliss to be this close to a man without any strings attached. She remained there for a good while, soaking it all in. Eventually responding, she sighed,

"Taran, you make me feel good about myself and bad about what I do. You're so different from the other guys. I don't know what makes you tick but keep ticking!"

Pulling in even closer to him, she kissed his chest.

"Careful, babe, I'm your friend but I'm also a full-blooded male. Have mercy on me!"

Trying really hard to respect his boundaries, she freed him from her grasp and kissed him on the cheek.

It was a sisterly kiss – the first kiss she'd given that wasn't a signal, in a long time.

Just at that moment, Blake walked into the room. Totally enraged by what he saw, he charged over and violently pushed Taran away from her.

"Get your own chick, Taran, don't steal mine!" His words were laced with expletives.

Taran leapt up, his eyes fierce.

"Danielle, leave now!"

It was a command and she instantly obeyed.

Not desiring to humiliate him, but rather to constrain him, Taran pinned Blake to the wall. He could have wiped the floor with him but his objective was to help him see sense.

Getting right into his face, he rasped, "Blake, come down off it! I'm not trying to take Danielle. You're out of control. You treat women like you're hanging out for the waves – pick one up, ride it in and wait for the next one to come along. People are getting hurt all around you. I wasn't touching her. I was comforting her, 'cause she's screwed up with people like you using her; and if you don't get that, it's because you can't see past her works of art."

Dropping him, he walked out of the room.

Chapter Nineteen

PROWLING LIONS

ERIN LEFT a message on Kes' phone.
"Hi Kes, when you come in tonight could you make it
twenty minutes earlier? I need to have a brief meeting with
you. Thanks. Catch you later."

Kes smiled to himself, he knew he was becoming hot
property at the club. Everything was working out perfectly.
His guaranteed regular slot would serve him well when
college started up again in a few weeks. Generating an
income from a job that he loved drove the fear of monotony
far from his door.

His music delivered, supplying energy from a great blend
of mixed beats and tempo. The dance floor was always

full during his set. The recent growth in the popularity of the night spot had to be attributed to him. Income had gone sky-high since he had been on the payroll. Jett was delighted with how well he was performing.

Erin knew Kes' worth.

Since she'd got her hands on the club, great improvements had been made to its infrastructure. She had then turned her attention to getting the best possible content.

Her degree in business management, along with her self-motivation, made her one of Jett's most valuable employees.

Rewarding her well, he had set her up in a plush town apartment and made sure she had a fine set of wheels.

Uncrossing her shapely, tanned legs, Erin stood up. Her black stilettos dug into the carpet as she whipped her phone from her handbag. Calling the doorman from her office, she sounded impatient. "Send Kes through the moment he arrives."

She was glad to be Kes' boss. Her position gave her an advantage – she could spend time with him under the guise of business. Many women would have loved to have had an audience with him; she could arrange to see him anytime she desired.

Kes was not unaware of her schemes. Reading her power games a mile off, he knew she enjoyed trying to entice and dominate him. Flattered, he went along with it, despite Taran cautioning him to be vigilant.

"She's like a lioness, Kes. Watch her, mate."

Whenever she phoned him or invited him into her office, he considered it harmless sport. Picking up on her seductive ways, he allowed her charm to entertain him. He loved frustrating her efforts by never giving much away.

He ignored Taran's warning that lionesses had a cunning way of creeping up on their prey; he believed he could outrun her.

When he entered the club that night, he looked fresh and ready for action. His healthy beach lifestyle meant he always had lots of strength and stamina. For entertaining clubbers into the early hours, it was needed.

The doorman informed him Erin was after him. "Her majesty's looking out for you. Very persistent she is. She's called me twice in the last fifteen minutes."

Kes' eyes sparkled with amusement. "Must be something urgent, eh?"

He popped down to her office, knocked on the door and went in.

Carefully poised on the leather sofa, she sat ready for the appointment.

Kes thought she looked staged and awkward, as if posing for a modelling shoot. Although her structured coral dress accentuated her curves, it looked tight and uncomfortable.

"Oh, hi Kes, thanks for coming in early, darling, I just wanted to see how everything's going for you as we plan ahead for the autumn months."

"Yeah, things are really cool thanks, Erin. Back to college in a few weeks, but doing my regular slot here will fit in well."

"That's great," she said, tipping her long brunette hair to the side and reaching down into her bag. "Let me check the dates leading up to Christmas with you. Do you foresee any clashes with things for college?"

"We get a few opportunities for showcasing our work at exhibitions, but I'll be sure to let you know if something's on the horizon. I'll try to give you plenty of notice."

Not being able to justify taking up any more of his time, she offered him a drink.

"Fancy a bourbon and coke?" Her voice was soft and caressing.

"Sure, one ice cube."

She strolled over to her mini bar, and poured two drinks. Passing him a weighty glass, she relaxed back on the sofa, fully conscious that her dress had slightly risen. She made no attempt to adjust it.

Sipping the smooth whiskey, he settled back into the chair. In the full knowledge of her pursuit, he rested his glass on his thigh and toyed with her.

"Saw you driving your hot wheels around town the other day. Nice little motor, Erin, it suits you."

"Thanks Kes, I think cars reflect our personalities, don't you?"

"That and our lifestyle; my blue camper van reflects mine. Carries my surf board and acts as a hotel."

She laughed. "Not my kind of hotel!"

"Oh, why's that then? I always get the best sea views and the bed is comfy enough. What else d'you need?"

She played with her hair and spoke slowly. "Waiters, cocktail bar... a good restaurant... bath oil... and crisp linen sheets."

He shook his head, grinning. "You're such an uptown girl, Erin. You ought to try downgrading a bit."

He couldn't imagine her walking back from a shower on a campsite. It made him all the more glad he was dating Ruby.

Her phone rang. It was Jett. Reluctantly answering it, she got waylaid for a good few minutes. As the call ended, Kes jumped up. His voice was full of life. "Well, I need to get the show going."

"Sure, off you go and fill the coffers. Keep me in my luxury hotels! Oh, how is the lovely girlfriend, by the way?"

Jealous of Ruby, she didn't give a hoot about how she was, but wanted to fish into his private life to check out the lie of the land.

"Ruby is one hot lady, Erin; she keeps me warm at night, especially in my camper van."

He winked at her and walked out.

Chapter Twenty

A LONG DAY ON THE BEACH

HERALDING ANOTHER GLORIOUS day, a blue, cloudless sky beckoned the masses to Trevanna Bay. The sea was balmy and its small waves were perfect for novice surfers.

Taran sat on the hot sand alongside a fellow instructor. A small group of youngsters were about to discover the joy of the sport for the first time. Each had been kitted out with a suitable board and waited in eager anticipation to enter the water.

Taran loved the process of mentoring. It was very rewarding for him to watch people's enjoyment of the ocean develop as a result of his teaching.

All the kids who attended surf school quickly grew to love him. He was very cool but also kind – a rich combination that made him everybody's favourite coach. It was easy for him to be enthusiastic. He regarded surfing as the most exhilarating outdoor pursuit anyone would want to take up.

Before he could get his class into the waves, he had to conduct a short beach session to explain technique and safety.

He put them through their paces, and his group were soon paddling out on their boards and catching some action. After a couple of hours, he brought them in from the waves, satisfied that they'd been given a great introduction to the sport.

As he walked up the beach to the surf hut, he noticed Danielle sunbathing.

Waving to her, he called across, "Soon as I've released the kids I'll be over."

Within twenty minutes he was lying next to her, sharing her towel.

She immediately examined his face for bruises and asked him how the scuffle had gone with Blake.

"Ah, nothing much happened. I just tried to get him to see some sense. He's living crazy at the moment. Doing a lot of drugs, partying too hard; he's looking really rough. Is he on coke?"

A faint smirk crossed her face. It spoke volumes. She rolled over and pretended to bury her head under her bag. She knew it was pointless trying to hide anything from Taran. He was always 'on the ball'.

Although she was used to being deceitful, she respected him too much to lie to him. "Yeah, he is, I've been with him when he's snorting coke. It passes around in our circles."

"Well, it's not doing him much good. He's so moody and agitated all the time. He hasn't spoken to me since the run in. There's a horrible atmosphere in the house, especially when we have to be in the same room. We just move around each other in silence, trying to keep out of each other's space." He ran his fingers through the sand, making patterns. "It's really sad to watch the change in him. He's such a brilliant photographer but he's shown no interest in getting out there and doing his thing with the camera. He's acting like a right loser."

Taran was shocked to see how quickly Blake had changed and lost the plot. Frustrated with the conversation, he changed the subject.

"Anyway, how are you doing since our little chat?"

"Could be better, but you got me thinking."

"Good. Make a go of it, Danielle. Don't let yourself be exploited. Show them you've got a bit of dignity."

"Yeah, I had a strange time the night after you spoke with me." She looked down. Although she wanted to talk, she felt uncomfortable getting this real. Avoiding eye contact, she continued, "I remembered being a little girl, watching beauty contests, seeing all the affirmation girls got for looking lovely and thinking 'I want that'. Funny, but I'm sure that's where it all started. That, and the fact my dad never seemed to want anything to do with me. Your dad's the first man in your life that you need to tell you you're beautiful. If he doesn't, you look for it somewhere else. Then it's too late because it all comes with conditions."

She rummaged in her handbag looking for her cigarettes. "Anyway, this is getting a bit too honest for me. I'm not used to baring my soul. D'you want an ice-cream, Tar?"

"No thanks, I need to head back to the house; gotta work on my surf website. Man, I had some little rebels in my class today!"

As they got up together, he was delighted that she put on her kaftan. Although it was very short and see-through, he knew it was her attempt at taking his advice.

"I do listen to you, Taran," she laughed.

Slipping his arm around her shoulder, he walked her up the beach to the kiosk. "At least someone around here does."

Kes was sitting alone, eating, when Taran came into the kitchen.

"Hi, mate, how did your surf class go?"

"Not bad, thanks."

"Listen, Taran, I've gotta whiz into town in a minute, but can we catch up later? I could do with a chat. Shall we go down on the beach tonight when everyone's gone home?"

"Sure, let's go about nine. It's packed out today. Most of them will have cleared off by then."

As the evening drew in, the pair of them lay out on the sand. The fading sunset gave way to the navy tones that replace light with darkness.

Kes had been mulling over the strained relationships in the house. At the beginning of the summer, everything had started out so untroubled and light-hearted. Now cracks were appearing. Left to fester, they could soon open up into a chasm.

"Blake told me you had a bit of a run in with him the other day. What was that all about?"

"Danielle – well, she was the catalyst. But it's a much deeper issue than her. I came back from the beach to find her in a right state; breaking her heart cause he's been at least triple timing her."

"She's probably doing the same to him!"

"Yeah, maybe, but he still needs to sort himself out; I took her in to try to calm her down and he went berserk thinking I was coming on to her. He's doing too many drugs, Kes. Danielle told me he's regularly snorting cocaine. It's making him paranoid. When it comes to women, he leaves his heart in the fridge. He's just selfish, mate."

"He told me a different story; he's mad at you, Taran."

"Well, I can't do much about that. I told him the truth and he didn't like it. It's definitely tense between us. Can we get off talking about him? It depresses me. How's everything at the club?"

"It's excellent. I love what I do and the money's good. It's not like I have to be there all the time either. Erin's divided it up well between me and the other DJs."

"Landed on your feet really, haven't you?"

"Yeah, it's a great venue, the regulars enjoy my set. It gives me a right buzz."

Taran was well aware of how popular Kes was becoming. People liked to be associated with him. Some of the kids down on the beach had been impressed that Taran not only knew him, but lived with him.

"Check out who your genuine friends are, though, Kes. It's really fickle out there, especially when you're the centre of everyone's attention – which you are, mate. Too many doors can open up for you and then suddenly, the choices in front of you will be overwhelming. You don't have to be a sacrifice to your own success or you'll find yourself split into little pieces. Ask yourself why people want to know you."

Kes laughed. "Tell me about it! Being the main man up there pulls all the groupies. And then there's the foxy lady! She keeps me entertained with all her strutting and feminine wiles. I catch her staring at me sometimes and she isn't afraid of letting me know that she's doing it – isn't that one of the signs of a woman being into you?" He rolled onto his side and took a big swig of beer. "You can pretty much guarantee she'll have something she needs to talk to me about, but when I get in her office it always turns into a drinking session. I just play along with it. She's wearing me down, Taran – she might just manage to catch me one of these days!" He sounded light-hearted, as if it was all a bit of a game.

Taran looked at him and shook his head. It bothered him that he could be so casual and flippant. "I'm serious man, when they pounce they tear everything apart! Don't let her do that to you, Kes. Ruby's a beautiful girl and I don't just mean her looks. She's nuts about you."

Taran often felt that Ruby's devotion to Kes was too one-sided. She was always willing to go the extra mile for him, putting herself out to please him.

Picking up on Taran's solemn tone, Kes changed the subject.

"What are your plans once surf school finishes?"

"I don't know yet. I just want to enjoy it 'til the very last moment. They'll keep the business going through the autumn at the weekends."

Staring up at the clear night sky, their eyes drank in the spectacular array of stars.

Taran whistled. "Wow, that looks awesome, doesn't it...? D'you ever wonder what life's all about, Kes? How we got here? Where we go when we die...? You know, what's the point of it all?" His eyes traced a constellation. "Looking up at those beauties and seeing the magnificence of the ocean, it's just amazing." Kes remained quiet but Taran continued to throw out his thoughts. "Don't you think it's crazy that the world is set up perfectly for us to live on? It's like a big daddy in the sky made a home for us, all fine-tuned to make life possible... I think evolution is a delusion – it's just a myth. Organisms are a product of design not blind chance...! D'you ever think about it, Kes?"

"No, Taran, I don't. I just think about what I'm having for my next meal and who's getting into my bed with me. You think too deeply, Tar. You're missing out on life, mate. You gotta grab what you can, when you can, and enjoy it. Let's walk back and pick up a Chinese; I need to call Ruby."

As they strolled off the beach, Taran felt restless. Everyone around him was so shallow. He was beginning to think he might need to move on. Why hang out with turkeys when you could soar with eagles? With the season drawing to an end, many of the lifeguards were moving to different countries to pick up an endless summer. Maybe he'd quit college and join them.

He thought of Kes trailing behind him on the path, through the dunes.

He really cared for him like a brother, but there was something destructive in Kes that concerned him.

Always living for pleasure and quick fixes, he wasn't astute when it came to building his life. He didn't think wisely.

Taran worried it might all come crashing down one day. It would be very hard to leave him but maybe it would work out for the best.

Jumping in the van together, they sped off to pick up a takeaway before it closed.

Taran was very quiet.

"What's up, Taran? Sorry if I dissed your philosophy, bro!"

"I might head out of here soon to stay with a mate in California. Catch the surf scene and shoot some pictures."

Kes hadn't seen any of this coming. Shocked, he turned to him and swore.

"Are you serious? What about college? What about us all living together? It won't be the same without you. You'd be leaving me with Flakey Blakey! I couldn't handle him without you being around. All joking aside, I'd miss you like crazy man! Don't go, Tar."

"I don't know for certain, but I'm definitely considering it."

As they sat and ate their meal together Kes was very subdued. He hadn't realised how great he felt being around Taran. There was a security he received from listening to his strong principles and ideas. Never in his wildest dreams would he have thought that Taran might leave. It had totally floored him and opened a gaping hole. Memories of feeling abandoned during his parents' divorce started to rise. Taran had once said something to him that seemed completely irrelevant at the time: "You never know the value of something until it's out of your reach. You never realise what you have in front of you until it's taken away."

It was beginning to make a bit of sense. Aghast at how depressed he felt, he went off to bed. He slept badly for the first time since they'd moved in.

Chapter Twenty-One

REVELATIONS

JETT LED THE last customers to the door. Bidding them 'goodnight' he locked up. Turning to his staff he thanked them for a great evening's work.

As Ruby started to assemble her things, he offered her a lift.

"I'm passing your flat, Ruby. I'll drop you off."

"It's okay, Jett. I'm meeting Kes at the club tonight. We're going back to a party at his place."

Jett smiled. Oh to have the energy to stay up all night. The distant memory didn't appeal to him anymore. "Then I'll drive you to the club."

His insistence persuaded her.

"Thanks Jett. I need to quickly change. Can you hang on a few minutes?"

He pulled up a bar stool. Having been married for twenty years, he knew how long a woman could take 'quickly changing'.

Ruby went off to the ladies' room and exchanged her uniform for a strapless red dress. She touched up her make-up and let down her hair. Weaving two tiny plaits into the front, she fixed them with a couple of bands. Slipping into a pair of kitten heels, she walked back into the restaurant.

Jett pretended to fall off his seat as she strolled over.

"Looking gorgeous," he laughed. "I hope Kes knows how fortunate he is. Come on, Cinderella, let's get you there before midnight!"

Always the perfect gentleman, Jett led her to his car and held open the passenger door. The vehicle reflected his character – strong, manly and reliable. As she settled into the boxy seat, she observed how the interior was also like him. It was very masculine and sophisticated. The gadget-packed dashboard and leather upholstery was typical of the quality he looked for in everything. It made her feel special to be sitting in such luxury.

As he swung in beside her and started up the engine, a feeling of safety and security swept over her. The scene was a cameo of his life. He was a man who was in control, knew where he was going and how to get there in style.

"Great car, Jett, I certainly landed myself in a carriage!"

"Kelly chose it," he grinned. "She's always got an eye for a good thing."

An image of his wife came into his mind. Her beauty had been burned into his brain. He knew she wouldn't be offended by him dropping Ruby off. There was no deficiency in confidence between them. Kelly completely trusted him and with good reason. When he'd made his marriage vows, he'd meant every word. If Jett set his mind to something he had the integrity to stick to it. He was a black and white type of guy. No messing. He hadn't achieved success in his personal life, or in the world of business, by being unfaithful or inconsistent.

He glanced at Ruby sitting there all young and pretty. A protective feeling rose up inside of him as if she was his own daughter. He was very fond of her and saw within her an innocent naivety. Her sweet nature reminded him of his Kelly – compliant and easy going. He smiled to himself. Well, she had been. She'd grown wiser with experience and was now very strong minded. They'd been through a lot, but it had all served to draw them closer together. Life's difficulties had strengthened them, resulting in a mutual respect for each other's willingness to battle through. They were both friends and lovers. He couldn't wait to get home to her.

Ruby unbuckled her seat belt as they pulled up outside the club. She smiled over at him. "Thanks Jett."

"Off you go then, honey. Have a great night. Tell Kes I'm watching him and that he needs to treat you good!"

Jett hated the thought of Ruby getting hurt. He wasn't blind when it came to Erin's manipulative ways. She was excitingly attractive and had the potential to be a snare. But he figured a man needed to stand on his own two feet, make his choices and take the consequences. He couldn't protect Kes from Erin. He only hoped he'd make wise judgements.

As Ruby started to get out of the car, she turned back. "Jett, I've been meaning to ask you something. Is there a chance I could do some overtime? It's Kes' birthday coming up next month and there's a special gift I want to buy him."

"You're a kind girl, Ruby. Yeah, I'm sure I can find you something extra. I'll sort the rota tomorrow and see what I can come up with."

The doorman waved to Jett and greeted Ruby.

Stepping aside, he welcomed her. "Looking for that man of yours?" he grinned. "He's in there somewhere. No one gets past here without me knowing about it."

Kes had finished his set an hour before but was nowhere to be seen. Ruby ordered a white wine and waited at the bar looking out across the crowded dance floor. Presently she shouted over to one of the bouncers.

"Where's Kes? Have you seen him?"

He came over and squeezed her shoulder reassuringly. "I'll try and find him for you."

A few minutes later Erin appeared. Walking straight up to Ruby, she planted a bright lipstick mark on her cheek.

"Ruby, my love, how sweet to see you!" Her perfume was strong and unpleasantly heady.

Ruby tensed up but managed to force a smile. "Hi Erin, can I get you a drink?"

"No thanks, love. I've had my quota tonight. Has a nasty way of clinging to the hips!" She ran her hands over her curvy lower body. Her tight fitted dress highlighted her figure.

Just at that moment Kes strolled up to the bar. He scrunched some of Ruby's hair in his hand and kissed her.

"Hi babe, ready to go? I've had a few drinks tonight.
We'll grab a taxi."
Ruby's eyes lit up. She instantly relaxed in his company.
He downed the remainder of her drink and led her out
of the club. Envious glances followed them. Many women
longed to be in her place, going home with Kes.
Jumping into the cab, they sped off.
Erin's perfume went with them.

When they arrived at the beach house the party was
pumping. It was a warm night and all the doors were open.
Bodies were everywhere – guys and girls, soaking up
the lustiness of the atmosphere. The music throbbed, soft
lights flickered, booze was flowing, mirrors smudged with
cocaine lay on the dining table and the sweet pungent smell
of weed wafted through the rooms. People lounged outside
on the patio amidst colour-changing solar globes.
Kes was already used up from a night DJing in the
same kind of surroundings. It didn't take long before
he wanted to get away from everyone. He'd recently
strung up a Mexican hammock between the outside wall
and his balcony railings. The thought of lying out on it
with Ruby snuggled into him was irresistible. He grabbed
a six-pack and a bottle of wine and went upstairs. Ruby
followed willingly; she was glad to be getting alone with
him.
Although the pulse of the music vibrated throughout the
whole house, his uncluttered room felt serene compared to
the chaos downstairs. The low level bed was neatly made

with fresh sheets. It was perfectly positioned to catch the
sea breeze floating through the open balcony door.

Kes went out and placed the drinks on the patio table.
Sitting down, he pulled the ring on a beer and tried to relax.

Ruby looked into his wardrobe and checked through some
of her belongings. She always kept extra clothes over there,
along with numerous bottles of toiletries and cosmetics.
Exhaustion from the hectic evening in the restaurant made
her long to slip between the sheets. Instead, her waitressing
skills were once more employed.

Kes called out to her, "Ruby, I'm gonna take a shower.
Can you be a love and pop down to get me something out
of the fridge? I'm starving but I can't face that crazy lot. It's
like a zoo down there!"

He no longer feared anyone getting too close to her.
Everyone knew she was taken and her devotion to him was
unquestionable.

Within twenty minutes, she was back in the room with
a platter of cold meat, cheese, salad and bread. Kes was
already out of the shower, sitting on the patio in a pair of
fresh jeans. He looked handsome and invigorated with his
hair hanging damp against his neck.

He sat swirling bourbon, having fetched a bottle from the
shelf in his room. Once home to a pile of art books, it had
recently become stocked up like Erin's office bar. Heavy
drinking was one of the consequences of working at the
club. He fiercely dismissed any suggestion of it being a
problem. But those close to him could see an escalation in
both quantity and frequency.

Taran had noticed and commented. "Kes, do you realise
how much you've been hitting the hard liquor recently?"

Laughing it off, he blamed it all on Erin. "She corrupts me after work, Taran. What's a man to do?"

"Well, watch it, bro, you'll think you're in control until it grips you like a viper."

A bonfire glowed into the night sky from down on the beach. The full white moon highlighted the crest of the waves.

Ruby looked out across the peaceful scene. "D'you want to walk down and catch up with Taran and the guys after you've finished that food?" She could tell he was uptight. "It might help you unwind a bit."

Kes reached for his glass and slurped back the whiskey as if it was water. It was a poor attempt at burying his thoughts about Taran. He felt uneasy about him leaving. The fear gave way to anger.

"Nah, I'm happy here with you, Ruby. Let 'em all get on with it. I've got you and the view. That's enough."

As he spoke, she detected a wavering in his speech. He stumbled slightly as he dropped down into the hammock. She climbed in with him and cuddled into his side.

For a few minutes, all seemed well with the world. Their warm bodies softly curled into one another as a gentle breeze rocked them.

If only they could have frozen time and held on to that moment. Such was the feeling of blissful content. Their lives would have seemed perfect. But external interruptions crowded in. As Ruby reached for her wine, the hammock tilted and she misjudged the angle. The whole contents of the glass tipped all over her dress. She excused herself and disappeared off to the bathroom, taking advantage of the mishap by getting ready for bed and stepping into a steaming hot shower.

Alone with his thoughts, Kes' peace of mind was challenged with all manner of intrusions – Taran possibly leaving, college looming, Erin pressurising.

His usual happy-go-lucky outlook was getting squeezed.

The sight of Ruby standing in the doorway wrapped only in a towel, served to relieve some of his stress.

"Time to hit the sack," he smiled, lifting himself out of the coloured meshing. He went over to the bedroom door and bolted it. It had been a smart move to attach the security fixture a few days before.

With hordes of people in the house, the probability of odd bods wandering in on them was very high. During parties, strays from Blake's menagerie of friends had often found their way into his room.

After such a long day, half an hour of unbridled passion left them completely spent. Ruby felt so in love with him. Their physical intimacy had unlocked her heart.

She made a risky attempt at bringing out her feelings. In doing so she tried to share a deeper communication than the language of their entwined bodies. Lying beneath him, feeling the strength of his embrace and the steady rhythm of his breathing, she dared to open up a conversation about how much he meant to her.

"You know that first night we got together...?" She paused until she knew she had his full attention.

As he softly kissed her face, she carried on, "I'd never been with a guy before, Kes. You're the only one. I don't ever want there to be anyone else."

She waited anxiously for his response, hoping it would hit him like some great revelation. Maybe it might draw out of him a desire for a more serious commitment.

She could play all the details of their first night together in her head like a movie, remembering every aspect.

To him, it was all a big blur. He'd slept with her so many times since then, he couldn't count and he certainly didn't keep track of any of it. The only thing that touched him from what she'd disclosed was his sense of being unrivalled and matchless.

The emotional pressure from her probing made him feel uncomfortable. He could tell that this was a calculated moment. Not prepared to give any ground that might make him vulnerable, he made light of her intensity by throwing out a casual joke.

"Hey, Ruby, your first time ever, huh? Well, babe, you chose good!"

It wasn't the response she'd been longing for but his flippancy was enough to satisfy her. She found his humour both amusing and seductive.

He turned away and she pressed up against his back, delighting in the fact she was so close to him.

Before long, she had fallen asleep.

A light flashed on his phone. Reaching over for it, he read an incoming text.

A little drunk and a whole lot lonely, Erin had moved in for the kill.

Her obsession with him spilled out onto the screen. "I've been thinking about booking a night in your hotel. Do you have any dates available?"

The spontaneous message caught him off guard. All these beautiful women desiring to be with him had greatly massaged his ego; he had been pushed into being impetuous. The dangerous mix of booze and careless superficiality made him feel invincible.

He acted rashly.

He messaged her back, grinning. "The bed at the beach house is better than the van. Which night do you want?"

Both irritated and flattered, he almost muttered out loud, "Okay lady, let's get this thing done and dusted. You've been asking for this and you just might get it!" Placing the phone back on the cabinet, he drifted off to sleep. He felt strong and in control.

The stark morning light woke Ruby first. Stretching, she rolled over and looked at the clock. It was 10am. Sensing the disturbance, Kes groaned and buried his head in the pillows.

Ruby got up, freshened herself in the bathroom and picked out a set of clothes.

Almost instantly, she started tidying up from the night before. It felt like second nature for her to clean. She went out onto the balcony and brought in the glasses, plate and cutlery.

Taran met her going down the stairs. They often cleared up together on the morning after a party. He smiled at her. "Brace yourself!"

Giving each other a knowing look, they stepped into the main living space.

The patio doors were wide open and bodies were scattered everywhere. Plates with discarded food, glasses, bottles, smudged mirrors and rolled bank notes littered every available surface.

"Okay, time to move on, party people," Taran called, shaking a few bodies.

As they woke up, he encouraged them to call for taxis. A large group of them went down to the beach and it wasn't long before they had all disappeared.

Ruby went around with a bin bag while Taran gathered the dishes. Between them they loaded the dishwasher, rinsed the rest of the crockery ready for the second cycle, vacuumed, polished the furniture and straightened out the settee. It wasn't long before the whole place was in order.

Blake was nowhere to be seen and Kes was still fast asleep.

Taran whisked up a smoothie and at the same time kept one eye on the surf; it didn't look very promising. The bay was like a millpond and the waves nonexistent. Ruby made a coffee and joined him on the sofa.

"How's everything in the wonderful world of Ruby, then?" he asked.

"Well, work's great. I love how Jett runs things. He's a good boss, very fair, fun to be around and steady. He leads from the front. You know, he does his share of things and rewards us when it all goes well. Everyone gets on with each other and really it's quite a family kind of atmosphere most of the time."

"That's brilliant. I feel the same with my work at the surf school. They're a great bunch of people. How's everything going with matey upstairs?"

Her eyes shone when he mentioned Kes, but she also looked pained. It was obvious she was devoted to him.

"It's amazing, Taran. Kes is a lovely guy…"

"And?"

"It's just…"

"What?"

"It's just… I'm not sure where it's all going."

Taran knew what she had come up against in Kes – his inability to go any deeper in relationships than the surface. He gave Ruby all he could, all he was willing to share, but no one could get past the wall he'd built up to protect himself. He was blind to the fact that although he didn't trust people, he was also untrustworthy.

Ruby knew she was safe to share her concerns with Taran.

"I get really worried when he's at the club; he's always got so many women around him all the time. Especially Erin, she's so forceful. I've seen the way she looks at him sometimes. I constantly fight my feelings towards her, but what can I do? He has to see her regularly. She's his boss. I get scared she'll move in on him, Taran."

He felt sorry for her. He knew she had just cause to feel threatened. "Do you try to talk to him about it?"

"Not specifically about her, but whenever I try to share stuff with him – you know, how I feel about things – he just brushes it off or makes a joke about it."

All the talk about Kes stirred her desire to be near him. "Anyway, I'm going to get him up. Watch this. It works every time!"

She went to the stove and put on some bacon and eggs. She smiled over at Taran and opened the living room door. "It's a sure way of coaxing him out of bed!"

Within ten minutes, Kes was sat up at the breakfast bar with a loaded plate.

Blake followed.

Ruby made him breakfast also. He'd just finished the last mouthful when a girl stuck her head around the door looking for him. Pushing his dishes aside, he left the room.

Kes tapped out a rhythm on the counter with his fingers. He appeared carefree and nonchalant. Eventually, he stood up, stretched and poured himself a strong black coffee.

"Taran might be leaving us, Ruby," he announced. "Isn't that right, Tar? Thought anymore about it?"

Even though he tried to sound blasé, they could hear the disquiet in Kes' voice.

"Yeah, I'm trying to make plans to head out of here in a few weeks."

Ruby looked stunned, instantly feeling a grave concern about him not being around. He was a good influence on Kes. "Where would you go, Taran?"

"California. One of the lifeguards I've been working with has invited me over. You've met Jayden – the guy who's always playing his guitar on the beach at night."

Kes looked disinterested and wandered over to the window to check out the surf. It was as flat as he felt.

"We'd miss you." Ruby spoke in a dampened tone.

"Thanks. I'd miss you all too, but I think it's a right move."

In Kes' world, everything suddenly felt unstable. He couldn't define why, but the elation he'd experienced when they'd moved in seemed to be slipping out of his grasp. "Everything was great a few weeks ago, but we've all changed since the beginning of summer."

Taran spoke up. "Have we changed, Kes? Or have circumstances just shown up what's really in us?"

Ruby caught an expression of annoyance on Kes' face. He looked angry, almost betrayed.

Chapter Twenty-Two

LAST SUPPER

A FEW DAYS later, Taran sat on the sofa with his laptop, uploading images onto his surf photography website. It had become a lucrative business for him alongside his coaching. When he wasn't teaching people to ride the waves, he'd been taking pictures of them in the surf. As the holidaymakers returned home, they were delighted to purchase images of themselves having fun in the sea.

Blake attempted civil conversation. "Great pictures, Taran, landed yourself a handy little nest egg there, haven't you? It was a smart idea to get them to sign up for surf lessons *and* photographs."

He was secretly jealous of him for being so industrious. Blake was very capable of producing excellent work but hadn't applied himself over the holidays. Instead of allotting time to develop his art, he had put it all on the back burner, hoping the deal with the calendar would come through.

He pressed Taran. "Are you still up for a joint exhibition later in the year?"

The largest gallery in town had expressed an interest in housing a presentation of their photography. The curator had studied their work at the college summer show. He thought their styles complemented each other and would work well displayed together.

"Yeah, count me in. It's just I probably won't be there in person."

"Why's that?"

"I might not be around."

"That's vague."

"Oh, come on, Blake, you're the King of Vague!"

"Surely you'll want to attend it. Think of the potential leads and opportunities that could come from it."

"I'm planning to go out to California."

Blake looked taken aback. He raised his voice. "Why? What about everything here – college, this place? We'd have to get someone else in. Kes might even try to replace you with Ruby! That would be so boring! She treats me like my mum does, always tidying up and looking at me disapprovingly."

Blake's phone rang. By a strange coincidence, it was his mum. He held the phone away from his ear and screwed up his face. After a couple of minutes he drew it back in and answered his mother's complaint.

"Sorry Mum, I've been really busy working on stuff for college, happy belated birthday anyway." He spoke as if he was smiling but his grimace gave away his true feelings.

He wriggled out of her verbal stranglehold by excusing himself. "Gotta rush, catch you later, Mum."

He stared at Taran in dismay. "Women, they're hard work!"

Kes had entered the room prior to the phone call. He was mad at Blake for his comment about Ruby and was amused to see him in discomfort.

"You've been doing too much pot and coke to remember Mummy's birthday, Blakey-Boy, not good!"

"Ah, shut it," Blake growled. He seized the opportunity to taunt Kes. "How come Ruby's always at the restaurant lately? Maybe she's enjoying that new waiter's company a bit too much. What's he called? Dominic? Or could it be Jett who's getting her attention? He's loaded and drives a flashier car than you."

Kes rose to his provocation.

"Not all girls are like the ones you hang out with, but you wouldn't understand that. I hate to break this to you, but Danielle changes blokes like she does her handbags."

Blake didn't care about Danielle's habits as long as she occasionally popped over. He carried on baiting Kes.

"Dreadlock Sam was hovering around Ruby the other night at the party. You know, when you'd sent her down to wait on you. You were doing your usual 'Mr Anti-Social' bit, but he was having a good old chat to her. I think he was admiring her plaits by the way he ran one of them through his fingers."

"Blake, you need educating, mate. Ruby's got class. It's a quality that's sadly lacking in your choice of ladies. She's a 'one man woman', so don't put your deranged thinking into my business. Guess what comes from soaking your brain in a paranoid fog of drugs? You get crazy notions! As for Sam, he's always out of his head just like you, but if he did lay a finger on her, I'll be having a little word with him not to touch things that don't belong to him."

Blake conceded and gave up the banter. He was well aware that his drug habit was getting out of control. Privately he valued the fact that they challenged him about it. At least someone cared. He slapped Kes on the back and gave a weak apology.

Taran laughed. "You two are as screwy as each other. Come on. Anyone want to walk on the beach?"

They all went down. Somehow they knew it was an attempt to capture what they'd felt together at the beginning of the holidays.

They abandoned themselves to fooling around – charging onto the empty beach, watching the seagulls flee before them. There was no intense conversation, no arguing; just happy, carefree friends, enjoying the great outdoors.

Blake pulled the ring on a can and passed the beer around. "I propose a toast. May we always have blue skies over us and beautiful birds under us."

After a couple of hours, they returned to the house, weary and hungry. Kes emptied the fridge of nearly all its contents and worked his magic. He quickly prepared a massive feast of leftovers.

Taran set the dining table. The unusual formality carried a sombre air, almost like that of a 'last supper'. As they sat together, restless waters churned beneath their jovial personas.

Taran knew he would be leaving soon. Having finalised his travel plans that very afternoon, he'd already booked his flight.

Kes secretly wrestled with Ruby's absence. Although he was illiterate when it came to reading his own emotions, somewhere inside he felt lonely and neglected.

Blake was skilled at putting on a front. Nothing ever seemed to affect him. Behind the deceptive veneer, he lived a life of quiet desperation. Often, when he was alone in his room, anxiety would so grip him that his whole body would go into involuntary spasms. Overwhelming panic would be followed by very strong, uncontrollable jerks and heart palpitations. He never told anyone and as long as he kept himself distracted from thinking too deeply, he could keep up the facade. Drugs and constant visits from girls served to divert his mind from his fears and bring temporary relief.

Chapter Twenty-Three

GOOD-BYES

DANIELLE SAT IN the coffee shop waiting for Taran. He was fifteen minutes late.

As she checked over her make-up, he strolled in and apologised.

"Sorry to keep you, just lots of bits and pieces that I needed to sort."

She snapped her compact mirror shut and dropped it into her tote bag. "That's cool, Taran. I understand. I bet you've had quite a few people to see before you leave."

He ordered a green tea and drew up a leather tub chair. "How's everything going for you, anyway?"

"Pretty good, thanks. I've got a big modelling shoot coming up soon." She fiddled with one of her gold hoop earrings. "It'll help replenish my bank account."

"Well great, but make sure they don't jerk around with you. You gotta ask yourself, 'How much do *I* pay for the money I earn?' A fat wallet isn't everything. Peace of mind is priceless. How are you doing in the relationship department?"

His question stirred a longing in her heart. She closed her eyes for a moment and groaned, "Oh, don't ask! Could be better; I need someone like *you,* Taran! That would sort things out for me."

She laughed. Although she would have loved to date him, instinctively she knew it wasn't so much Taran she needed as something he carried within him. Going out together would ruin their relationship.

Smiling warmly, he looked her straight in the eyes. "You know what I think? You should keep away from all the poser guys you hang out with and get yourself a *real* man. A good, honest builder or painter-decorator type – someone who knows how to work hard with his hands, spend his energy on something worthwhile and would value coming home to you at the end of a long hard day. You need a man who'd cherish you and not want you as a trophy date to be seen clubbing with."

She checked over her nail extensions, examining them for damage. "Can you imagine me at home making pie and chips for someone's tea?" She giggled, quite liking the thought of what he was saying.

He leant forward, resting his arms on his thighs in an easy relaxed manner. "Yeah, I could. It would do you the

world of good to be a bit normal. Become someone's
Mrs and live a quieter life. You've made enough
money already with your modelling. You could go
off and make cupcakes; set up your own business doing
something completely different!" He screwed up an
empty sugar wrapper and threw it at her playfully. It
bounced off her pendant and rolled down the front of
her gaping vest top.

"Slam dunk, Taran," she laughed.

A joke flashed through his mind. "I could hit that target
with my eyes shut," but he thought better of it. He wanted
to steer her away from her grand frontage always being the
centre of attention. He hadn't meant the paper to land where
it did and she was already on the receiving end of much
ridicule.

"Seriously, Taran, thanks for your friendship over the
summer. I don't know what I would have done without you.
You've seen me at my worst and you're still happy to hang
out with me. Keep in touch won't you? I hope you have a
fabulous time in California."

Days turned into weeks. College started up again and
Taran left for other shores.

It wasn't a big send-off. Kes said he was too busy at the
club to do much. He hated 'good-byes' and wanted to avoid
any awkward moments.

He walked into Taran's room as he was packing his last
few bits.

"Well, have fun, mate. Keep in touch."

"Yeah, Kes, it's been a good time. Look after yourself and that girl of yours. Keep an eye over your shoulder for what's stalking you."

With that he was gone. Kes looked down from his balcony as the front door slammed and a car pulled up with a couple of the lifeguards in it.

He poured a whiskey and surveyed the bay. The weather was turning. There was a chill in the air. The heat of summer and all of its promise was fast fading. The house was going to feel empty without the fullness of life that Taran exuded.

Kes went back to college for three and a half days of the week. He also put in three nights at the club but his usual joie de vivre had taken a big hit.

Chapter Twenty-Four

SECRETS

RUBY SETTLED WELL into the time-consuming rota at the restaurant. Much to Kes' annoyance, she worked every hour she could, putting herself forward as the first port-of-call if any member of staff was absent. She was happy for Jett to contact her at the last minute but this only added to Kes' frustration.

"Why do you need to work so much? Ease up on it, Ruby."

He was irritated with her lack of availability. She excused herself by saying Jett was under pressure and she wanted to show willing.

Jett rewarded her dedication by slipping her the odd twenty pound note. He admired her effort and only hoped Kes would value it too.

With his birthday looming, Kes tried to fix something up with her.

"Don't work next Saturday, alright? Tell Jett there's no way you're going in. If you don't, I will!"

"It's fine. I've already booked it out." She acted in a cool manner. He didn't have a clue she'd been planning his big day for weeks.

She wanted everything to be perfect – a birthday that would be beyond compare.

"What do you want to do, Kes? I could come over and cook your favourite meal? How about we put the patio heater on upstairs and sit out on your veranda? In any case, I'll be staying over and making you a special breakfast on Sunday morning. We can have a lovely lazy weekend together."

"Come over to my place all day," he urged. "Blake will be working this Saturday at the hotel and then he'll be partying all night. I'll tell him to stay out. We could cook together or I could take you to that new French restaurant that's just opened in town. Erin says it's really good."

The mention of his glamorous boss instantly got Ruby's back up.

"We don't have to go there just because *Erin* likes it." The thought of showing up at a place where Erin hung out didn't appeal to her.

The tone of his voice was intense and agitated. "Okay, steady on; let's go there because *I'd* like to try it."

He cast his eyes over her.

"You really ought to take it easy, Ruby. You're looking exhausted. I need you around more. Blake is so morose. He's taken to playing really weird music lately and he hardly ever comes out of his room. The other day I found some strange ancient symbols drawn onto pieces of paper scattered around the dining table. Since then there's been a heavy atmosphere in the house."

Ruby yawned. She was shattered. The past few weeks had been a long haul. The punishing shifts would soon be over and Kes would realise why she'd been so busy. Her pretty eyes still managed to shine. "Don't waste your time thinking about Blake. Saturday is going to be perfect." She drew in close to him and kissed his lips. "I promise you, I'll make sure it's a day you'll *never* forget."

The week leading up to his birthday saw Ruby turn her attention from work and the restaurant, onto all the arrangements that were going to make his day special.

Jett cut her some slack from the hectic rota she'd been working and extended her breaks so she could run around town sorting all the details.

"He must have more than his good looks to make a beauty like you charge around after him! Tell me his secret, Ruby?"

She'd already bought a lovely dress a fortnight ago. The high street had an exclusive boutique called *Annabelle's*. Ruby had gone in and tried on several cocktail dresses. The owner had been very helpful and complimented her on her final choice. "You look beautiful in them all, but with a

169

figure like yours, the mini black taffeta one is amazing and shows off those legs!"

Now all she had to do was bring together her accessories. An androgynous guy sprayed her with mandarin and bergamot as she passed the fragrance counter in a department store.

"Try that, sweetie. It's light, fruity and full of fun."

She kept getting delicious wafts of it as she went around the store. After choosing some pretty, lacy lingerie, she eventually went back and bought a bottle.

"Lovely, isn't it, darling? Drench yourself in scent, I always say!" He squirted her other wrist with a liberal amount of the perfume and took an elegantly packaged box up to the counter.

"Here are some free samples of the matching body lotion. Smooth it on your skin first and you'll get a long-lasting layered effect – wraps you in an invisible veil of sweetness!"

She picked up a few replacement pieces for her cosmetics bag, so her make-up would be in tip top condition. Now that she was all sorted, she set her mind on all the tiny elements that would show Kes how much she cared.

The manager at the French patisserie showed her the huge variety of celebration cakes that could be made to order.

She opted for a two-tiered, double-chocolate gateau.

He raved about it. "It is magnificent. Pure chocolate indulgence – a chocolate lover's dream! I can add your personal message in icing and our chocolatier can make you any style of decoration you can imagine."

She asked for a chocolate surfboard to be placed sideways on top.

"Just write 'KES' on it please."

Next stop was the delicatessen. An old fashioned bell tinkled as she rushed inside. "Hello Ruby, what can I do for you?" Ricardo, the owner, knew her well. He regularly supplied bits and pieces to the restaurant.

"I'd like to order a fine selection of your best ingredients for an antipasto lunch. I need it for Saturday."

"No problem. Say what you want."

"It's for two, so some of your best mozzarella, stuffed olives, Parma ham, salami, artichokes and vine-ripened tomatoes, please."

"Yes, Ma'am, and I'll throw in a couple of freshly baked ciabatta's. They're complimentary." He winked at her with a big beam on his face. "What time do you want to collect it?"

"Nine-thirty would be great. Thanks Ricardo. See you on Saturday then." She turned to leave, but suddenly remembered something else. "Oh, I'll need a bottle of Prosecco as well."

With all the fussy things sorted, she went off to buy Kes' main present. It was a top of the range laptop. She carefully selected some wrapping paper and a card. The sentiments were deep and meaningful with plenty of space for her own special message.

Kes had offered to pick her up from her flat on the morning of his birthday but she insisted he stay home and relax.

"I'll get a cab over." She wanted all the exciting parcels to remain a surprise until the very last minute.

On the Friday night she stayed home doing her nails, assembling everything, wrapping his gift and writing a heart-felt message in his card.

The big day finally arrived and all was going beautifully to plan except for picking up the cake. There was a delay in the delivery to the patisserie which threw her schedule by nearly an hour. She arrived at the beach house loaded with bags and packages and just managed to ring the doorbell by balancing the cake box on her thigh.

As Kes opened the door everything got off to a bad start. Glaring at his watch he protested. "I thought we were gonna spend the whole day together! What time d'you call this?"

"I know. I'm sorry, Kes. I had a lot to arrange." She tried to soften him up with a myriad of tiny kisses. It half worked but he still seemed strangely distant. She couldn't put her finger on it but he'd changed recently – hardened up. She reasoned it was probably because Taran had left.

He'd been watching a film before she arrived. He didn't attempt to turn it off, but kept his eyes fixed to the screen while she unpacked some of the bags.

She placed the Prosecco in the fridge, set up the cake on the kitchen counter and put aside the items from the deli ready for lunch. Dressed in her usual casual chic style, she lifted a clothes bag with her cocktail dress carefully hung inside. She hoped to wow him with her matching high heels when she got ready for their date at the French restaurant. He had swayed her by insisting that was what he wanted to do and suggested they book a taxi to take them into town and then back to the beach house. They planned to spend another long, restful day together on the Sunday.

She ran upstairs to lay out her clothes and to arrange the present for him to open at the end of the day. She wanted the gift and card to be the crescendo of the evening, the finishing touch before bedtime.

His room was in an unusual state of disarray. It took her by surprise. He was normally very tidy. The bed was unmade; the floor scattered with his clothes; used glasses on the shelf. She sighed. "Oh Kes. This will need a good sort out before we leave tonight."

Placing her clothes on his storage chest she went back downstairs and set lunch out on the coffee table. They ate in relative silence and then she cuddled up next to him on the sofa. Apart from playing with her hair he was quite unresponsive.

He seemed completely engrossed in his film. She waited patiently to talk to him, knowing it was nearly over, but when the time came he just put on another one and asked if she'd make him a coffee.

She contented herself with lying beside him, despite feeling he was preoccupied and purposefully ignoring her. She glanced at her watch. 4:45 pm. The restaurant was booked for 8 pm. Her mind settled on the bedroom – it needed a lot of attention. Once that was in order, she would take a long bath, get changed into her lovely outfit and place his gift and card beautifully in the centre of his freshly made bed.

Getting up, she told him her plans. "I'll go and sort everything in your room and get ready. If you grab a shower at quarter to 7, we can leave for the restaurant at 7:30. I'll book the taxi. Does that all sound good?"

He nodded, half listening to her, and she disappeared upstairs.

≈

Kes flicked off the TV and looked at his watch. Shocked that it had gone seven, he leapt off the sofa. Why hadn't Ruby prompted him?

He rushed upstairs to his room expecting to find her looking stunning and the place in perfect order. Instead he discovered that nothing had been touched.

The bed remained dishevelled and Ruby was sitting on the balcony still dressed in her jeans and top. She hadn't even been in the bath and his present and card lay on the floor amidst his discarded clothes.

"What the hell's going on?" he shouted pushing past the balcony doors. "You should be ready. You've had ages! Don't you know what the time is? What've you been doing?"

She didn't even look up at him. Her gaze was fixed out towards the ocean. It was as though she couldn't hear him.

He stood directly in front of her, barefooted in his faded jeans and unbuttoned shirt. "Ruby, what the hell's up? Why aren't you ready? What have you been doing?"

Her expression was beyond anger. She avoided looking him in the eyes. With tears rolling down her cheeks, her tone was husky and fierce.

"What the *hell* have you been doing, Kes? Or more to the point, *who* have you been doing?"

Surprise and shock swept his face as it reddened. "What d'you mean?"

"Kes, don't play stupid games with me. You know very well what I'm talking about. It's Erin, she's been here, and don't try to deny it!"

He looked stunned, glancing around for whatever possible evidence Ruby could have that Erin might have been there.

"Oh, don't look so astonished, Kes. It's not blatant like she's left her high heels in your wardrobe or anything like that. No, it's much more up-close and personal." She marched up to his bed shaking with emotion. "Your sheets reek of her perfume and there are long brunette hairs all over your pillows!"

He tried to protest. "Oh damn it, Ruby. So she slept over. She came around to talk about the club. It got late. She'd been drinking. I said she could stop here for the night. She took my bed. I slept in Taran's old room."

He sounded convincing. Ruby barged past him and raced off to Taran's room. He followed her.

"Almost believed you, Kes," she screamed looking down at Taran's perfectly made bed. She had changed the sheets herself when she'd cleaned his room after he left. Her special style of folding the bed linen was her signature. No one had slept in the bed since she'd made it.

"I was drunk. Maybe I slept downstairs on the sofa."

"You were drunk. Maybe you slept in your own bed with Erin, Kes!"

She stormed back to his room sobbing. Leaving his gift and card in the middle of the floor, she picked up her bags. The taxi they'd called for their special date had pulled up in the drive, without looking back she left the house, slamming the door behind her.

Instead of feeling contrition, he was mad at her for messing up the evening. His seared conscience did not allow him to consider the severity of the situation. He had no idea of the extent of her effort to make his birthday special.

He opened the gift but avoided the card. He couldn't cope with sentiment. No doubt it was full of tender emotive words – they would just heap guilt onto him by the truck load.

Convinced of Ruby's devotion, he reasoned she'd soon get over it and forgive him.

As for Erin, she didn't figure at all in his affections. He had no intention of pursuing a relationship with her. It had been a one off, purely physical expression of lust – a bit of a power play to curb her domineering ways.

Ruby meant more to him than that. He'd leave her for a while to calm down and then go and repair things.

Sullen, he went downstairs and put the TV on.

His phone rang.

It was the restaurant. "We have a table booked in your name, Sir."

"Yeah, sorry, my girlfriend got sick at the last minute."

He clicked 'end call', went to the fridge and ate the leftovers from the Italian buffet. Taking the chocolate off the top of the cake, he bit into the surfboard and poured himself a whiskey.

The remainder of the evening was spent flicking through TV channels. He hovered around some adult stations for a few minutes and then settled for an action thriller.

Before turning in for bed, he caught the end of a wildlife programme. A lioness had just outrun a wildebeest and was tearing into its belly. Fascinated, he turned up the volume and listened to the commentary: *"Lionesses are persistent hunters, pacing themselves to seize the moment. They hide behind the tall grass, waiting until their prey has lowered its head. Then they stalk, crouching motionlessly, inching in, until they leap and break the creature's neck with their paw. Then, turning it over to expose its underbelly, they rip out its tender guts."*

Taran's warning flooded into his mind. It was the first inkling of trouble he had felt all night. A little disturbed about the possible consequences of his behaviour, he went off to his messy bed and reluctantly wrapped his body in Erin's toxic scent.

Chapter Twenty-Five

OUTCOMES

THE FOLLOWING TWO weeks saw Kes and Ruby's positions polarise – each waiting for the other to make the first move. Instead of being able to understand Ruby's pain, Kes just felt mad at her for walking out on him. Erin meant absolutely nothing to him. He had just wanted to put her in her place, stop her dominating him. He'd seen her as sport and never intended to sleep with her again.

Erin had other ideas and pushed persistently to see him. Her constant texts and calls made it hard for him to ignore her. He did his best to avoid her by getting into the club minutes before his set and slipping out quickly when he was done.

One of the waiters at Jett's restaurant also worked the bar at the club. He proved a valuable source of information on how Ruby was coping.

"How's Ruby been lately, Adam? Have you seen her?"

"She's in a dreadful state. What's happened between the two of you? She's been so depressed. We're all shocked because she's usually so bubbly. She was completely buzzing during the time leading up to your birthday. She put so much into it. She loves you man. Whatever's gone wrong, you need to fix it fast!"

Kes didn't give him a hint of what had happened, but was left in no doubt about Ruby's feelings towards him. He'd give it another week or so and then move in to restore things.

It was torture for Ruby, constantly checking her phone. She was always left disappointed with no messages or missed calls. As more and more days passed, she convinced herself that he had completely fallen for Erin. How else was she to read his silence?

Ruby's conclusion couldn't have been further from the truth. The ruins in Kes' life from the trauma of his parents' divorce gave him very little hope of pursuing reconciliation. Broken relationships didn't get fixed; they just crumbled within you like treacherous bomb sites. Somewhere he had been left disarmed emotionally; he was paralysed when it came to being able to defend and fight for what he knew to be of value. The rejection he had experienced made him dismiss and exclude any semblance of love that might expose his brokenness. He didn't want to own up to having caused Ruby any pain, but he *did* want her back.

Eventually, Erin tracked him down. One night at the club she called him into her office. He knew he couldn't keep putting off facing her, so went reluctantly to the meeting. As soon as he entered the room, she came onto him – walking up and running her hands over his chest. He wasn't having any of it. Clasping her fingers firmly in his, he removed them from his body and pulled them down to her side.

"No Erin, it's not gonna happen again." The flirty varnish that summed up their relationship had peeled off. The teasing and tempting no longer promised any fun. He had bedded her and now everything had changed. She didn't have anything he wanted. The game was over.

In his haste to get away, he left his phone on the coffee table, providing her with an excellent excuse to drive over to his house later that evening.

The irony was, Ruby had finally caved in that same night. Not being able to take the torment any more, she'd ordered a cab to drive her over to see him. As the taxi's headlights flashed onto the beach house driveway, Ruby died a thousand deaths; Erin's sports car was parked on the tarmac. The situation was cruelly misleading. Kes had no idea how the tender underbelly of his life was being ripped out from beneath him. Ruby told the driver to turn around and take her back to her flat.

What was happening inside the house was not the nightmare Ruby was imagining; a completely different scene was playing out. Erin was crying, begging Kes to get intimate with her, but he refused.

"No, Erin. It was a mistake. It would be best if you left now. I need to get off to bed. Thanks for returning my phone."

In all the commotion Blake came down. He overheard Erin's pleas as Kes showed her out. Kes closed the front door and stood against it, relieved.

Blake goaded him. "She is *seriously* sexy. What's the matter with you?"

"She's not my type. She's a dominating control freak and what's more, she's my boss. It's not a great idea to lay your boss. It gets too confusing. In any case I want to be with Ruby. At least one good thing has come out of this mess. I know what I want."

Blake reached into the fridge and glugged back a litre of milk. "Variety is the spice of life, mate. I know what I would have done if I was you and it wouldn't have been to send her home."

"But you aren't me, Blake. You're not in my head. Erin is bad news. The sooner she understands I'm not interested the better."

A month had been and gone since his birthday. Kes had often wanted to get in touch with Ruby but a mixture of pride and guilt caused him to hold back. The truth was he didn't know how to approach her. As the days drifted by he grew anxious as to why she hadn't come running.

Late one afternoon, he sat on his balcony with a coffee. In his mind he was reliving that awful moment when he had walked into his room with high expectations of everything being in order. He still recoiled with the shock of finding her staring out to sea, when he had anticipated her being all dressed up for their special night out.

Slowly, he allowed the truth about the mess he'd made to seep under the wall around his heart. Of course it wasn't her fault. How could he have been so selfish as to play around with Erin? He'd agreed to sleep with her while Ruby lay cuddled into him, blissfully unaware of the scheme.

Taran had been right – he'd acted foolishly, playing with a lioness that had suddenly pounced and torn into him.

Ruby was so sweet and kind – a tender-hearted, beautiful woman. What had he exposed her to? He'd behaved like a complete idiot. He'd had everything a man could possibly dream of. It had all been given freely for the taking. Why hadn't he been able to access it? It wasn't her issue. It was his. It was as if a starving man had been taken to a table loaded with the choicest food but he was on the outside of the room looking in. Shut out. Yet in *his* hand was the key.

As his heart began to soften, he decided to risk opening her card.

The envelope itself spoke of quality, the feel of the paper thick and textured. He ran it between his hands anticipating the contents. He was afraid to rush. He wanted to read it slowly, let it all affect him, try to receive her heart towards him.

Gently peeling back the flap he discarded the paper and studied the contemporary image on the front of the card. He smiled at the black and white photo of two hearts formed in the sand.

The simple message read *I Love You.*

As he opened it up there was a short printed birthday greeting. Underneath lay a handwritten message from the pretty blonde waitress he had fallen for a few months back:

Kes,
I love you more than words can say.

Thank you for the best few months of my life.

I am truly one of the luckiest girls on the planet.

Hope you have the most beautiful birthday ever.

I am so happy to be your girlfriend. (Even saying it gives me goosebumps)

Enjoy your present.

I have another very small gift for you – opening it will have to wait. I'm afraid you can't have it for another seven months.   PTO

He turned the card over.

It's wrapped up inside of me –

You're going to be a daddy x

All my love forever

Ruby xxxxx

He dropped the card, then picked it up again and re-read it several times. A hot, almost nauseous sensation flooded his stomach as he took in the full scale of the implications.

He was shocked at the joy that he felt.

He had to see her immediately. A phone call would serve as an instant way of connecting with her, but he quickly dismissed it. No, he must go in person. This was too important.

He drove urgently, as if he was racing an ambulance to an emergency. He had to catch her before she went to work. A dreadful feeling overtook him, worse than guilt – poor Ruby, whatever must she have made of his silence?

As he pulled up outside her flat he knew that he loved her and wanted to be with her.

Just at that moment she stepped out of the front door. He leapt out of the van and ran after her. Taking her firmly in his arms he gripped her shoulders, channelling all his strength towards her. She looked down at the ground.

"Look at me, Ruby," he pleaded, "I've only just found out! I hadn't opened your card."

She stood frozen stiff, like iron hammered into the earth, gazing down as if she wanted to be invisible.

"Ruby, look at me, let's make a go of it! I'm sorry about Erin. She's *nothing* to me. I just got beyond myself. I was an idiot. *Please...!* I'll quit the club. I want you to move in with me... Let's start tonight. I'll begin packing your stuff while you're at work. I'll tell Blake to leave. It'll just be you, me and our baby."

Eventually she looked up at him.

There was something strange in her eyes that he'd never seen before. Her soul was missing – her pupils dark and blank, like no one was at home.

With tears streaming down her face she stared beyond him, pushing him away with all the strength she could muster. The physical force shocked him but not as much as her words.

"There is no baby, Kes. I've had an abortion."

As she walked off he realised she was no longer the bright, naive girl he had dated all summer. Something had changed, irrevocably. Her soul had died along with their baby. All her hopes and dreams, the essence of what made her dance through life with passion and energy, had been killed off – the real person inside that pretty body, wilted and barren.

Jett noticed a massive change in her. Her brokenness spilled out into everything she did. Eventually her Doctor put her on anti-depressants. They acted as sedatives and masked the pain but could never heal the root of her breakdown.

In late autumn, a desperate, fragmented young woman quit work, gathered her few belongings and left town.

As the coach pulled out of the bus station one cold grey morning, a lonely girl sat gazing lifelessly out of the dirty window. Ruby left Trevanna Bay with a shattered heart.

Chapter Twenty-Six

SAND WOMAN

KES CRASHED INTO a state of grief. The finality of the separation threw his whole life off its axis. Initially he was in denial as he absorbed the shock. The numbness that protected him from the intensity soon gave way to guilt and anger. It became all encompassing. He felt hopeless, helpless and worthless. His lush, carefree lifestyle dried up like a wilderness. He couldn't cope with anything and lost sight of all his daily routines. He withdrew from attending college, had difficulty sleeping and hardly ever ate. He rarely saw Blake; the odd occasion drew them together in the living area.

One afternoon Kes was standing looking out of the window when Blake came in and put on the TV.

"Don't, Blake. I don't want any noise in here." He spoke slowly and quietly.

Blake was well aware that he had split up with Ruby.

"What the hell's the matter with you, Kes? Eat something. Move on. She's only *one* girl."

Kes didn't want to bare his soul to Blake. He knew he would stomp all over it. Instead, he gave him the hard facts.

"Ruby was pregnant."

"Was?"

"Yeah, she had an abortion."

"*So?* You're free then, aren't you? Don't give it a second thought." He grabbed his face and pointed his gaze towards the horizon. "Look at that ocean, that magnificent sea. That's what we evolved out of. You shouldn't worry about a cosmic blob of jelly being removed from a woman's body."

"Shut up, Blake!" he screamed, letting out all the pent up tension. "That was my son or daughter! It's too damn convenient just to believe it's a cosmic blob. Suck it out. Throw it away in some incinerator. A fifteen minute screw is easy, but then there are the consequences. Taran's right, you shouldn't separate sex from love. I should have cared, thought about what I was doing when I shot my seed inside her body!"

"Yeah, you prat, you should have used something."

"You're right I should have used something. I should have used my heart. That's the only part of me that didn't get involved."

He stormed out of the room and went and lay restlessly on his bed – the precious bed where he had taken Ruby's virginity. There on the soft mattress their baby had been conceived. It was also the place where he had made out with Erin.

He turned and groaned into the pillow.

How arrogant had he been to suppose he could gather fire into his lap without getting burnt?

He had entered her not knowing that it was his soul he was forfeiting. How could one careless night change his life forever – one thoughtless moment when he had made a foolish choice and let his guard down?

The torment was unbearable.

The booze did nothing to ease it. He rushed to the bathroom, flung up the toilet seat, dropped to his knees and vomited into the bowl. He emptied the bile from his stomach. If only it could be that easy to remove the agony from his heart.

Glancing in the mirror, he ran his hand across the top of his head. In his remorse he'd even shaved off his hair. He wasn't fully aware of why he'd done it but it was a kind of attempt at showing contrition.

He took a shower and slowly dressed for his set at the club. He had no motivation and decided it would be his last night before he called Jett and quit. As he walked in, one of the bouncers greeted him by pulling him aside. His intimidating arm hung heavily around his shoulder as he led him down the corridor to a quieter spot.

"No more visits to Erin's office. *I'm* seeing her, alright mate?" he winked.

Kes shrugged himself out of his grasp, squared up to him and intently locked eyes. "Yeah, mate, that's *fine* by me." A derogatory comment about Erin surfaced but wisdom shut his mouth. She'd already caused him enough trouble.

Wearing a heavy attitude, he walked off, glad that Erin wouldn't be coming on to him anymore. As the evening progressed he realised that his spark had left him; it was as if someone had torn out his plug. He went through the motions but his heart was no longer engaged. When groups of pretty girls came up, he was blunt and didn't even manage to smile. Ruby and his baby had paid too high a price for all his casual messing around.

Late autumn gave way to winter. The beach was often desolate during those cold December days.

Kes stirred in the middle of the night. As his thoughts orientated, he wished he could have stayed asleep. At least there was some comfort in not having to think too much. Consciousness brought with it the reality of his circumstances. He took a tablet and within half an hour dropped off into a fitful dream.

Ruby was sitting on the balcony with a toddler on her knee. As Kes walked into the room, she turned and smiled at him. The child wriggled free from her lap and ran to him excitedly, shouting, "Daddy, Daddy, Daddy!"

He woke, startled, in a cold sweat. There was a strong chill blowing through the open veranda door. He stepped out and stared down at the beach. Pulling on a pair of jeans and a hoodie, he left the house and wandered to the edge of the sea.

The moon was high and full, the wintry air, brutal. He welcomed the biting wind's punishment upon his body as if it were penance.

The tide was a long way out and a line of white foam traced a path across the wet sand.

His despair was dark and bottomless. Nothing could appease it.

Suicidal feelings gnawed through his soul like a devouring worm. He felt powerless to change his circumstances and there was no one in his life that he could relate to.

The reality of his failure seemed unsolvable and he hated what he'd done. It was history repeating itself. He'd vowed not to turn out like his father but had produced the same bitter fruit of unfaithfulness.

Death offered a release.

He stepped a few metres back from the water's edge and dropped down onto the moist sand.

There he sculpted a woman.

He formed her lying on her side, her beautiful contours soft and feminine. Long strands of hair splayed out framing her delicate face. Removing the keys from his jeans pocket he etched her fine facial details. The finished work of art looked stunning and remarkably like Ruby.

He lay down beside it, pulling his body into its back.

As he turned on his side he wrapped his arm gently around it.

There, he remembered the times Ruby had unreservedly given herself to him.

He shut his eyes and ran his hands over the sculptured curves, imagining and reliving the closeness he had taken for granted.

His hand slipped down to where the soft mound of her stomach would have lain. His fingers lingered over the womb.

Clenching a fistful of sand, he wept.

Wasn't it true that we had been formed from the dust of the earth? His little child's ashes would barely have filled half an egg cup.

He lay there for a long time. So weary from endless nights of sleep deprivation, he drifted in and out of consciousness.

A wash of icy water trickled over his foot, signalling the sea was returning to claim the beach.

He continued lying there exposed to the elements as a gentle flow of water gradually ate into his woman.

Numbness developed on his face, ears and fingertips.

His dangerously pessimistic outlook, coupled with the onset of hypothermia, would have seen him surrender his body to the sea.

Suddenly a surge of warmth enveloped his freezing right hand and a body pressed up against his back. Someone's cheek rested upon his face and an arm wrapped around him in a strong embrace. Thinking he was hallucinating he remained there unresponsive for several minutes, eventually turning into the face of the only man on earth he trusted.

In disbelief he gently murmured, "Taran, I wanna die. Nothing matters anymore. Nothing!"

Taran gathered him up into his arms. Holding him firmly, he pulled him close. Together they wept.

Taran knew that he needed to get Kes indoors quickly. Dragging him to his feet he led him hastily off the beach and up to the house. He helped him change out of his wet clothes, fetched him a warm drink and wrapped him in a duvet. It didn't take long for his body temperature to rise and colour to come back to his flesh.

"Taran, how come you're back? How did you know where to find me?"

"I've always been good at treasure hunting, mate," he grinned. "We need to talk but not now. We'll have a big catch up later in the morning. You look dog-tired!"

A glow had reappeared on Kes' countenance that had been missing for months. He felt secure for the first time in ages. It was so comforting to have him home.

Kes spoke in a husky whisper. "I know this sounds a bit weird but will you sleep in my room? I can't believe you're here. I feel safe with you around. I haven't slept properly for days. Even if I've managed to nod off it's only been for a little while and then I get the shakes."

"Of course, mate," Taran laughed softly, "but I'm not getting in your bed. I couldn't begin to explain it to Blake if he walked in on us. You know what he's like!"

Taran dragged a mattress in and laid it next to Kes' bed. He closed the blinds – daylight would break in a couple of hours.

As they rested in the dark, Kes quietly questioned him.

"D'you know about me and Ruby?"

"Yeah, mate, I'm really sorry. I heard about it."

"How did you find out?"

"Blake – he's been emailing me about the photography show."

"Is that why you came back?"

"No, I came back for *you*, Kes. I don't care about the show. I knew you'd need me."

Kes rolled over and slept for the first time in weeks.

Chapter Twenty-Seven

CONFESSIONS

THE COMFORTING SMELL of hot buttered toast caused Kes to stir. Taran held a tray in front of him with two soft boiled eggs and neatly cut soldiers.

"There, get that down you." He had been shocked to see how lean Kes was looking. His facial bone structure was more pronounced and he had dark circles under his eyes.

Kes sat up slowly, his gaze fixed on his homecoming friend.

"It's flippin' freezing over here compared to California!" Taran exclaimed as he pulled a duvet over himself and sat on Kes' bed.

"You're looking good, mate," Kes smiled. Taran had left with a golden tan. It had only got richer. He looked handsome and healthy. "So Blake told you everything that's been going on, did he?"

"Pretty much, I know what happened with Erin and all about Ruby getting an abortion."

After swallowing three quarters of an egg and half a toast soldier, Kes pushed the food aside.

Taran's presence drew out his confidence. It was time for confession. He wrapped the bedclothes around himself, lay back against his pillow and spoke slowly and deliberately. His usual chirpy fortitude was not evident and there was a broken tone to his voice.

"All I wanna do is die. I don't care about anything anymore. Not college, not my art, I don't want to DJ. All I long for is Ruby and our baby, but I can't have them. I can't rewind it all to the night before I slept with Erin."

Taran didn't attempt to jump in quickly with an answer. There was nothing in him that wanted to score points by saying, 'told you so'. It wasn't right to kick a man when he was down. It didn't need to be said. Kes knew he'd blown it and Taran had no desire to rub his face in it.

He sat in silence for a while and then offered his counsel.

"Right now, you can't see any future and death seems like a release from the pain, but to throw your life away would be crazy... Yeah, you've messed up, but at least you own it as *your* wreckage." He stared at him with kind, warm eyes. His voice was earnest. "We all mess up, Kes. You've just got to learn to live life better from now on; let what you've been through mould and change you." He paused and reached for his drink. "Listen to me carefully, because you need to get this. In a way, you *do* have to die, but not the kind of dying that would snuff out your life to suicide. Die to your selfishness. Die to keeping that fortress up around your heart. Allow the agony you're in right now to tear it down so you can live in the fullness of who you really are underneath."

Kes clenched his fists so hard they turned white; his eyes looked haunted and fierce. Angrily, he gave vent. "There's nothing there underneath! If I have to try to describe it to you, it's like a burnt out ruin – a smouldering black hole. When my parents split, my heart got ripped out of me. Aren't your parents supposed to model what life's all about, you know, teach you how to live it well? Show you what love is meant to look like? I watched the demonstration Taran, and all I saw was vicious quarrelling, fighting, anger and frustration.

"My mum was – still is – a beautiful lady, but Dad was completely blind to it. Why couldn't he have been content with her? Given to her, instead of looking elsewhere? She was so in love with him, but she was always upset 'cause she could never get through to his heart. Eventually he left her for Stephanie, but he's still not happy. Neither is Steph, she fights with him all the time just like my mum did."

Taran attempted to pull him out of his hopelessness.

"It sounds like one hell of a crazy mess. Your dad's way of doing life wasn't a good model to follow and yeah, I can see you've put on the same show. But we don't have to stay victims 'cause of other people's botch ups. We're always quick to blame the other person in the relationship for the problems, without looking at our own behaviour."

Still wrapped in the duvet, Taran got up and walked over
to the window. The waves looked awesome. For a moment
he felt a selfish desire to be out there riding them in. It
made what he said next even more fitting. He came back to
the bed and dropped down beside Kes. "We're all lacking in
the love department, man. Love ain't some mushy feeling –
it's a committment to a lifestyle. It's being kind and patient,
putting others before ourselves, being happy with truth,
being faithful, not lying or cheating. You know, I'm just
thinking about what you said about your mum, but it could
apply to any other woman for that matter – we guys have
a lot of power in relationships. Women want to feel secure
and cared for. We've gotta be careful with that power 'cause
when they make us their king, they'd do anything for us –
anything! That's why we've got to be responsible with their
hearts."

Kes groaned. He looked contrite and serious. His whole
body language showed signs of anxiety. Taran's words were
honing in on a soft spot.

"I've failed on all those counts. I completely missed
Ruby's heart. I think the only clue I've got as to what
real love could be, is when I watch how you treat people.
You've proved to me that I'd be wise to listen to you, and
my track record shows that I don't listen hard enough!"
A bewildered expression filled his soft grey eyes. "I had
everything and nothing, didn't I, Taran? When other people
looked at my life, they probably thought I had it made, but
there was always a massive void. I thought I loved Ruby,
but I was just on the take. I never really gave anything
to her. You saw what I was like; you warned me loads of
times."

He drew his legs up and folded his arms tightly around them. Dropping his head onto his knees, he slowly rocked himself to and fro. "I've got to share this with you 'cause it's been tormenting me – it's eating me up. Look at what my arrogance has cost: I've brought about my baby's death and Ruby's lost to me now... But this is what's *really* doing me in – I can't face what my selfishness has done! I've let some guy, I've never seen before, put a sharp instrument into that special place within Ruby – that beautiful place that she'd surrendered to me, and I've caused him to tear down my son or daughter. That gift we'd been given! Just cut down, violently torn away, and thrown into a bin to be burnt with the rubbish... D'you know what they do? They have to piece the baby together to check they've got all the bits! They make a jigsaw out of your baby! I can't live with myself, mate. God help me! I've wrecked three lives through my own blindness."

They sat in silence for a long time.

Eventually, Taran shook himself loose from his duvet, drawing attention to his chest.

"Look Kes, you know I've got these scars around my heart. We like to joke about it and say it's because I survived the 'men in grey suits' coming after me but we both know this didn't come from a shark attack. It was from surgery when I was a kid." He looked down at the marks on his flesh. "We all carry scars, mate – some outside, most inside. When it comes to Ruby, you'll always have scar tissue. You can't get rid of it. But you can determine to let it change you for good. She gave you so much of herself and it all got mangled up through your lack of care and her willingness to trust a crazy, imperfect guy with her most precious stuff." He leant in close to him. "That burnt out place inside you, Kes, is the reason sex is so powerful for you. Sex is an awesome thing, but if you forget love and commitment, it just becomes a pleasure kick that people get used in. It wasn't designed for that. It's not supposed to be a one dimensional lust outlet; you've got to engage your heart, spirit and soul, as well as your body. You can't do that outside of a faithful commitment without ripping yourself and other people apart in some way."

Kes thought about that night with Erin. Lust had certainly been in evidence by the bucket load. How come a few hours could screw your life up so easily? When it came to Ruby, lust had *also* been the driving force of him getting together with her. It had looked like it meant more than that, but his greedy appetite had been the real motivation. If he refused to face it now, it would dog him for the rest of his life. Taran was right – he didn't know how to give himself in a relationship.

"Taran, I don't *really* trust anyone on this planet. Maybe my mum, a little bit, and definitely you; I trust you more than my old man."

"Well that ain't much is it? Going by his performance, no wonder you don't trust anyone. He's never been very responsible and reliable. His lying and cheating was what made you set up your fortress in the first place! You need to look at that wound you carry there – it affects how you see yourself, your motivation, your hope for the future. You don't realise your own value, Kes. Not when someone that close to you treats you like crap."

Taran rolled over onto his side. He got right up into Kes' face. Choosing his words carefully, he spoke slowly and gently. He knew what he was about to say was going to be a hard pill to swallow. "Until you see that you're worth something, you won't understand other people's value either. You'll always be guarding and defending yourself with a fierce pride. Your dad should have been building you up and affirming you, not ignoring you and rejecting you. One day you're gonna have to forgive him in order to see that wall around your heart come down."

Kes held his forehead in both hands and scrunched up his face. "I don't wanna go there, Taran. I can't afford to. I watched my mum go nuts."

Without realising it, he did begin to 'go there'. Things he'd bottled up, that he'd never shared with a soul began to spew out.

"She hit the booze big time when dad walked out. It was like a bomb had gone off and we were just left in the ruins. I can still feel the trauma when I look back on it. We had to get on with it. But we were stunned. We couldn't share our feelings with each other. We just argued, swore, screamed, slammed doors, got drunk and high but nothing helped... Yeah, I built a wall. I had to. I'd been betrayed. I was never gonna let anyone into the 'real me' again. That's why Ruby couldn't get through and that's why separating sex from a true relationship is easy for me to do. Erin was nothing to me except a sexy body. She was purely a good lay. It wasn't like she was a human being, just an object for sex. I didn't want to see her again. I know Ruby wanted more from me but I didn't know how to give it."

Taran hated seeing him like this. He could tell he hadn't slept properly in ages. Extreme fatigue had sapped him of his usual high-energy.

He gently reasoned with him. "You can't give to another person what you haven't been given yourself. I *know* you can't afford to deal with the mess of your life, Kes, not if when you've finished looking at it, you're just left with a heap of broken pieces with no solid foundation to rebuild them on… You say you trust me, man, but I'm gonna ask you to do a really brave thing: will you trust me to find the real you – that guy that you think is lost in a black hole? Trust me, that when we've looked at it all, I can help you find a firm rock to build your life on again?"

Kes breathed out a deep laboured sigh. When Taran had mentioned the rock, it reminded him of the night before on the beach. He immediately thought about his sand sculpture. "Did you see the woman I crafted out of the sand?"

"Not really, I was more interested in my mate lying beside her. But admittedly, you're a brilliant artist and if she was anything like your paintings of women, she must have been stunning."

Kes suddenly seemed a bit more relaxed. He was beginning to feel safer about sharing his true thoughts.

"I remember the day I first fell for the image of a woman big time! I'd gone into my parent's bedroom. I was tossing a coin and it rolled under the bed. As I reached my hand in after it, I drew out a glossy mag. I must have been about thirteen years old, just beginning to get hormonal reactions and man did I get one. I studied those beauties like works of art. They completely mesmerised me. It was the first time I'd laid my eyes on a fully naked woman. This gorgeous blonde was unveiling all her loveliness to me. The strength of the lust was overwhelming. I fell in love with that stuff.

The invitation, the vulnerability, the comfort a woman's form offered. I felt this weird warmth rush through my body and from that day I've been hooked."

Taran smiled at him. "Yeah, it's been pretty obvious for a long time that you worship the image of women." He glanced around at some of Kes' paintings. "It's easy to do. They were created to get our attention. And if you just go for the outer packaging, an image doesn't give you any grief. It doesn't demand anything except a physical response and it's never got a headache!"

Kes was on a roll. The honest conversation was doing him good. "I've loved the way they look as a source of fulfilment and pleasure for a long time now. It makes life easy for me, because I don't have to build any deeper than the surface. When a woman slips out of her clothes and into my bed, she fits that idol. But it's what happens after the sex – I'm just left unable to relate because of my crappy emptiness."

Taran loved how much Kes was opening up. He could see light coming back into his eyes and occasionally he broke into a boyish grin.

"Yeah, you're right, Kes – you need to learn how to build a relationship that has more dimensions than the horizontal. You can't go through life with a one-legged stool, mate! You've got to break into the fullness of life's adventure to find the real colour. I tell you what I've discovered – women out there are longing for guys to stand strong and show some character. They want to be pursued for more than their looks. That's what really turns them on. I reckon if I asked Danielle to marry me tomorrow, she'd throw herself at me because she knows I'm not seduced by her.

She understands I'd want way more from her than just her body." He laughed. "And, in case you're wondering, I'm not thinking of asking her! I don't think she'd fulfil me. Making idols out of each other isn't a good idea. We were never meant to be gods. We can't get out of another human being what we can only get out of our Creator."

Kes smiled and threw a pillow at him. "There you go again! You've got even deeper into your spiritual journey since you've been away, haven't you? Did stuff go on in California?"

"Yeah, I hung out with some interesting, like-minded people and we had lots of late night chats on the beach. It completely rocked!" His eyes shone and Kes knew Taran had found what he'd gone looking for.

"I'm glad for you. You look really stoked. I think I'll go and take a shower. Then maybe we could make a bit of lunch."

"Sounds good to me." Taran walked out onto the balcony and studied the waves. They rolled consistently into the bay in long lines. He would have loved to have hit the beach but Kes obviously wasn't up for a vigorous surf session. There was no way he was going to leave him by himself. Instead he went downstairs and put some food out. He was delighted Kes' mood had lifted slightly and that his appetite seemed to be returning. It was a good sign.

Over lunch, they continued their conversation. Kes was obviously wrestling with getting more off his chest. He ate half a sandwich and discarded the other piece. Avoiding what he really wanted to say, he made small talk.

"Danielle's been dating Dave Chapel since you've been in California."

"Oh, I heard there was someone on the scene. We kept in touch while I was away. Is he the guy who owns the scaffolding company?"

"Yeah, she seems quite steady with him. She still goes out on the town with the girls. Blake sees her on the party scene, but he says she's not so easy any more. He's a bit miffed."

"Well good for her. I hope she makes a go of it and enjoys cooking him pie and chips."

"What d'you mean?"

"Ah, nothing, it's just something I said to her before I left. I'll try to catch up with her soon. She knows I'm around... anyway... come on, Kes, what's really pressing on that heart of yours?"

Kes pushed his chair back, put his hands behind his head and closed his eyes. After sitting quietly for a couple of minutes, he slumped forward and looked down.

"I feel terrible about what I've done to Ruby. She never did anything to deserve what happened. I was always flirting with Erin, even when she'd come down to the club after working so hard in the restaurant. She must have been aware of the situation, though she didn't say much." He looked Taran in the eyes. "She'd never even slept with anyone except me. It meant so much to her, but when she told me, I just laughed it off, because I was afraid of making any commitment. I'm gutted at how I've wrecked her life. There's no doubt she would have made a beautiful mother. I must have flipped her over the edge because it looked like I couldn't give a toss that she was pregnant... The truth was, I only found out when it was too late.

"The scariest thing about all of this though, was the look in her eyes when I went to try to reason with her. It was as if she'd disappeared into a bottomless pit, Taran. She must have broken somewhere inside – denying her tender heart in order to cope with her decision. It wasn't in her nature to do something like that."

When Taran had lived at the beach house, he'd been well aware of the dynamics between Kes and Ruby. Because he'd seen things from both sides, he was in a great position to offer Kes some comfort.

"Ruby is a lovely girl, Kes. She must be devastated. I used to have lots of conversations with her, especially on the mornings when we'd clear up together. From what she told me, I was in no doubt she adored you and feared Erin. You're right to care about the part you played in what went wrong, but that isn't the whole picture. She put you on a pedestal and you fell off. Remember, she did choose to give herself to you. It's not like you raped her. You guys had only known each other for a few hours before you began to get it on. I saw more than the heat of the bonfire that night down on the beach! You both left in a rush and went off and slept together. Don't forget, I went surfing with you the morning after, and you were going on about what a crazy night you'd had. If you're gonna find a balance in this, you'll have to get your head around the fact that Ruby wasn't perfect either. You were her idol, Kes. You're a very good looking guy and you would have easily fitted into her dream of Mr Perfect."

"Yeah, until all my selfishness took over... and that would have been on the first night!"

"She was also getting something out of it. It wasn't a one way street."

Kes reached for his sandwich and finished it up. He sat quietly for a while, absorbing his friend's advice.

"Thanks Taran..." He hesitated. "I mean, thanks for everything; I don't think I'd be alive if you hadn't found me last night. Talking with you today is beginning to clear my head, and if you keep on pushing me, you just might find my heart!" He had a twinkle in his eye and managed a smile.

Taran playfully locked his arm around Kes' neck as he got up. With his other hand he rubbed his knuckle into his scalp. "What's with shaving all your hair off, eh? Seriously, it's good to be back with you. Let's watch a movie tonight, shall we?"

అ

Chapter Twenty-Eight

THE PECULIAR VIBE

THAT EVENING FOUND them settled on the leather sofa munching through a large packet of crisps. A selection of DVD's lay scattered across the coffee table. Kes picked one up.

"Are you sure you want to watch that supernatural thriller, Kes, in your current state of mind? Perhaps a comedy might be better for you?"

Taran had seen the film before and knew it was intense. He was aware it could stir things up that were beginning to come to rest. "The devil does a good PR job with these movies. He likes to make himself look *all* powerful."

Kes turned to him. "D'you believe in angels and demons, Taran?"

"Yep." His simple answer was clear and affirming. It carried with it an invitation to explore.

Kes pressed ahead, knowing Taran wouldn't knock what he was about to say. "It's just something's been going on with Blake lately that has brought a strange atmosphere into the house. I noticed that he started doing things after you left."

"What *kind* of things?"

"Well, I came in from the club one night and there were all sorts of ancient symbols drawn on bits of paper. They looked like a handmade set of cards, and were lying all over the dining table. There's been a peculiar vibe in the house ever since." Kes sounded jittery.

Taran looked around the room. "Yeah, come to think of it, there is a heavy feeling in here. I thought it was because of all you're working through." He stared over at the table. "I've got no doubt that what he's done has opened a door to a demonic presence. Blake's such a hothead. He never thinks about the consequences of his actions. He doesn't know anything about being responsible when it comes to personal governance. He probably doesn't realise the power he's got in the choices he makes. He's given his will over to *something*, and invited it in."

Kes seemed confused. He lowered his voice. "What d'you mean, 'invited *it* in'?"

"Every one of us has an inner door. It's connected to the heart of what we're really seeking in life. Who, or what, we welcome in, is what makes all the difference. You can see from Blake's lifestyle, he's not really in control. He might like to think he is, but he's given himself over to stuff that dominates him. It's more powerful than he is. He's addicted to porn and drugs and now he's getting into the occult."

The main light that hung low over the dining area suddenly went out.

They sat for a while in the dark and then it came back on, almost as if it had a will of its own.

Kes raised his eyes to the ceiling. He looked startled. "*Man*, what do think that was? It's a bit spooky considering what we're talking about."

"Seriously, mate, don't worry about it." Taran sounded confident and unfazed. "I'm certain it's a demonic display connected with what Blake's been doing, but more important than the manifestations in the house, is what he's opened his soul up to. Trust me, *that's* where the real trouble will kick off – whatever he's given his control to, will master him. You can't play around with that stuff without handing over the driver's seat."

Kes fixed his eyes on the light. "It's freaky. Why would he do that?"

"Well, look at your own struggles with the things you're dealing with. We're influenced all the time by forces of good and evil. None of us have the luxury of sitting on a fence in life. There's no neutral zone. There's always something to battle. It's our choice what we entertain and who we give our authority to."

Kes got up and walked over to the window. He rubbed his forehead and then rested it against the glass. "Everything's *mental* at the moment!"

Taran looked at him with sympathy. It had been an extreme twenty-four hours. He figured a little light relief wouldn't go amiss. Opening a bag of marshmallows, he threw one at him. "There you are, mate, let *that* in!"

It didn't take long for a wide smile to break across Kes' face. Taran could always bring him round.

They fooled about chucking the sweets into the air and trying to catch them in their mouths. The place was soon littered with pink and white blobs. Taran started to collect them up.

"Ah, leave it, Tar, we can do it in the morning. I'm shattered actually. I think I'll hit the sack but there's *no way* I'm sleeping alone tonight, not without you in my room!"

Chapter Twenty-Nine

THE WAKE UP CALL

A REPEATED RINGING of the bell was followed by a heavy banging on the front door. Kes awoke abruptly and glanced at his phone. It had just gone 5 am.

As he stepped onto the landing in his boxer shorts, he could see Taran was already ahead of him, racing to answer the urgent caller.

He went back into his room and pulled on a pair of jeans and hoodie.

A terrible din rose from downstairs.

He could easily make out Danielle's voice. She sounded uncontrollable, wailing and howling. He reasoned that she was either off her head or Blake was up to his old tricks again.

Kes sprinted downstairs looking towards the front door. Danielle was collapsed in Taran's arms, screaming. Taran looked ashen. His words were shocking.

"It's Blake, Kes. He's *dead*."

As he led Danielle into the house the nightmare unfolded. Through violent sobs she managed to get out a few words.

"After clubbing, we all went back to Gabi's and he suddenly passed out. The paramedics couldn't bring him round. He'd had a heart attack. They took him to A&E, but after about an hour, they pronounced him dead!"

Kes poured out some strong drinks. The other two didn't touch them, but he took a large gulp. It was so early in the morning even he couldn't stomach it. Chucking it all down the sink, he put the kettle on and made some coffee.

After exchanging a multitude of questions and comments for a couple of hours, they all sat in silence. The news was horrific but it hadn't caught any of them completely off guard. Each of them had been well aware of Blake's destructive habits.

Poor Danielle looked frightful. Her bright make-up was smudged all over her face and her tiny dress barely covered her. She looked slutty, cold and uncomfortable.

"Why don't you take a shower?" offered Kes. "There's a load of Ruby's toiletries and cosmetics in the back of my bathroom cabinet and a few of her clothes in my wardrobe. D'you want something to eat? I'll make you some breakfast if you like."

Danielle had calmed a little. Her voice was quiet and broken. "Thanks Kes. Yeah, it would be good to grab a hot

bath actually. I'm really chilly. It'll warm me up. I'd love
a bite to eat afterwards." She got up and headed off to his
room. She was still wearing her big heels but he passed no
comment.

"Help yourself to fresh towels," he called after her.
"They're in the large cupboard on the landing."

Taran observed how kind he had been. He'd always
treated her harshly before. "Good on you, mate, Danielle
needs a bit of TLC. She gets enough of all the other kind of
affection."

Kes glanced towards the door to check she'd gone
upstairs. He screwed up his face. "*Man*, is it just me or does
she feel really unwholesome? She needs more than a bubble
bath to scrub her down."

"Yep, the stuff that makes her dirty is never gonna wash
off with soap and water. But she's still a treasure worth
finding underneath it all."

Kes' phone rang. It was Blake's mum. She was hysterical.
He paced the room listening to her frantic outpouring for
nearly half an hour. Occasionally, he punctuated the one
way conversation with a few gentle platitudes. As the call
finally ended he flopped down onto the sofa sighing deeply.

"She's blaming us! She thinks we led him astray. She
presumes we were all doing drugs. I couldn't get a word
in!"

"We'll have to suck it up, Kes. It's just the shock of it.
She's got to vent the pain somewhere. Maybe there'll come
a time when we can justify ourselves and explain that Blake
was a law unto himself. But until then, try to think about
her. His dad isn't around and the poor lady has had it really
rough from what Blake told me."

Kes knew Taran was right. He always saw things from the other person's point of view.

Taran held his head in his hands. "I did see this coming. It was always a possibility in the back of my mind. I often tried to talk to him, but Blake was so reckless. He never considered the danger or consequences of what he was involved with."

"Yeah, but he was so funny as well. Remember when we first met each other doing our 'A' levels? He was even surrounded by girls then! I thought, 'that guy's got something to gather all the chicks around him'. Then he opened his mouth and I knew why. He had the gift of the gab, his humour was charismatic and he always had a vulnerability that made all the girls want to mother him. He had that distant, 'lost boy' thing about him." Kes choked up.

After a while, Danielle came back into the room. She hadn't put on much make-up and she looked softer and sweeter in Ruby's clothes – although tight, the jeans and top were more appropriate for daywear than her usual outfits.

Kes swallowed hard. It was very difficult for him to see her dressed in Ruby's stuff. The garments had been hanging in his wardrobe with almost shrine-like reverence. Every time he'd gone to get something out, they'd confronted him with her absence.

Taran could see the agony in Kes' gaze. He caught his eye with a knowing look, attempting to reassure him.

Kes passed Danielle a plate of food. "Blake's mum called. Have you ever met her?"

"Yeah, Pauline, she's really heavy duty. How's she taking it?"

"Badly doesn't come close! She thinks it's mine and Taran's fault. I couldn't get a word in edgeways."

Danielle protested. "That's typical of Pauline, blaming you guys. You never even went to the parties. I haven't seen either of you take drugs. Someone will have to set her straight."

Taran spoke up. "Give her a break, Danielle. She doesn't know how we've been living here. I can understand her presuming we all do drugs. She's just lost her only son."

Kes added his piece in Pauline's favour. He was getting used to admitting his shortcomings. "Yeah, and babe, I'm not that clean. I can't sit back and let you paint me whiter than white. Just because I never did anything with you lot... my balcony's seen a few joints smoked on it."

She suddenly went silent and pushed her breakfast away. A weighty sense of guilt and shame pierced her conscience. If anybody had encouraged the use of cocaine in the group, it had been her. She had made the original contact and been the door through which it flowed; it had been her own purse that kept everyone's habit undergirded.

Not being able to face it, she picked up her handbag and excused herself. "Listen, I'm going to make a move now, guys. Thanks for everything. I'm so sorry for you, too." She reached for her phone to call a cab.

"I'll drop you home," Kes offered, getting up. "I haven't had much to drink. I'll just go grab my keys." He left the room.

Danielle looked down. Taran lifted her chin. Nothing got past him.

"What is it?"

She burst into tears. "It's my fault!" she wailed. "I introduced him to cocaine!" Taran held her tight as he led her through the hall and into the van. She left sobbing. As Taran waved her off, he sighed. He rested his head wearily against the doorframe. It was a good job his shoulders were broad.

Chapter Thirty

PAULINE COMES TO STAY

WITHIN A FEW days and after several phone conversations, Taran had persuaded Pauline that he and Kes had neither encouraged nor condoned Blake's heavy drug habit. On the contrary, Taran, especially, had attempted to get alongside him and dissuade him. The outcome of his accountability was that a bridge had been built. On the night before the funeral, Pauline came over to stay.

Kes had made the suggestion, although he found it all extremely awkward. He wanted to follow Taran's lead of being friendly and accommodating.

The invitation to spend time in the house that Blake had called home was very comforting for her. It would act as a kind of pilgrimage to the place where he had lived out his last days. She arrived with a small suitcase in the early evening.

The guys had discussed trying to make it as good an experience for her as was possible, given the circumstances. They both made an effort to consider little details that would make her feel welcome and cared for.

Kes offered her one of the spare rooms but she asked if she could sleep in Blake's.

"Yeah, of course," he said climbing the stairs. He shot an anxious glance to Taran as they both showed her in.

She wept as she looked at all of Blake's personal belongings. Taran whizzed off to the kitchen and brought her up a cup of tea and some biscuits. Kes went and fetched a box of tissues. The three of them sat on the large bed and slowly went through Blake's things.

It was harrowing for all of them.

Kes was only glad that the walls couldn't speak. That room had seen a bit of action and it wasn't anything you'd want your mum to be privy to.

Taran was gifted in making people feel relaxed and at ease. He studied Blake's photography with her and told her how the tutors at college had highly rated his work.

They all found it nearly unbearable packing up his clothes.

Pauline offered them first choice before they bagged it all up for charity. Neither Kes nor Taran accepted anything. They politely said that it would be best going to a good cause.

When his favourite surf hoodie came out of the wardrobe there wasn't a dry eye in the room. Taran remembered that Blake had been wearing it when he'd pinned him to the wall. He thought better of telling Pauline his last memory of seeing him in it.

Taran emptied the drawers onto the bed as Pauline packed up the laptop. Kes only hoped she was IT illiterate. Searching through his history or favourite sites would probably curl her hair quicker than her styling tongs.

There were a few items on the bed that the guys tried to shield from her eyes. They were of little monetary value but spoke of his lifestyle. They attempted to gather them discreetly but she saw what they were doing.

"I know Blake was no angel. You don't need to do that. I appreciate you're trying to protect me but I'd rather see the truth of how he lived."

"Let's just say he liked the ladies," Kes grinned, relieved that he no longer had to hold the excruciating fear of what they might come across.

After several hours, everything was pretty much sorted. Taran mentioned that there were a couple of surfboards and wetsuits downstairs that had belonged to Blake.

"Do whatever you like with them," she said.

"I could donate them to the local surf school. They'd get good use and it would be kind of fitting since Blake loved Trevanna Bay."

He couldn't believe what he was saying. It all seemed so surreal.

He'd only popped back from California to support his friend and he'd found himself in a four car pile-up – Ruby was in meltdown, Kes had nearly drowned himself on purpose, Danielle was falling apart and Blake was dead.

Chapter Thirty-One

GREY SKIES

THE DAY OF the funeral arrived with grey skies. Taran got up early and set the table attractively for the three of them to have breakfast. Nobody was that hungry, but they tried to eat a little, knowing they needed plenty of energy for what lay ahead.

After she'd finished her second cup of strong coffee, Pauline went out onto the patio to have a cigarette. Her prematurely lined face spoke of a life of anxiety and stress. She obviously lived on her nerves. She was a wisp of a lady who chain smoked and used swear words in the place of adjectives.

Taran joined her as she stood in the cold, wintry breeze. He couldn't bear to see her standing out there alone. Although she smelt like an old ashtray, he extended his arm towards her. At first she was stiff and tense. He could tell that her tiny frame was not used to receiving tactile affection. As he gently squeezed her shoulder, she yielded to the warmth of his gesture. She could feel that the physical demonstration was coming from his heart and soul. It wasn't needy or abusive. It just wanted to comfort and share. Sensing its purity, she crumpled into his arms and wept. He held her for several minutes while a little bit of her grief spilled out.

Kes marvelled at his friend's capacity to give beyond himself. As he watched him holding Blake's broken mother, he caught a glimpse of what true love was all about. Taran displayed rare qualities. He genuinely cared for people and they knew it. Thank God he was around.

Kes had given the beach house to be used afterwards for grieving friends and relatives to come back for refreshments. The living area looked flawless once he'd cleared the dishes. He set out paper plates, serviettes and glasses. Outside caterers would soon be arriving with a buffet of sandwiches, pastries, cakes and nibbles.

The doorbell rang. A florist delivered a beautiful bouquet for Pauline. It was from Taran and Kes. They had chosen it online – delicately scented roses and lilies were arranged in a glass vase. She was very appreciative.

"You boys have thought of everything. Thank you very much."

There was nothing left to do except get themselves ready. An hour before the cars were due to arrive, Taran and

Kes came downstairs, freshly showered and shaven. They looked impeccable in their hired black suits.

Pauline commented, "Wow, I'm going to feel like I've got two movie stars either side of me." As she left the room, Kes muttered to Taran, "Well, this is as smart as it's gonna get! All of Blake's girlfriends will be wearing their one inch dresses."

"One inch?"

"Yeah, one inch from their pants! I mean, what do they think we'll be imagining when we're trying to be all dignified and send our mate off? It's not even like they're handing it to us on a plate – those girls force feed you!"

Taran laughed. "Well that's the point. They want our attention and they know how to get it. But think about why they would dress like that on such a freezing day. They believe their only worth is in what they've got under their skirts; blokes like you and Blake have done nothing to make them think otherwise. You better be nice to them. Don't you dare play up or I'll be kicking you."

Despite the jesting, it hit Kes hard. Taran's words had given him a good spanking. He was starting to understand that he needed a change of attitude. If he was truly sorry about how he'd been with Ruby, the process had to start in situations like these. The way he treated any girl mattered.

It was a sombre sight as three figures stood on the driveway to greet Blake's remains. An immaculate silver hearse parked up beside them. The shiny wooden coffin carrying the body was crowned with two floral tributes. Pauline and the boys stood quietly and read the messages before getting into a chauffeur driven executive car. It slowly wound its way down the country lanes towards the town, following the hearse.

As they pulled into the cemetery they saw a large group of mourners gathering around the crematorium. Pauline, Kes and Taran went in first, along with Blake's uncle, aunt and a few of his cousins. Once they had taken their seats at the front, all of his friends filed in and took up the rows behind them.

Classmates from college, photography tutors, old school friends, work mates from the hotel, groups of girls and an assorted mix of party animals intermingled on the pews.

They all stood as the coffin was brought slowly down the aisle and laid out on a platform before them.

The order of service carried a lovely picture of Blake's head and shoulders. His bright smile lit up the page. Kes fought back tears as he looked at his cheeky grin. Although he had often clashed with him, Blake had still been one of his best mates.

The service was led by a member of the pastoral team from his previous school. There was hardly a dry eye in the place as he recalled facts from Blake's life that Pauline had informed him of. His father had been absent for most of his life, but he had enjoyed spending time with his grandad as a young lad. It was through this relationship that his interest in photography had grown.

The message was short and as sweet as could possibly be, given the circumstances of his death. A couple of his friends were called upon to pay tribute. One girl got through her first paragraph and broke down in floods of tears and the other message came from Dreadlock Sam. Unfortunately he looked slightly stoned and gave a garbled account of having met Blake through college. Everyone was left in no doubt that hard partying had been Blake's favourite pastime. Although it seemed a little inappropriate, it was very truthful, and in that sense, a fitting eulogy to the wild friend that most people in the room knew Blake to have been.

As the committal approached, a piece of Blake's favourite rap music rang out through the old chapel. It played before the climax of the whole service – the moment when the sweeping velvet curtains closed and the coffin was hidden from view.

A distinguished looking funeral director led the small group of close family and friends out first. These were followed by a steady procession of mourners. Pauline and her brother thanked them all for coming and an opportunity was provided for people to look at the floral tributes and read the messages. A large heart of cream roses had a card attached from his mum. The handwriting was erratic and hard to decipher.

His uncle had sent a small wreath. The message read:

Blake, you were damn trouble coming and damn trouble going. RIP, much love, Uncle Ronnie, Aunty Sue, Dave, Pete and Fiona.

Pauline lit up a cigarette. She found it very hard to engage with any of Blake's friends. That job fell to Taran and Kes.

The weather was so bitter, it made it even harder to make polite conversation. Taran suggested they all move on to the beach house as quickly as possible. He turned to Kes and was shocked to find that he was fuming. Drawing him aside he asked him what was up.

"You look like you're about to go ballistic, what on earth has happened?"

"Dreadlock Sam was mouthing off about why I wasn't seeing Ruby anymore. I could punch his lights out."

"Kes, just calm down a bit, a fight ain't gonna work here, mate."

"Yeah, well you better make sure he doesn't come back to the house 'cause I can't handle him being around. It'll end in big trouble, Taran, I'm warning you."

Taran went and talked to a couple of guys who had come with Sam. He persuaded them not to show up afterwards. He went back to Kes.

"It's sorted. He won't be coming to your place." He planted a firm hand on his shoulder and led him briskly to a waiting vehicle.

"Get in and stay in. I'll be over here in a minute with Pauline."

As the car left the cemetery, Taran took a deep breath. Fortunately, this was one occasion when Kes had listened to him.

Pauline packed her suitcase and said 'good-bye' to the boys. Her brother had arranged to take her home in his people carrier. They waved her off and went back into the empty living room to finish up the food. As they sat with full plates, they reflected on the day's events. The gathering at the beach house had gone without a hitch. About forty people had turned up; Dreadlock Sam had *not* been one of them.

Danielle had brought Dave. It was Taran's first proper opportunity to catch up with her since he'd arrived back – when she'd come around to tell them about Blake's death, their conversation had been about nothing but the tragedy.

He chatted with her as she piled up a plate of cocktail pasties and sausage rolls.

"Hey, watch your figure."

"This is for Dave. I've found my pie-man," she winked. "You were right, Taran. I needed someone more down-to-earth. I have such a laugh with him and he treats me good. He's very protective. At first I thought he was a jealous control freak but now I can see he's just caring for me."

"That's great, Danielle. How's your modelling going?"

"It's interesting really. When I first met Dave I took him along to a fashion show I was doing for a swimwear company. It was down at the rugby club in the marquee. I really wanted to impress him. I thought that if he saw me up there on the catwalk doing my thing it would keep him hooked. But his reaction wasn't what I expected. At the end of the show, I went off to find him but he looked really cross about what he'd seen. He said if I was doing anything else like that, he didn't want to come. I was shocked and thought he was crazy. But when we left, he said I made myself look cheap and he wanted more for me than that. It reminded me of your little talk with me on the settee."

Taran smiled. "Yeah, I won't forget that day easily. I came up from a fabulous surf session to find a blubbering beauty, didn't I?"

She lowered her eyes. "Well, you were very kind to me." Brightening, she added, "Anyway, you'll probably be glad to know I've decided to be a bit choosy what stuff I model from now on. I love it, Taran. Dave makes me feel that someone's looking out for me. We're already talking about our future together. His brother breeds pedigree dogs and he says he'll talk to him about getting me a puppy for my birthday."

Taran looked over at Dave. "You've got a good one there, treat him well and whatever you do, girl, don't cheat on him!"

She had an excited sparkle in her eyes that Taran hadn't seen before. He was glad to see her happy about something good for a change. When she turned to walk away, she whispered in his ear, "I'm really gonna try to stay off the coke as well."

As early evening approached, Kes brought down his guitar. Blake had always loved it when he played. It seemed poignant to strum away and sing some of his favourite songs. A group of scantily dressed girls gathered around and listened to his rendition. He was genuinely moved as they broke into tears and passed a large box of tissues amongst themselves. After Kes laid the guitar aside, Taran noticed him embrace a few of the girls in a kind, brotherly manner. He seemed sincere and caring. Judging by the state of his white shirt, a lot of the girls had cried on his shoulder – much make-up and mascara had rubbed off on him. He'd discarded his jacket and tie a long time back. His unbuttoned shirt was now smeared in black lines, with patches of lipstick and foundation. Taran was proud of him.

"You survived it all, Kes," he commented.

Kes sighed. "Yeah, it all turned out the way it should've really, didn't it? I owe you one for stepping in and dealing with that situation with Sam. It was right on the edge of blowing open. I nearly lost it." He laughed. "It would have been hectic to say the least. That dope head has got some mouth on him. I'm glad you shoved me in the car when you did. Hey, how d'you reckon I did with those girls? I tried really hard to behave myself. Did you see me? I had to hug them all."

"Yeah, I was smiling away to myself. It was a nice touch when you brought down your guitar. It kind of mellowed out the atmosphere a bit... Danielle seems well into Dave, doesn't she? He looks like a strong guy."

"He'll need to be, to rein her in! I wouldn't wanna try it." He suddenly felt a horrible dart of pain over Ruby. When everything was busy he could consign his distress to the back of his mind. It was harder when he had to slow down and give himself time to think. Taran could read his mood-swing instantly.

"Kes, you're doing pretty well, considering the state you were in when I found you on the beach. Give yourself a break."

He poured out a couple of glasses of red wine, and they rested on the sofa. Kes looked uneasy and pensive.

"Where d'you think Blake is now, Taran? I remember what you said to him once. You know, that stuff about our bodies being our earth suits. I've thought a lot about that since. Sometimes, I look at my body and think, 'Surely I'm more than flesh and bones?' I mean, how weird is it, that when you break us down, we're just a small heap of dust and a bucket of water? We're definitely more than that, as human beings, aren't we? This body's just a tent, isn't it? It houses the *real* us. A house is empty when a person leaves it, but they're still alive. They've just gone somewhere else. But where do they go? I find it all really freaky." He took a large slurp of wine. "What did you think when you looked at that coffin today?"

"Seeing it lying there just reinforced what I always think – life's a gift. We've got to be grateful for it and treat it with respect. We didn't create ourselves. We have free will and we all have to make our choices as we go through the journey – whether that's for good or evil. Then the time comes when we will all have to meet our Maker and give an account of how we lived down here. Did we respond to love or did we align with rebellion and hatred? There will have to be a separation. Light can't mix with darkness; oil can't mix with water."

"But where's Blake? He could be a right pain but I wouldn't say he was evil."

"We can't judge his heart, Kes. Look at what you're facing in yourself at the moment. You're getting deeply into what's really at the core of you. I wonder, what was going on at that level in Blake's life? He'd certainly made many choices. It's not for us to say why he responded to things in the way he did. The truth is he found it hard to face his own selfishness. We can only deal with our own responses and leave Blake to his Maker."

Kes knocked back his drink and poured another one. "D'you wanna know something, Taran? If I'm honest, death scares the hell out of me."

"Well, let it."

"What?"

"Scare the hell out of you. Once the hell is out of you, you won't be scared about it any more... Hey, this is great wine. What is it?"

Kes reached for the bottle and read the label.

"It's from the Beulah estate. I found it in the back of Dad's drinks cabinet. It's amazing, isn't it?"

They finished off the bottle and turned in for bed. It had been a long, testing day.

Chapter Thirty-Two

THE PHONE CALL

EARLY THE NEXT morning Kes' phone rang. He didn't respond but left it to go onto voicemail. Hours later he recalled the message while sitting at the breakfast bar with Taran.

"Kes, I need to speak to you. Call me back as soon as you get this, please."

It was from his dad.

He uttered a disapproving groan. "Oh no, my dad's trying to get hold of me. I really don't want to talk to him right now."

Pressing ring-back, he was soon on the receiving end of a brusque download of information.

"Hi Kes, how come you've been so long getting back to me? I called over three hours ago. Don't you pick up your messages?" He gave Kes no chance to respond before launching abruptly into the reason behind his call. "Listen, I'm coming back to live at Trevanna for six months or so. Steph's going to be doing some writing, so it will serve us as a good base for her to get on with that. I'll need you to leave within a couple of weeks." It was blunt, matter-of-fact, with no room for negotiation. "I hear things haven't been going well lately. A friend of mine from the Trevanna Bay Golf Club told me about that guy Blake. Kes..."

Kes held his breath in anticipation – maybe a word of compassion might come from his father at last? Surely he could understand what an awful time he was going through and offer some kindness?

Not surprisingly, there was no diplomacy or tact forthcoming. Instead, he ended the call with a heartless instruction. "Kes... make sure you leave the place in immaculate condition."

As the call ended, the years of absorbing his father's emotional incompetence boiled over. He channelled the noxious energy into his fist and punched the kitchen cabinet so hard that his knuckles bled. Torrents of choice swear words spewed out of his mouth. He glared at Taran, as if wanting him to share some of the pain. "That guy is so hard and dysfunctional. He's a complete genius at screwing my head up! The only thing that ever draws my old man's attention to me, is if I've got a beautiful girl hanging on my arm. Then he acts like a pervert, lays on all the charm and tries to get off with her. I hate him

Taran. He's got no ability to see things from my point of view." He spat out the last few sentences with real angst. "He's just told me I have to get out within two weeks. He's coming over to live here, so *Stephanie* can write. It's typical of him, he'd do anything to keep his tart happy, but stuff his son. And don't even try to give me any of that forgiveness crap. Now you can see why I live behind a fortress. I have to!"

He stormed out and went down to the beach.

Taran flicked through a surf mag. He didn't take Kes' outburst personally. After giving him plenty of time to cool off, he went looking for him.

He soon discovered him, slouched against a rock. The glint in his eyes said 'sorry.'

"Look, Kes, I'm planning on going back to California soon. Jayden's folks have a place in Redding. They let him use it as he wishes. It's not on the coast, but it's pretty cool and there's a good highway with a beautiful scenic route that eventually gets you to the sea. All the guys that hang out with him are really laid-back. Why don't you come out with me?"

Kes didn't need any persuasion. "My insides are like a car wreck, Taran." He scanned over the whole panorama of the bay. "This place is really beautiful, isn't it? It seems so calm and restful, but it doesn't give me any real peace – not deep down inside where I truly need it. A bit of pretty scenery can't heal my shattered messed up soul. You've found something that I want. If you can help me discover it in Redding, I'm game for that... Thanks Taran... Thanks a million... You're a true mate and I love you with all my freakin' broken heart!"

Taran squeezed him so hard it nearly winded him. Lifting him off the ground he reciprocated Kes' sentiment. "Come on, let's go dig out your passport and book our flight."

Chapter Thirty-Three

BACK TO BEULAH

I T TOOK KES four evenings to share the significance of
the scripted tattoo with Alice. He'd come over after work
and stay until the early hours.

Most of that time was spent lying out on a rug beside her
caravan.

There was one occasion when they had walked through
the grounds of Beulah. It had started to rain and they'd run
into a small thicket – there, under the canopy of trees, he
had exposed the agony of his final weeks at Trevanna Bay.

He'd opened his wet shirt and uncovered his chest. The
word 'life' ran over his tanned flesh in Celtic lettering. It

stood as a bold, overcoming statement, defying the ugly encounters he'd experienced with death.

"This reminds me of how close I came to the edge. When Taran and I got out to California, we settled in Redding. After a few days we headed off on a road trip with Jayden. I had the sentence etched onto my arm in Sacramento – at the same time, I had this written across my heart."

His disclosures had laid bare his soul to a young woman shrouded in darkness. His eyes often searched hers for a response. The intensity of the detail had brought to the forefront ghosts from his past. Despite the pain, he didn't mind sharing his brokenness. He'd grown to love honesty and had come to see that superficial relationships were dangerous.

"These tattoos are only skin-deep, but before they ever appeared on the surface, they were first carved into my heart. I've been through hell and hell's been through me. That's why I ain't ever going back. I've got to live for something deeper that doesn't hurt everybody around me."

Alice was both fascinated and scared. No one had ever been real about themselves with her before. Although his authenticity showed him to be trustworthy, it also meant he wouldn't tolerate pretence. She had spent her whole life hiding in the shadows of deceit. Her artfully cunning ways were set for a head on collision with his candour.

When Kes was hard at labour on the estate, Alice had plenty of time to think. Impressed and affected by his story, she pondered many aspects of it. In doing so she invariably arrived at the same impasse. Whenever she thought about Ruby and Erin her mind froze with jealousy. She'd linger on thoughts of his intimacy with them and longed to be on the receiving end of his affections. Somewhere she yearned to be written into a chapter of his life with the same amount of impact and significance that these women had commanded. She felt painfully aware that Ruby had possessed his thinking and had an advantage over her by being part of his history. She still didn't know where she stood in relationship to him, often feeling like the little sister he visited because there was no one else to talk to.

Her desire to know what Ruby and Erin looked like grew into an obsession. All she could do was imagine them from his descriptions. She wanted to be able to compare herself to them and longed to know if she was as attractive. Ruby's hair was long and blonde, Erin's brunette, hers raven. Did hair colour matter to him that much? Hadn't he fallen in love with the image of a blonde as a young teenager? As she wrestled with self-examination, she allowed herself to accept that her feelings towards him were very strong.

With so much time on her hands, she planned a way to test him.

Melantha had trained her in all manner of witchery. When it came to the fine art of seduction, she could have achieved an A*.

Overwhelmed with a longing to be desired by him, she devised a trap.

The primary law of enticement was location, location, location. The first thing she had to do was to choose a place.

In order to create a suitable, romantic atmosphere, she needed somewhere with few distractions. It must be secluded and full of mystique.

She was spoilt for choice on this one. As she contemplated ideas, she felt anxious. Every time she'd been with Kes it had been in isolated, undisturbed settings and she'd always had his complete attention.

Her plan already looked to be off to a shaky start and she'd only just begun to think about point number one.

Suddenly, she remembered the thicket where he had opened up the deepest recesses of his heart. It was already marked in his memory as a special place where the two of them had shared intimacy.

She would take advantage of his vulnerability.

Melantha's sultry voice spoke from a distant memory, "Never scorn the power of soft candlelight." She would furnish the whole area with hot, melting, vanilla tea-lights.

Next, was the question of what she should wear.

Her mind examined the moment his hand had reached out towards her and lifted her fallen sleeve to cover her bare flesh.

Perhaps it might be best to show a little, but make sure much was hidden. Melantha had given her an outfit that she'd once worn on stage during the *Fairy Fay* performances. It oozed Victorian Gothic sensuality. The top was a bustier corset, tightly fitted and strapless with lacing at the front. The long skirt was made of black mesh and had a short, frilled overskirt in velvet. Alice had worn it with the burgundy silk corset to a Halloween party and received no end of compliments. With a few gold bangles and accessories, she could easily achieve a romantic, vintage look. It would suit the setting perfectly.

The potent influence of the right scent would stir his senses below the threshold of consciousness. She would dab exotic blends of rose and sandalwood on every pulse point on her body. It would increase her attractiveness and serve to enhance his pleasure.

Finally, she needed to play a game with him, so as to heighten his anticipation. It must draw upon his manly desire to be heroic and adventurous. She would send him a cryptic invitation that would be both mysterious and whimsical. It would arouse the explorer in him and lead him to her luscious den.

Kes discovered her letter as he returned late from an intensive time of heavy lifting. It had been a beast of a day, clearing vast amounts of overgrown vegetation. As he ran the envelope through his mud-stained fingers, a lump lodged hard in his throat.

That dreadful afternoon, when he had eventually opened the birthday card from Ruby, had been a monumental moment. There was an altar in his heart that marked the spot.

His hands trembled as he turned the piece of parchment. Alice had placed a wax seal over the flap, which instantly appealed to his artistic nature – it was unusual and spoke romantically of days gone by. Its presence made the invitation look more alluring and secretive.

As he broke it open it made a pleasing 'snapping' sound. He drew out a piece of cream paper with ragged edges. In beautifully styled calligraphy there lay a short message. He scanned over the hand-written request:

Meet me in the thicket at midnight. Fortune favours the brave and courageous.

Alice

At first he smiled to himself. There was a similar text on the weights room wall at the beach house. He could never see why his dad displayed such a statement. To Kes, it was a macho message with not much substance. In his opinion fortune hadn't favoured his father. Although he was pumped with an expanded chest and large muscles, he was a wimp when it came to character issues. He was never reliable or trustworthy, always self-centred and hard.

Kes never thought of him as being strong and manly, instead he viewed him as an ineffectual coward. His dad's decal might read *Fortune favours the strong,* but when it came to spiritual strength, he'd be a liability in a girl's tug-of-war team. If they wanted support, they'd be best to relegate him to the sidelines.

Kes felt a stirring of anger. He remembered his dad not even being able to offer him a word of comfort over Blake's death. No, he wasn't brave or strong. He had no emotional testosterone.

"Oh, Alice, what are you up to?" He spoke out loud, in a tone of affection and care.

Yes, he'd go. Check out her little scheme, unveil the enigmatic game. But he wouldn't go unguarded. He'd put on wisdom as well as his fresh jeans and T-shirt.

He soaked his tired muscles in a long hot bath, and then grabbed a plate of food. When he'd finished eating, he rested on the sofa for a while.

As the night drew in, he picked up an art book that was lying on the coffee table. Taran had recently sent it to him as a gift. He opened the first page and read the scrawled message from his best friend:

> *Kes, enjoy the journey, stick close to the one who loves you the most, Taran.*

He flicked through some of the pages. It was unusually styled, as a sort of picture book for grown-ups. Twelve beautiful oil paintings illustrated a rich poetic text. Readers were encouraged to embark on a bold and engaging journey in the quest to find true love. The road ahead was dangerous and difficult but it eventually led to a place of fulfilment and rest. His eyes lingered on a particular page. The revamped image was based on a famous painting. It depicted a man nearly ensnared in a woman's grasp. The accompanying words read:

> *A letter, a text message, an email, could negatively change my destiny. A moment's decision! I was on course, travelling in the right direction, when the dark clouds started to gather and swirl ominously. Suddenly a rush of the purple heady scent, a glimpse of the veil, a beguiling captivating voice is provoking me to come off the narrow road, to lower my guard, to drop my sword, to become entangled. I feel the intense strength of the desire. I feel the magnitude of the moment. Yet, another*

voice cries out within me. Wake up, run, flee, and get out from this barbed and thorny den. Take the lead for a far greater adventure.

He laid the book aside carefully, and glanced at his watch. It was ten to twelve.

He picked up his keys, drove towards the thicket, parked up and strolled down over the bank.

Chapter Thirty-Four

IN THE THICK OF IT

I T WAS a hot, sticky night. A thick covering of cloud held
in the heat of the day. Although the moon was blocked
out, plenty of soft light glistened in front of him.

As he drew near to the thicket an exotic bouquet of spices
hit his senses.

A magical aura of sorcery hung in the air.

Alice was positioned in the midst of a circle of trees as
if she was on stage. She looked almost like a statue and
appeared to be in a dazed trance.

As he beheld the stunning artistry of it all, he experienced
an uneasy tension within his soul. It was as if a lasso had
been thrown over him. It was not yet tightened but he could

sense its presence. A strong thought entered his mind that sought to flatter him: *"Alice has done all of this for you. She has dressed provocatively to delight you – only you."*

Like a woodland nymph, she sat in all her loveliness. Her raven hair hung to one side in cascading waves. Though much of her body was clothed, she revealed tender hints of radiant skin. The warmth, the scent and the candlelight all worked together to create a soft, sensual atmosphere.

She looked like she had come from another world – this perfect image of womanhood called to him to receive her. What harm would it do to lie with her? It would be sheer delight. What more could he wish for, than this stunning beauty offering herself to him on a woodland floor?

He entered the thicket and stood in front of her. The tight lacing on her bodice emphasised her tiny waist but caused the top of her breasts to curve and spill over the bustier.

He dropped to his knees, pressing in towards her, so close that his chest brushed hers. His lips were less than a breath away. He pushed his mouth under her hair towards her neck; it swept across her skin sending tingles down her spine. Catching the beautiful fragrance of her hair, he whispered in her ear, "Alice, I want you to get naked with me, stark naked."

As a surge of triumph ripped through her soul, she started to untie the lacing on her bodice.

His strong hand met hers, arresting and firm; he stopped her from going any further.

With eyes blazing with anger, he raged, "How could you do this to me? You know full well what you're doing! I've completely bared myself to you! Didn't you hear a word that I said to you over the past few days?"

He withdrew his hand but remained close. His voice was still scolding.

"Did you *listen* when I told you about Erin and how stupid and selfish I was? My baby was mutilated because of this seductive crap – sacrificed to the god of pleasure. Ruby's lost her mind and I nearly committed suicide!"

He stood up and paced the thicket.

"What's this all about, Alice? You knew I needed a big break from this stuff, yet you've piled it on! You don't want to *give* anything to me. There's something ugly inside you that just wants to steal and destroy."

He strode back to her, knelt down and got right into her face, so near that she could feel his breath on her skin.

"I could take you, girl! I could have you freely on this forest floor, but then what? What happens afterwards, Alice? You'd get used like a bargain-basement whore and both of our insides would lie in tatters, torn to shreds by vice."

Alice looked dismayed and stunned. She hadn't foreseen this sort of reaction at all.

She relaxed from her stiff pose and drew her knees up to her chest. There was something strange happening that she couldn't quite fathom. Despite his fury, she never once felt threatened or intimidated. Somewhere deep inside, she actually liked what he was saying.

Kes sensed her give way and yield. He sat down in front of her and took on a gentler tone.

"Look Alice, I want to be married one day and have children. What have I got to give my wife and kids if I can't give them faithfulness? I owe it to them to be able to resist the power of all of this. If I fall for your temptation now, it will just wear down my soul to do it again and again. I'd be helpless prey to any beautiful woman who comes on to me – weakened to the wiles of every bit of seduction that heads my way. D'you know what it's like to have an unfaithful father? It rips your heart out! You have to watch your mum go through hell and you're left feeling worthless, tossed on the refuse dump of life with no identity – I want my kids to have better than that, I want my wife to be able to trust me!"

He ran his eyes over her and slid the satin ribbon of her bodice through his fingers. Looking back into her lovely, hazel eyes, he groaned softly. "It's true, Alice, I want you to get naked with me."

She stared at him. By now she knew some of the things he said were conundrums – mysteries waiting to be revealed.

He let go of the ribbon.

"Who are you underneath those sexy clothes? And I don't mean what does your body look like? Who is the real girl deep inside you? Strip for me and show me who you truly are. 'Cause, I tell you what I see – not a young woman with a glossy pout and exposed breasts, but a lost, lonely little girl who's bound in fear!"

He lifted her chin. He was firm but not rough.

"Come on, Alice, get real with me. Let's talk about you. Risk letting down your walls! Tell me why you do the things you do? Show me how messed up you are. That's the kind of 'getting down and dirty' I want to do with you."

She looked like she wanted to cry, but still refused to say a word. Her lack of honesty frustrated him.

"Is that really what you want me to do? Undress you and make out? It would take twenty minutes at most, but it's not what you really need. We'd both be left with nothing." His eyes flared up again with strength. "You insult me, Alice! Is that all you think you're worth to me – a cheap screw? Now, blow out your silly candles before you set the woods on fire!"

He sat on a rock watching as she blew out the flames of her little tea-lights. He felt compassion for her as she collected them up and placed them into a tin bucket.

She did actually look very beautiful – exceptionally delicious.

He could have easily made a meal out of her on that leafy bed, but this wasn't about him or his appetite.

This was all about her and hoping she'd grow to realise that she was a treasure worth finding.

Alice wrapped herself in a shawl and sat on a rock opposite him looking down. She was shocked when he walked over and gently took her hand. His grasp tightened as he led her firmly out of the thicket.

She ventured the first comment she'd made throughout the whole episode.

"Kes, I thought that's what you would want from me."

"Did you, Alice? Is that really why you put on such a performance? How about trying to be truthful with yourself? Because I think tonight's little show came out of insecurity. And as for it being what we guys want, it might be what we think we want. But actually, we need much more than that. We need someone who can stand alongside us in this crazy battle of life and be a true friend as well as a lover."

Walking quickly and purposefully, he almost marched her back to her caravan.

"There, now, off you go to bed. Sleep tight and we'll talk tomorrow… Oh, and Alice, think hard about this one – I'd never be willing to share you with another. You already have a lover – Darcus!"

With that, he set off across the meadow to retrieve his van.

Chapter Thirty-Five

THE PURPLE VEIL

WHEN KES CAME in from work the following evening, he found Alice sitting in his living room. She was reading through the book he'd left out on the coffee table. Having studied Gothic literature at college, some of the images and text fascinated her. The expression on her face was one of complete astonishment.

He chucked his keys down on the side and leant up against the counter. "Hi Alice, what's up? You look dumbfounded."

She fingered the glossy cover. "It's this image on the front of your book."

"Great, isn't it? I just love it."

"Yeah, it's beautifully painted, but it's not that, Kes..."
She hesitated. "Look, after what happened in the thicket,
I can see this is only gonna work if I get honest. I'm not
used to doing that. I've spent my whole life hiding what I
really feel about things." As she continued to speak, she
avoided any eye contact with him. "I've never shared with
anyone the motives behind the things I do. I've hoarded all
my inner secrets, stashed them away, buried them. I'm very
skilled at doing it because no one's ever been interested in
the *real* me before. It's as if that person has been entombed,
and is lying there voiceless, almost dead... Your talk last
night disturbed me, probably in a good way. It was as if I'd
heard someone calling to me for the first time in my life."

Although it was difficult, she managed to look up at him.
"All day, I've been wrestling with how you treated me last
night. When you resisted me trying to get off with you, I
know you were looking for something deeper than sex. It
was like you came down into a prison and shook the bars. I
didn't ever think anyone would come for me. I'd given up –
just wasting away on the floor in my fetters and chains...
I want to try to get real with you. But you need to
understand something – this is alien to me. I feel vulnerable
and exposed. And all this truth stuff is weird."

He smiled to himself and walked towards his bedroom.
"This is cool, Alice. I'm gonna grab a shower, then you've
got my full attention."

He disappeared for fifteen minutes and came back into
the kitchen. Opening the fridge, he pulled out several bits
and pieces. "Say whatever you need to."

Fighting tears, she tried to explain the effect of his
challenge upon her. "Can you imagine how it feels to a

person who lives in a windowless, lightless room, when after years someone arrives with a blazing torch in their hand? It hurts, Kes. I'm nearly blind when it comes to seeing truth and if you're asking me to walk in it, I'm almost paralysed – I'm good at lying and being dishonest. I'm not used to being sincere. You'll have to be very patient. Take it slow. Be gentle with me."

He looked at her for the first time with a hint of real attraction in his eyes. He liked what he was beginning to see.

"Well, Alice, you're off to an excellent start. To be able to say you're a good liar shows that you're already beginning to be truthful. This kind of talk turns me on!"

With a plate of sandwiches in hand, he came over to the settee and dropped down next to her. Usually, when they were in the cottage together, he sat opposite her with his guitar.

Surprised by his closeness, she picked up the book again and stared at the picture on the cover. Two young people were dressed in pale clothes and bearing armour. They were breaking through a dark veil which was hanging on a wooden construction in the middle of a field.

Alice pointed to the image. Her voice was quiet and troubled. "You see this place? I went there last night in a vision. It was twilight, and I was walking up a hill in open countryside. There on the horizon stood this strange four poster structure. Draped with purple fabric, the soft material was billowing in the wind. It was magnetic. I felt dominated as it pulled me forward. It was so attractive and possessed power that started to overcome my will. As I drew close, I knew I should pass through it and continue on my journey, but its beauty called to a hunger within me. It cried out to my emptiness, offering me rest and sanctuary. I wanted to bury myself in its sensuality and stay there forever."

Kes didn't say anything, but he wondered if she understood that she was identifying something within herself. What had happened in the thicket last night had sprung from this place. She had manifested the essence of the purple structure. Its spirit was embodied within her and had tried to seduce him.

He wanted to question her, "Does it sound familiar?" But he respected that she'd asked him to go easy on her. He knew all too well the power of this stuff. He'd been a prisoner to it himself.

She continued to describe what she'd seen, "As I went inside, there were sconces dripping with purple candle-wax and a strong, poisonous scent came from some poppies that were twisted around the frame. The whole place was full of people. They were stoned and enjoyed the pleasure they found in each other's image and sexuality. Sounds were rippling out – beautiful, heady rock songs. The lyrics promised that fulfilment, identity and intimacy could be discovered in human love. Everyone within the veil had pain in their souls, but their anguish was superficially numbed as they got wasted. There was a scattering of velvet floor cushions and I sank down into them, not wanting to move on. I loved what the place offered. It relieved my loneliness."

Almost unconsciously, she ran her finger across the scabby scratches that marred her pretty wrist.

Kes rested back on the sofa with his hands behind his head and drank in her beauty. She stretched out her legs and re-arranged her skirt. Ruffles of netting from her petticoat softly enveloped her form. She looked at Kes sadly. "The whole purple veil is just a fake, fantasy of love and not the real thing, but I've been addicted to the hope that it promises. When I was sitting on those cushions in the vision, a faceless phantom came to me. I lay in the embrace of this being, and its countenance became the face of a man. His appearance was a lot like yours, Kes, but it wasn't you. It was Darcus. I've never seen him properly before – he's always been hooded, but he came to me last night. As he held me I felt dissatisfied and I heard your voice say, 'If only you would dare to believe that there's a love that's real and true, you could awake from this counterfeit and flee from this compromising place.' "

Kes instantly fathomed the full interpretation of the vision, but he felt she wasn't ready to hear it.

She'd already told him that she would need time to adjust to truth. The searchlight that he wielded might be too overpowering.

He wondered whether to risk probing into why she self-harmed. What caused her so much mental suffering that she would physically damage herself in order to release some of the stress? He understood this was at the root of Darcus holding such a prominent position in her life.

Something had opened the door for his entrance.

Once she became empowered with that revelation, she'd be able to break out of the purple veil.

He pulled himself up. "Well, Alice, that was some vision! I'm glad I figured in it and said something cool. My first impression is it sounds a bit like the action going on in the thicket last night. But don't let's go there." He walked over to the kitchen area. "D'you want a piece of chocolate cake?"

He purposefully played down the intensity. Darcus was a massive issue for her and he knew he needed to tread carefully.

He watched as she finished up a large slice of the moist sponge. He was pleased to see her eat it. A couple of weeks ago she would have taken the tiniest bit and nibbled it like a mouse.

Another surprise awaited him.

Completely out of the blue, she started to expose a secret. Putting down her plate, she threw caution to the wind.

"Kes, d'you want to know my deepest fantasy?"

He sank down onto the sofa beside her. "Huh? Yeah, Alice, I would *really* like to know. Go on, lay it on me."

Chapter Thirty-Six

ALL ABOUT ALICE

KES WAS DELIGHTED at how much Alice had opened up in such a short period of time. She was stripping off her inhibitions before his very eyes. His 'reading of the riot act' the previous night had obviously had a big effect on her.

"Okay, here goes, my secret fantasy is lying in the arms of a man forever. It's not even sexual, just lying there would do it for me."

"I could help you fulfil it right now, if you like," he smiled, pulling the ring on a can of cider, "not forever though." He glanced at his watch. "Would three hours count?"

Alice felt very strange as Kes settled back onto the cushions and pulled her into his arms. He gently folded them around her and she lay like a child snuggled up next to him. Occasionally he stroked her hair, lightly, tenderly. Their eyes didn't meet; she rested against him, looking away.

He knew what this was all about. She needed a daddy, someone in whom she could feel safe and secure. She wanted to belong, to know she had someone's unconditional love, devotion and attention. Not for any reason, not so they could get anything out of her, but just because she was worth caring for.

Cradled into Kes' warm body, her own words lit the candle that began to lead her out of her dungeon.

"My dad left home one night after a massive argument with my mum, and I never saw him again. I was just four years old. I used to wake up and hear bitter rows, but that one topped the lot. Day after day, I'd fantasise about him coming back to see me, but he never came.

"As I grew a bit older, I heard rumours that he lived nearby and had another family. I was so jealous. Often I would cry myself to sleep, but I never shared how I felt with my mum. I would overhear her saying bad things about him, but to me he was still my dad and somewhere deep inside I loved him.

"When I started school, I would scan the faces of all the men waiting in the playground, wondering if one of them was him. I even ran up to a man once and asked him if he was my daddy.

"I remember a policeman coming into our classroom and warning us about 'stranger danger'. We had to fill out worksheets to help us be on guard if a stranger approached and started to talk to us.

"But d'you know, Kes, the place that I felt most in danger from strangers? It was my own home. Mum was always bringing men back. It's not that she was a prostitute or anything, but she was constantly looking for a relationship to fulfil her.

"I hated having these odd guys show up. I felt tiny, voiceless and defenceless. I was angry with them for getting all her attention. Most of the time they'd ignore me – it was as if I was always in the way, spoiling things for them.

"She never found a guy who would cherish her. It wasn't for lack of searching – she had a string of relationships over a period of fourteen years. Some were brief encounters with fly-by-night types, but most moved in for a good few months.

"We had a lovely cottage and I knew that nearly all of the blokes were more in love with the roof over their heads, the food and sex, than her. They'd come in, eat their tea whilst reading their newspapers, ogling the images of half naked women, and I'd think, 'my mum's nothing to them. They just live here in a mindless existence of TV, sex and chips'.

"She'd always end up with the 'going nowhere guys'. To me, they were fat, lazy, lust buckets.

"Mum worked late shifts, and sometimes I'd go downstairs and peep in on them watching all their porn whilst she earned the cash to keep them in pizza.

"She was so bubble-headed. Most weekends, she'd be out down the local pub, pretending to have a good time. How come it's having a 'good time' getting wasted? When

I eventually got to see her she'd be fighting a hangover or was high and out of it."

Kes reached for a sandwich. "Oh, that sounds familiar, my mum has her issues too. What's your mum called?"

"Lyndsey," Alice smiled. "She's very sweet, the sort of lady who'd do anything for anybody but in a self-effacing way. She tried to be kind to me, at least I had a home, food and clothes, but she never asked me how I was or how I felt about what was going on. She wouldn't have wanted to hear the answer. There's no way she'd have been willing to change the way she was living. So she carried on in denial and avoided anything from me that might challenge her."

Kes got up and put the kettle on. "Yeah, abandonment isn't just getting chucked out on the street, is it? Parents can't build into you what they haven't even got themselves. We look up to them thinking they're the big people with all the answers, but a lot of the time, *they* haven't even found what they're looking for."

He made her a hot drink and resumed his position holding her. He knew Alice was getting to the crux of her insecurity and fear. She was so relaxed that she visibly melted into him. There was great freedom in feeling protected. Sensing his lack of guile, she continued to open her heart.

"It was always risky and unpredictable at home. I was powerless, lonely and frightened most of the time. I lived a very secluded life, in that I would just disappear into my little box room most nights. I was very withdrawn and detached. If I ever came out of my bedroom, it felt really intimidating.

"As I grew up it got worse. I remember going into the bathroom one night. I walked in on this guy I'd never seen before. It's horrible to come across a strange bloke in your house in the middle of the night. To be aware that he's in a room next to your bedroom and you don't even know who he is. He looked at me all lustfully and tried to grasp me, but fortunately I wriggled free from his grip. I was so scared. I piled up books and furniture against my door but I knew I was really vulnerable. I'd have been completely defenceless if he'd made any attempt to get in.

"Mum was all giggly in the morning. As she flirted with him in the kitchen, she introduced me, 'Alice, this is Colin. You'll be seeing quite a lot of him in the future.' I thought 'thanks Mum – I nearly saw quite a lot of him last night.' But how could I tell her?

"She gave him a key to the house and he pretty much moved in with us for a few weeks. Whenever I'd go off to the bathroom, I would wrap myself so tightly in my dressing gown I could hardly breathe.

"The surprising thing is, I never actually got abused by any of them, but the fear was bad enough. It kept me awake, always alert and on guard. I'd be shattered by the time I got to school and then I'd get in trouble for not being able to concentrate.

"The worst guy of the lot of them has to be the one who lives with mum now. Jimmy Griffin! He's the reason I'm here. I couldn't take it anymore being under the same roof as him. He's a biker and has moved in with his dogs. He's filled the place with all his pot plants and leather gear. He's completely taken over our pretty little home. It was all stylish with painted furniture and country chic bits and pieces. Now it reeks of his Rottweilers and cheap, homemade booze. I clash with him all the time. He does

nothing to help Mum and he's turned our place into a drug
den. There's always a steady stream of people coming
by the house, day and night. Taxi's pull up, and off goes
Jimmy, popping out with his little package for the driver.
We get all sorts of mean and menacing types dropping in
for a few minutes. Mum can't or won't do anything about it.
For some crazy reason she's hooked on the slob."

Alice curled up her legs.

"Before I moved out, the only sense of peace I ever
experienced was when I managed to get some sleep – I
used to have a repetitive dream that I lived in a tree house.
Although there was always a pack of wolves encircling me,
at least I was safe off the ground!"

Kes didn't say a word. He knew she was allowing him
to look at the core of her soul. It was a revealing exposure.
They sat for a good half an hour in silence.

Alice had begun to unpack her life for the first time. It
was raw and real. Kes felt proud of her. She'd been brave.

It wouldn't be a good idea to send her back to the caravan.
With so much having been opened up, it was better for her
not to be alone. He remembered needing Taran to stick
close by him when he was at his most vulnerable.

She could stay over and have his bed while he slept on the
couch.

He whispered to her, "Alice, stop here tonight, you can
have my room."

When she didn't respond, he realised she was fast asleep.
Her countenance looked less tense than usual. He didn't
want to disturb her.

Staying put, he rested beside her. Eventually nodding off,
he held her all through the night.

Chapter Thirty-Seven

COMING CLOSER

A S ALICE WOKE the following morning, she found
herself next to Kes. His right arm was wrapped around
her waist. Gently slipping free, she went off for a shower.
Refreshed, she pulled on her crumpled clothes and went
back into the main room.

Kes stirred and smiled at her. "I'm not going to work this
morning. We're gonna fetch Vanda and your caravan and
bring them up here. I think you should be closer to me."

It took them a couple of hours to carry out the move.

Alice brushed Vanda down and harnessed her while Kes
packed up the make-shift bathroom. Her little tin bath
looked very feminine surrounded by a carpet of daisies.

He lifted all the pieces into the van and secured the door. It wasn't long before her brightly coloured home made its way to the meadow next to his garden. Soon, Vanda was settled into her new location, happily munching a variety of greens from the hedgerow.

Kes seemed satisfied with the arrangement. "This is gonna be so much better for you. Now you can use my place without all the trekking to and fro."

Alice looked troubled. She was concerned that she'd been brought out of obscurity. It had felt safe being hidden away in the wooded area. Now, no longer covered by the leafy canopy, she was wide open to view and to questioning. "What about the fact that I'm still an illegal trespasser? What would your employer, Mr Brunswick, say about that?"

"It's fine, trust me," Kes reassured her, "you won't get any problems from him."

She gazed towards the big old house. "Kes, what actually goes on in Beulah? I've heard strange stories about the way it's decorated and furnished. It sounds really eerie and bizarre."

As they sat down on his door step, Kes picked up a stick and fiddled with it. Peeling back strips of bark, he tackled her question. "Eerie and bizarre happenings are not so much about places as they are about people. A locality can act as a vortex for the metaphysical, but when you study what made the area like that, it always boils down to something *people* have done there – I mean, I could have added a few vibes to Trevanna Bay if Taran hadn't found me that night I nearly committed suicide. What we tap into, opens up realms and portals. Powers from the spiritual world can then manifest their personalities through our minds and enter the physical dimension. Once they have access, they then impact our souls and affect the way we live. They influence everything – our mindsets, our belief systems, the things we get into, what we gather around us. All that we express on the outside extends from within us. So, the art we display, how we treat ourselves and each other..." He would have continued but something started to manifest in Alice.

She suddenly hardened. Her eyes grew dark. A migraine sprung out of nowhere. Nausea swept her stomach and she started to shake.

"Kes, I need to spend some time alone. I feel really rough. I've got no energy. It's like it's been drained out of me. I'm going back to my caravan."

As she walked off down the path he caught up with her.

"Alice, there's a turmoil inside of you that won't get fixed by you running away or by smoking your weed. You can't keep putting this off. We need to talk about Darcus."

"I don't want to," she glowered, feeling an aversion towards him.

The strength and resistance of her retort was not spoken with her consent. It was not self-commanded but originated somewhere beyond her choice.

Kes knew she was mastered.

He held her face firmly in his hands. The steadfast look in his eyes washed through her, speaking into her soul beneath the gross blackness. "Alice, keep walking towards the light. Put your will into climbing up that staircase inside of you. There's a door at the top and someone is coming to rescue you."

"I think I'm going to throw-up," she muttered, urging.

Kes fetched a glass of water. He found her leaning up against the garden gate.

"Have a few sips of that." He brushed her hair aside. "Listen, you'll get through this. Go and lie down and we'll spend some time together this evening. You're gonna have a dream this afternoon. Things will come clearer."

He led her to the caravan, helped her into her bunk and tucked her in. His lips skimmed her forehead with a hint of a kiss. "Now get some sleep."

Chapter Thirty-Eight

THE DOOR

ALICE DID HAVE a dream that afternoon – vivid and memorable. She rushed to tell Kes as soon as she awoke.

They sat on the porch step in the early evening sunlight.

"I heard someone knocking on a door deep inside of me. It was the entrance into my heart. A huge iron bolt lay across it. I wrenched it back and let the caller in. It was a guy. He came in laughing. His presence flooded the whole place with light.

"At first I felt ashamed and guilty because so much chaos was being exposed. The place was filthy. Bins were overflowing and garbage was everywhere. There was no way you would want to invite anyone into that foul place. It needed sanitising.

"I apologised, but this man said that he didn't mind the mess. He'd come to help me clear it up and change the atmosphere." Alice smiled. "He was obviously picking up on the constant distress and agitation I live under!

"He'd even brought food to share with me. I tasted it, and it was better than anything I'd ever eaten before. It immediately started to nourish and heal me.

"He had the kindest eyes I've ever seen. I felt totally safe in his company. I knew I could tell him anything about myself and that he wouldn't be shocked – all my dark secrets!

"I was convinced he knew me, *really* knew me, everything about me! But it didn't scare me, because I sensed he had the power to sort out all the bad stuff and make it come good.

"He stretched out his arms and told me he wanted to take me on a journey. I noticed some strange marks on his hands. His palms looked bruised. When I asked him how he'd got injured, he told me it happened while he was constructing a road. He'd forged a way for me to be rescued from the things that haunted me.

"He'd taken a big hit for me.

"I marvelled at his endurance because the scars looked very deep and painful. I sensed he'd known extreme affliction and self-denial to open up a route for my freedom.

"I headed for the door, but he just laughed and called me back. I went over to him and he took my face in his hands saying, 'You can't run out on your own heart. It has to be changed from within. But I tell you, Alice, something beautiful is taking place here. Everything is becoming new.'

"Oh Kes, I was so excited, he told me my heart would come to peace as soon as a couple of squatters had been evicted. Two brutally oppressive rulers had taken over and were dominating me. They had stolen precious stuff that belonged to me and were wrecking my life. He said that because I'd welcomed him in, a change of government was taking place. A dark kingdom was being overthrown and a new kingdom was becoming established."

None of what she'd described was a revelation to Kes. He knew prophetically what she was going through and why. He drew up one of his legs and pressed his back against the doorframe. He could get a better view of her from this angle. He thought how lovely she looked with her flouncy skirt gathered up around her knees. Her long slender limbs now carried an olive glow from soaking up all the sunshine. Her physical beauty stirred him, but what got him more excited was how she was so perceptive about the things that were being uncovered. Her vulnerability was releasing a soft womanliness that was beyond sexy. He reined in his thoughts as his eyes followed her jet black hair all the way down her back. "Hey, Alice, this is stunning. What happened next?"

"I saw that inside me there was a throne that overflowed with all the sensuality of the purple veil. Because I'd never known good fathering, a stronghold had developed around the tender beauty of my femininity. That wonderful gift had been crushed and defiled by a provocative spiritual force."

She picked up a tiny wild flower that was growing out of a crack in the step. "What should have blossomed lay barren. There was toxic bitterness in my heart; such was the anger and pain. I'd absorbed it from all the behaviour of the men in my life that had used their manhood in a negative way and hurt me. It made me grow haughty and arrogant.

"I despised men and looked down on their weakness. I hated them for treating Mum and I the way they did. I realised that was why I'd tried to seduce you, Kes. This area in me wanted to control and dominate you.

"When you resisted my temptation but didn't reject me, you proved that you wanted the real me – the little girl who was locked away, buried underneath the licentiousness – the one whose dad had walked out.

"No one had ever sought her before.

"Your actions started to unlock my true worth and value. You didn't want to use me for something you could get. What you did began to heal me.

"You led me well.

"When I think of people like my mum, I know that so many women are crying out for men to act in the way you did. We want someone who can direct the course. Guys who can cover and protect us, be tough-minded but tender-hearted – warrior-poets!

"I was so shocked when you stopped me undressing. Something evil in me hated you, but the little girl in the dungeon rose from the dead. I was delighted you had battled for me. I knew you were showing me true love.

"Kes, I'm really sorry for the way I came on to you. I know I hurt you."

Her eyes watered over. Kes knew she truly meant it. He reached for her hand and ran his fingers through hers. He was deeply moved by what she'd said. "Carry on, Alice. This is beautiful."

The warmth of his touch caused a reaction. She constantly battled her feelings towards him and wondered if he realised he was as smokin' hot as he was kind.

Taking her eyes off him, she tried to concentrate on what she was saying. "I don't know what's beautiful about it. From now on it gets even worse! I've had a lot of input from a spiritual mentor called Melantha. She lives in a village nearby and runs the Three Castles pub. She epitomises the spiritual force in the purple veil. Vanda and the caravan belong to her. She lent them to me when I told her that I couldn't stand living around Jimmy anymore.

"I was moaning on to her about how much I hated him. I obviously hit a sore point because out came one of her many 'I despise men' stories.

"As we shared half a bottle of vodka, she gave me a lecture, 'Alice, let me teach you something from my experience. Some day Jimmy will get his comeuppance! Men think they carry the power in this world. But it's *so* easy to usurp. When you turn it on, you can get *anything* you want! They're simple prey. Especially the guys in top positions – the power goes straight to their heads and they overstep the mark. *We* end up holding the reins and calling the shots. You can even change government strategies with a bit of seduction… I dated an ambassador once. It's a typical 'same old' story. He thought he was 'the big guy' with all the clout. He gave me the wink at a hotel bar. I happily went up to his room for the night. He had a really

important meeting the next day. Loads of people had flown
in from all over the globe, but *I* decided to change the
course of events with a little flattery. He never showed
up for that meeting... We have power, Alice! It was music
to my ears to hear the excuses he made to his PA. He
lied, by saying that he was ill, and she had to tell *all*
his colleagues that the meeting was cancelled. It was
exhilarating for me! But as we made out under the sheets,
the most amusing thing was letting him think he was in
control. We can take their authority. Cut off their heads.
Women rule the world, Alice. We just let men think they
do.' "

Kes let out a deep sigh. Alice's story-telling had drawn
a thought about Erin to the surface. He remembered that
night before his birthday and the conflict he'd felt as he'd
unzipped her out of her tight shift dress.

Alice looked deeply into Kes' eyes and unfettered herself
with honesty. "It's all very well being manipulative and
conniving towards men, but there's a huge price to be paid
in your soul. I hate the hardness in me. I know why it's
there. It grew because of my need to self-protect, but the
walls I built to defend myself have become the prison that
locks me away. I want out, Kes. I want this stuff that rules
me to be overthrown."

Kes got up and stretched. He appreciated her explaining
how Melantha had encouraged the 'femme fatale'
approach towards guys. When he'd been DJing in the
club, his popularity had always made him a prized catch.
Instinctively he'd known it was the position that he held
that carried the 'pulling power'. Everyone who'd frequented
Attic had loved being associated with him because of his

success. It was like the groupies had wanted to make love to his image but not the real him.

He remembered something Jayden had said when they were driving through LA on a road trip. Having once played bass in a rock band, he had good insight into the pitfalls of being sought-after. 'Kes, it's like this, mate – although celebrity gives you a passport into stranger's bodies, you end up whoring yourself out in no-man's land. You'd be a fool to think it's you they really want. The people who throw themselves at you just want to validate themselves by basking in your perceived glory.'

Pulling himself back from his memories, he turned to Alice. "Shall we go for a stroll? Everything you're saying is brilliant. But what about Darcus, what else have you found out about him?"

જી

Chapter Thirty-Nine

EXIT DARCUS

A S THEY WALKED down over a grassy bank, Alice brought into focus the character that had dogged her life for months.

It cost her to expose him; he'd been such an important object of her affection. Yet something within Kes compelled her to want to divulge the truth about him.

"During my dream, I came across another room marked 'spirit guide'. It was full of mirrors, like a dressing room in a theatre. A mask was hanging on the wall – used as a disguise, it bore the features of a handsome man.

"A hooded being stood in the middle. As it lifted its face towards me I knew it was the real Darcus. His countenance was that of a vile demon, full of wickedness and malice. He had masqueraded as an intimate lover, but the play-acting soon dissipated to reveal the truth – a cruel, destructive force.

"He doesn't love or care for me, Kes. He's a liar and deceiver. He wants to rob, kill and destroy my life. He's always angling to drag me into Hades, a place of misery and eternal torment."

She started to pick at the skin around her nails, lifting them up to her mouth to chew. Kes gently took her hands and pulled them away. His voice was urgent, encouraging her, almost as if she was giving birth. "Keep going, you're nearly there."

"Darcus has been a strong presence that has continually sought my company. Always menacing, filling my mind with disquieting, harmful thoughts. He's occasionally manifested a pseudo affection that has charmed me into thinking he's fond of me.

"I opened a door that let him in and I'm powerless to remove him.

"He now sits like a squatter within me. He knows I can't evict him. I just have to bear the harassment of his spontaneous coming and going. He haunts me and his voice wears me down with his threatening suggestions.

"Although I've been terrified, I've become resigned to the situation. There's been nothing I can do to change it. I've had no option but to be subservient to him."

Kes squeezed her hand. "Listen, I believe there's always a light at the end of the tunnel. Good news can break into this gloom. D'you believe that?"

"I do, but I need to tell you something else that I learnt while I was asleep. I became aware of the reason that

Darcus had been able to enter me and gain so much control. I'd given him my consent by participating in Melantha's night of magical rites and incantations.

"I knew there was power in what I joined allegiance with. I surrendered my authority – gave my approval and agreement to whatever fiend was evoked by our actions. Looking back on that dreadful night at the Three Castles, I can remember the fear and daring anticipation that we felt as we conjured up the spirit beings.

"I knew I shouldn't have been doing it. My conscience told me it was forbidden. I was looking for power but what came through was illegitimate and renegade. It wasn't authorised for good. I didn't care that it was outlawed and slipping in through the spiritual black-market. I wanted to have the ability to affect things around me, to exercise an advantage over others, but I was the one who ended up becoming a slave. Darcus had a steel hand in a velvet glove. The essence of his being is that of an impersonator and soul-stealer."

Kes was relieved that she had come to understand this for herself. It would have been no good him telling her. He could sense there was an air of optimism in her voice despite the ugliness of the situation. Somehow a hope had been kindled that spurred her on to unmask Darcus, showing him up for what he really was. He could tell by her attitude that the fear that used to overwhelm her was breaking up.

"How did it end, Alice?"

"It was awesome. I was sorry that I had to wake up because this incredible peace broke into the hell of it all.

"The lovely man who had come to help me clean up my house said he wanted to introduce me to the ruler of the new kingdom. He presented me to his Father. He was the spitting image of the son in character and nature. This tender revelation of his fatherhood wrapped around me like a warm blanket of love that enfolded my shivering body.

"I had lived my entire life feeling like an orphan; I never knew what it was to be loved or cared for. I suddenly felt that I belonged as a daughter. I began to have hope and I didn't feel a slave to fear anymore.

"The father said that because his son had come into my heart, those evil forces could easily be driven out of me. He said his son was *all powerful* and had total authority over every principality and power."

Kes smiled at her. His whole face lit up. "D'you know who the son is, Alice?"

"I haven't got a clue. Who is he?" she asked curiously.

He laughed. "It's Jesus. I met him in Redding. I had a massive spiritual encounter that changed my life. Taran led me to him. He's all powerful. Darcus has to leave you, if you want him to. Just ask Jesus to tell him to exit. The only thing you've got to do is give the permission. It's easy for him! The hardest part has already been done by the way you've got real with him. He's conquered hell and death – ain't that good news, kid?"

Alice's eyes glazed over. Looking faint and weak, she grabbed Kes hand.

"Alice, you don't have to panic, just renounce the occult and ask Jesus to remove Darcus from your spirit. This isn't gonna be difficult. You should have seen the stuff I was released from!"

They stood under the towering oak tree where they had met for their first date. Kes gently held her shoulders as she asked Jesus to drive out Darcus and free her from Jezebel's seductive stronghold.

It wasn't a big fuss.

As Kes prayed, she felt a force lift out of her. Something was ebbing away. A divine exchange was taking place. As the evil left, there came an infilling of the sweetest spirit she'd ever encountered. She bubbled over with joy and ecstasy.

"Wow, Kes, this is more beautiful than the best weed I've ever smoked. I feel amazing!"

"Yeah, I'm with you on that one. It's better than any high I've been on."

As they strolled back to his cottage, he was delighted to see her looking so radiant and peaceful. "Couldn't buy what's just happened to you even if you had a billion in the bank! It's just a lavish, free gift from a dad who adores you!"

Once inside, Alice picked up Kes' art book while he made some tea. She read out the title poem:

The Purple Veil (Beyond Eros)
Take me beyond the purple veil into the field of innocence.
There we can run in purity untainted by the crimson stain
The purple fabric allures the eye outstanding in its garishness
Its heady scent has drugged those sleeping underneath its spell

Awake, awake from slumbers deep
And images of naked hope
For it stirs desire, arouses passion
But never fulfils body soul and spirit
Emotions still scream out for healing
The brave and courageous pioneer beyond Eros' thicket
strong
Daring to believe that there might be
A better way of intimacy.

"That kind of sums up everything you've been leading me through for the past few days." She smiled up at him. "Thanks Kes, the whole time I've known you, you've been a brilliant friend."

He placed some food on the coffee table. "Tomorrow, I'm gonna take you to Beulah, Alice. I'll show you what I get up to when you're sitting out in the field making daisy chains and jumpers."

Later that night, he took her over to the caravan.

Once she was safely inside, he walked back, whistling.

Alice flopped into her bed with a peace that transcended anything she could have ever hoped for or imagined. It took her a long while to get off to sleep. Her inner house was going through an awesome makeover and the little girl inside was having a party.

Chapter Forty

INSIDE THE HOUSE

THE SOUND OF an early songbird rang out across the meadow. It was as bright and clear as Alice's spirit. For the first time in her life she woke up feeling light-hearted and not in fear of what the day held.

The absence of dark, oppressive thoughts was mental bliss.

Everything was new.

She showered in the cottage and went back to the caravan to change out of her satin chemise.

Choosing what to wear proved difficult. Everything she picked up didn't really appeal to her anymore. None of it reflected her mood. It all reminded her of Melantha. She had no desire to shroud her cheerful spirit in that miserable sackcloth. Out of the corner of her eye she saw one of Kes' shirts flapping in the breeze. He'd left it out on the washing line overnight. The soft white cotton looked appealing. She was sure he wouldn't mind her putting it on. Teaming it up with a beige belt and matching ankle boots, she prepared herself for the big day out at Beulah. She was so excited and couldn't wait for him to surface.

When he stepped out of the cottage, she walked over. He was very impressed with her outfit. She looked fresh and lovely. The shirt reached midway down her thighs.

"Suits you better than me, you look really cute," he smiled. "I'm gonna drive us over in the van. Jump in."

He always looked happy, but today there was an extra glow about him. His blue-grey eyes twinkled with sincerity and natural charm. Alice found him so handsome that sometimes she had to look away. She feared that what he ignited within her might spill out and cause her to behave in a clumsy, embarrassing manner. She loved everything about him – his spirit, his character, his wit and his physical appearance. He definitely had the full package.

Pulling up at the front of the house, he helped her down onto the crunchy gravel. The two lion statues stood either side of the steps.

Alice stroked the head of the one that had been restored. "Melantha came here once with her boss."

"Yeah, I know. She's a tall model type with hennaed hair, isn't she? I was in the house when they broke in."

"Why didn't you say something to them?"

"Beulah has an interesting effect on people. It was important for them to look around. They discovered something about themselves in the furnishings and decor."

He led her up to the grand entrance and got out a weighty bunch of keys. The wooden doors opened into an old hallway. A sweeping staircase rose in front of them. As they stepped into the magnificent space he had a change of mind. "Ah, come on, Alice, let's do this some other way – how about we retrace your last visit to Beulah?"

"What, and scramble through the side window?"

"Yeah, it's quick and easy access to the bell tower from that side."

She remembered the whole experience as being a scary, frustrating time. But things were very different now. "Okay, let's do it. But you go in first and shut your eyes because this shirt is going to ride up, clambering in there."

They trailed around to the side of the house and found the small, unconventional entry point. Sure enough, the latch was not across and with a bit of leverage it gave way easily.

Kes climbed in and then helped pull her through. He honoured her request and glanced away as she smoothed down her outfit.

As they followed the route to the cellar, Alice delighted herself in the peace that bathed her mind. Last time she had walked that corridor and staircase, all she had known was intense torment.

Stepping into the ancient, carved stone chamber felt like a sacred pilgrimage.

"What is it about this place, Kes?" she asked, marvelling at the sense of wellbeing in the atmosphere.

"It's sanctified, consecrated ground," he replied. "The cornerstone of Beulah, its foundations and basement, can never be polluted. What gets built on *top* of it can be impure. But nothing can ever spoil the integrity of the bedrock."

The twelve hallowed gemstones that had been crafted into the table shimmered in the soft light. They inspired reverence and respect. Alice pulled out one of the heavy chairs and sat down. This place spoke of a higher cause than the temporal. Instinctively she knew that life had been laid down in order for her to know complete peace. Sitting there, quietly, she could feel within her the absence of agitation. A contentment and wholeness filled her entire being.

After a few minutes, Kes led the way through to the bell tower.

"I'm gonna take you right to the top. There's something I want you to experience. You never got there last time and it was just as well."

As Alice climbed the steps, she recalled Melantha's description of the mayhem that emanated from the great bell – a sea of destruction and hatred.

On reaching the upper platform, Kes unveiled a gleaming new bell. "The previous one has been replaced. Rebellion won't be summoned by this."

Alice read the Latin text engraved in the metal – *Salvus.* Kes instructed her to close her eyes and meditate on its meaning.

Within seconds, a fearsome vision entered her mind – a child standing on a circular mound of sand. Encompassed by an incoming tide, this tiny patch of dry land was slowly being eaten into, inch by inch. There seemed no hope of survival.

The mighty bell chimed and instantly a helicopter became visible. A winch hauled the little girl out of danger. The mission of rescue was soon accomplished – a life had been saved.

The whole sky lit up with the sense of wellbeing that a bright sunny day brings. Health and prosperity flowed out upon the earth.

With each peal, ripples of goodwill, hope and soundness of mind saturated the masses.

Fear and prejudice were washed from men's thinking.

Quarrels stopped.

Wars ended.

Tears, grief and vexation vanished.

Plagues and diseases lifted off creation.

Death ceased to be anything more sinister than a ford to cross.

Alice's face shone. "That's what happened inside me yesterday."

"Pretty cool, isn't it?" Kes laughed as he led her back down the staircase.

He stopped mid-way, at the small arched door. Alice remembered all too clearly the frustration she had felt at being locked out. Kes sat down on the step and passed her his keys.

"There you go, you open it. Look for the little copper one."

He knew it was important to empower her to breakthrough into what lay beyond. She was about to encounter something very special.

ॐ

Chapter Forty-One

THE BOX

ALICE EXAMINED THE heavy bunch of keys and selected one that was old and ornate. Placing the small antique in the keyhole, she turned it. As she grasped the handle, there was great pleasure in feeling it give way.

The first thing that hit her as she entered the circular bedroom was the fragrance. Pomegranate, rosemary and lemongrass fused with a rich pepper. The walnut four poster bed stood dressed in the purest linen, so white it dazzled. The curtains surrounding it hung wispy and light in silver organza.

In the centre of the bed lay a recycled cardboard box tied with a simple cotton ribbon. Alice became aware of

Kes' eyes burning into her. He was staring at her with a confident yet soft look, smiling gently.

"D'you wanna see who the gift is for?" He leant up against one of the posts and gestured for her to read the tag.

She turned the small label over. It read:

To Alice, a sweet and noble lady x

She flushed with embarrassment – the intimacy was really awkward. To open the gift with him in such close proximity was stifling.

He could tell that she was struggling with the situation and broke the ice. "Hey, go for it, Alice, this can't be too hard for you. You're made of feistier material than that. It must have taken some nerve to lay on the show for me in the thicket the other night."

"Yeah, I was high then. I've never liked opening presents in front of people."

There were subconscious reasons that barred her from being relaxed when it came to receiving something. Disappointment from her mother's bizarre choice of gifts had left her anxious when packages were presented to her. She had often forced a smile and said, 'Lovely, Mum, thanks,' when inside she'd been screaming, 'How could you even consider I'd like this? You haven't got a clue about my taste. You don't really know me at all!'

Kes lay out on the bed on his side. His elbow pressed into the cover as he supported his cheek on his fist. He watched her hesitate for a few minutes and then got up. "Okay, this is painful. I'll tell you what I'll do – I'll go and sit with my back to you on the spiral steps and you can open it in privacy."

He laughed and went and positioned himself so that he was turned away from her.

A little less inhibited, Alice pulled the bow on the ribbon. It slipped open easily. Lifting the lid, she found a sticker holding together the edges of a sheet of tissue paper. As she broke the seal, she grimaced and clenched her teeth.

She needn't have been afraid of anything. Her hands reached in and unfolded the fabric of the most beautiful garment she had ever seen.

It was the prettiest, most delicate of dresses – almost lingerie.

Attached to a pure white, laced bustier hung dainty layers of soft muslin, trimmed with a few white feathers. It was her style totally – feminine and full of vintage charm.

A small card had been placed within its folds. She sat on the bed and read it.

Whatever he'd written caused a reaction. Immediately walking over to Kes, she dropped down behind him. Pressing her body against his back, she wrapped her legs either side of his. Her arms folded around his shoulders as she buried her face into his neck. Brushing her lips into the warmth of his hair, she wept.

He didn't move. He just let her hold him for a long while. He couldn't even see her apart from her bare legs, which his strong hands gently caressed.

Eventually she kissed the back of his neck and whispered, "Yes, I will."

His card lay on the floor. Its message read:

I would love to spend the rest of my life getting naked with you. Would you wear this on our wedding night?

As they rose from the floor, all that had restrained her and held her feelings in check broke free from her soul. For the first time, her eyes met his without fear of him knowing how much she adored him. He pulled her close but didn't kiss her. Without having to say anything, they both knew it would be dangerous. If they started it would be virtually impossible to stop.

"I want to marry you before the summer's over," he said resolutely.

Just hearing those words made Alice feel giddy with delight. She was used to the sensation of extreme pumping adrenalin and butterflies in her stomach, but never for such a pleasant reason. "That gives us about a month then. We'll have to move fast."

"There's no reason why we can't keep it simple and uncomplicated. I'm sure we can sort it all out easily. We'll crack open a bottle of Beulah's best tonight and get things going."

Alice loved the fact that he knew his own mind. He was determined and always followed through what he said he would do. He made her feel secure and that was the best foundation for building their lives together. Squeezing her hand tightly, he led her down into the grand hall.

Chapter Forty-Two

RESTORATION

THEY STOOD TOGETHER looking out of a massive window. The extensive grounds of the house lay before them.

"I still don't quite understand this place, Kes. How does this house relate to you? Why are you here and how did you come to be doing it up?"

A portrait of Mr Brunswick hung in the hall. Seated next to him were an attractive, elegant woman and a young child.

"Those are my grandparents, and see that cute little girl? That's my mum, Cara. There she is, all grown up."

He pointed to another picture of a beautiful woman with dark hair.

Alice looked astonished as she was hit with all the ramifications. Struggling to take it all in, she blurted out, "She's very pretty, Kes."

"Yep, she's also very messed up. She's been in and out of rehab several times. She now lives in Italy with my grandad. He prefers a warmer climate. When Grandma passed away several years ago, he bought a place out there. After my parents' divorce, Mum went out to look after him, but in many ways he takes care of her."

"Wow, so Beulah is your family's ancestral home?"

"Yeah, it's a rambling old house but there's lots of interesting stuff here. The fine art, marble structures, furniture and tapestries all have meaning and significance. When Melantha and her boss broke in, the state of the place very much reflected my heart. I was living a life of total rebellion. Everything was undone. It didn't matter to me who I hurt. I was the centre of the universe and I just used people for my gratification. But that's all changed now and I'm really glad about it. It's so freaking miserable being self-centred and detached."

He turned and showed her the elaborate paintings on the walls.

"Recently, when I've not been working outdoors, I've spent most of my time restoring these panels." He walked towards the six large frescos that had been covered over with images of the Greek mythological sea-god, Proteus.

"I couldn't bring back the original images but I've painted over the graffiti. So now you get to see my modern take on the creation account."

Kes' artwork was superb – his contemporary interpretation of the six days of creation swept across the wall in lavish colour and detail. The mural that had desecrated it had been completely wiped out.

A simple, black and white, geometric image depicted night and day. This stood alongside an abstract painting of water.

Kes had used a soft blue-green palette – turquoise, aqua and many other shades rippled and flowed into each other.

"I loved doing this," he said, pointing up to the third picture, "there's something about dirt, dust and the ground that really appeals to me."

His landscape was partly covered with all sorts of vegetation. It looked fresh and fertile – ready to inhabit.

A mass of stars littered the fourth panel. The sun, moon and planets hung in space, gracing the inky background with their splendour.

"There is no way this orderly, systematic universe came about by some random, chaotic accident." He ran his hand over the painted surface and led Alice to the fifth image.

All manner of fish and birds covered the sea and sky. The painting teemed with life. Swordfish, crabs, stingrays, bright tropical fish shared the space with flamingos, parrots, skylarks and sparrows. The vibrancy caused Alice to linger. She studied the detail of the tiny brushstrokes.

"It must have taken you ages to do this."

"Yeah, but most of the time I'd work through the day and night. I'd hardly stop. I was so focussed. I'd blast out my music and go into 'the zone'. There were no distractions, only the odd pit stop for something to eat. It was fun."

The sixth image was the most elaborate of them all. Many different kinds of animals showed their unique qualities in an abundant display of fur, stripes, shape and texture. Mankind appeared as the crescendo of creation in the handsome form of a man and a woman.

Alice laughed. "She looks a lot like me and he has got to be modelled on you."

"You'd just arrived at Beulah as I was finishing the last painting. Yeah, you did provide me with the inspiration for her hair and face. The rest I had to make up from my imagination."

She tipped her head to one side and studied the naked form of the woman. He wasn't far off. Kes reached out and drew her towards him. "D'you know what God instructed them to do after he'd made them?"

Alice shook her head.

"He said, 'Be fruitful and multiply.' I'm looking forward to obeying that commandment. It was his idea! He knows why we get attracted to each other. He put it in us to have that strong drive for procreation. He's so awesome."

Alice scanned over the six paintings. "I remember you saying that Taran talked to you about all this stuff on the beach one night at Trevanna Bay. At the time you told him you never gave it a second thought. I know you went through hell but what made you change your mind?"

"The truth is I always knew we were created, really. I just refused to thank God or worship him. I wouldn't acknowledge him because that would have meant I had to be accountable to him for my choices and actions. It was a lot easier to pretend he didn't exist because then I didn't have to face my rebellion. My mind became darkened and I hardened myself against the truth. He's flippin' gracious! "

He looked up at the last image and a huge smile broke across his face.

"I argued a lot with Taran and his mates in California. We would have lengthy discussions about it all… Jayden came up with a good illustration that helped me. He said that if he stood for a hundred years outside a house, willing his arm to grow so that he could paint the top, nothing would happen and then he'd die. His son would certainly not pass on adapted genes for an arm extension to appear in future generations! Yet people say that's what happened to a giraffe so it could reach the leaves on the top of trees. No, a giraffe was created as a giraffe. End of story. I then spoke with some guys who have studied loads of scientific evidence. I was left in no doubt that the theory of evolution is *seriously*, scientifically flawed. We are fearfully and wonderfully made. The study of anything on earth or in the heavens shows precise design."

"Yeah, I agree with you, Kes. I used to get so frustrated having that theory presented to me as fact. It doesn't ring true at all. I love what you've painted. It gives me peace of mind."

She sat down on the chaise-longue and rested against the pillow. The cluttered array of items that Ethan had discovered had been removed. The seventh station of the creation narrative was now restored as a place of relaxation.

As she lay there, Kes wandered over to the window. He looked deep in thought as he stared out across the gardens. His eyes shone when he turned back towards her. "Are you ready to see my favourite room?"

He pulled her up and led her down a corridor. "I'm gonna show you the nursery."

On the way, they passed the bathroom where Melantha and Ethan had discovered the mass of drowned creatures. The door was wide open.

Alice stepped inside and noticed the Noah's ark was no longer in the bath but had been placed on the window ledge.

A simple drift-wood cross hung on the wall. Kes stared up at the twisted, bleached twigs. "That's the ark we find refuge in now. What Jesus did on the cross, will see us through the storms of this life. He'll lead us safely into eternity, without any fear of judgement."

Alice smiled. This whole experience was so uplifting. Everything she was encountering served to reinforce the freedom that she felt inside. With all of these wonderful discoveries, plus the fact that Kes had asked her to marry him, she could honestly say it was turning out to be the second greatest day of her life.

Of the many rooms that Melantha had described to Alice, the baby's bedroom had impressed upon her the most fear.

Now, completely transformed, there was not a trace left of its former decor or contents. Kes had torn out the previous nursery and remodelled it from scratch.

Instead of the dark, forbidding room, draped with the ugliness of death, he had created a calm oasis.

Using a neutral palette, he had changed it into a serene, peaceful space. The oak floor had been sanded to a smooth finish and layered with a soft ivory rug. Soothing, bright-white furniture was crafted in high quality wood.

The cot, wardrobe, dresser and storage unit spoke of love, care and preparation. It was the perfect canvas to welcome a precious life into the world. A small crystal chandelier had been fixed with a dimmer switch and blackout blinds hung in the windows. Textural details made it feel cosy and inviting. Cream linen upholstery and plush quilting softened the look of the furniture. A fleecy blanket lay over the side of the cot.

Kes had already added several accessories. A large ornate mirror had been painted white and hung on the wall, alongside a collection of sweet art prints. On a shelf stood a pile of classic children's books – new editions in pastel jackets. Beside them rested a pair of knitted booties.

A pale, wooden rocking-horse was posted in one corner of the room and daisy-chain bunting hung as a banner, celebrating innocence and new life.

"Oh Kes, this is beautiful, you've got great taste. Did you do it all by yourself?"

"Well, it's the first room I started to work on when I arrived. It took a long time. I spoke with Mum about the colour scheme and together we chose the furnishings to kit it out. She sent bits over from Italy. I'm really pleased with the end result. It's ironic though, because no kid of mine will ever be bundled off into a room like this all by themselves. They'll be in a crib, right by our side."

Alice felt happy. She agreed with him. Although it was a stunning room, it was too remote. For intimacy and security to be cultivated, a more hands on approach would be essential.

Kes gently pushed the rocking horse, making it sway to and fro. "And you won't have to work either, not if you don't want to. I want you to be free to enjoy nurturing our kids. Make them woolly jumpers, build snowmen, run in the fields together, climb trees, have picnics, play in the brook and catch minnows – give them an amazing childhood. I'm gonna enjoy working and coming back home to you all. They'll have grazed knees and dirty fingernails but they'll know how to have fun."

Alice loved the idea. "It sounds perfect. Would we live up here or back in the cottage?"

"We could start out in the cottage, keep it all close and snug. Then we could see how it all pans out. We don't have to live at Beulah. We could go out to Italy for a while if you like. But the first thing we've got to sort is getting married. Let's pick up a bottle of wine on our way through the cellar and go and talk about things."

He closed the nursery door and took her back to the circular chamber. She gently folded her special white dress into the tissue paper and placed the lid on the box. Fixing the ribbon, she carried it back through the small arched door and down into the basement.

Kes had gone ahead of her and was crouched down selecting a fine wine. He spent some time deliberating – only the very best would do. When he eventually pulled one out, they climbed the two staircases and exited the way they had entered.

Chapter Forty-Three

PLANS

BACK AT THE cottage, Alice could not believe what she was doing. The sheet of paper in front of her was rapidly filling up with a long list of things to consider for their special day.

Kes glanced down at it. "Enjoy yourself. Be creative. Think outside the box. This is an opportunity for you to be limitless with your dreams. We already have the perfect venue. Tell me what you'd love to have; don't worry about how much it'll cost."

Her eyes widened. She could give her imagination free rein without thinking she'd be building a castle in the air.

There was real hope that any idea she could come up with had the potential to take on substance and certainty.

She pondered the many things on her list.

"Read it out to me," he called.

"Well, there's the dress and all that goes with it for my outfit… Then who would be bridesmaids…? What they would wear…? There's so much to think over, like the colour scheme, all the food, the guest list, your outfit, who you'd like to be best man…? The photographer…"

Looking over at him, she threw down her pen and sighed. "I don't want all of this. Getting married isn't about all this stuff, is it?"

"I'm with you on that one," he grinned. "Let's break the mould. Forget all about that crazy pressure and keep the main thing the main thing."

"Which is?"

"Let's arrange the legal bit at the local registry office. We only need two witnesses. It won't take long to book it in. Then we can get on with the real marriage – you and me coming together as one flesh before our Creator."

"Yeah, perfect, that's what I want too. Who shall we get to be the witnesses?"

"To be honest, Alice, I don't care who they are. How about your mum and what's he called? They're local. They'll do."

"Jimmy? D'you honestly want that dude there?"

"I wouldn't mind. It doesn't bother me meeting him. We won't be with them very long. If we're gonna ask your mum to come, she'd probably like him to be around. Let's keep it all low key. Tell her it's not a big deal. She's gonna get a shock anyway. You've run off with your mate's caravan and a few weeks later you're marrying the rich boy from Beulah. It would make a good movie."

"Yeah, but remember the last time I spoke to Jimmy, we were both yelling at each other. Even if he does come along, he'll be stoned and dressed in his biker garb."

She had a flashback to her last encounter with him. He'd just walked in from having 'Lyndsey' tattooed on the back of his neck. Alice had eyed it with contempt. It was all very well bearing her mum's name as if he loved her, but actions spoke louder than words. If he really cared about her, he'd stop making their cottage the centre of attention for all the wrong reasons.

"Give your mum a call and let her know what's been going on with you. Check out the lie of the land, and see if she'll be a witness. We need to book an appointment in town to start to set things up. I'll sort that tomorrow."

The following day Alice managed to get through to her mum. Although they were used to being superficial with each other, the circumstances demanded an honest language. It was tense to start with – Alice had absorbed a lot of pressure over the years. Lyndsey's emotional neglect of her daughter had caused much to lie hidden and unresolved. Once Alice had broken the initial barrier of surprise, her mum softened.

When Kes came back from work, he was pleased to hear that Lyndsey was actually delighted for them both.

"She was astonished, but excited at the same time. She's a sucker for romance. I know that secretly, she would love something as 'whirlwind' to happen to her too. She asked what your dad was like and if he was free!"

"Oh, poor old Jimmy, not good news for him is it? As for my dad, even when he's with someone, he likes to think he's not tied down. He's nothing but trouble. We'd have to steer them well clear of each other if she looks anything like you!"

"Mum's always been the same. She rides on the swing ready to jump onto the roundabout. She can't be without some action. She's always looking for the next guy to come along, hoping that things will get better. She's in love with the idea of being in love, but doesn't have a clue what it is. She wants someone to embody her fantasy. I'll have to lend her your Purple Veil book! I'm sorry, Kes, but she's really fickle, she's in awe of your family and Beulah. She kept asking me if I was on a trip."

"Is she okay about helping us out at the registry office?"

"Yeah, I told her how simple our wedding is going to be, and that we have private plans for afterwards. She was disappointed that we weren't having a grand do at the house, but I think she feels really special to be asked to be a witness. She said she'll tell Jimmy he *has* to come along."

"I'm beginning to feel sorry for the guy," Kes laughed. "It sounds like your mum leads the show – I couldn't live like that."

"He's rock hard when it comes to all his drug dealing but in other ways he's so weak. I know she takes advantage of that and dominates him very subtly. I hate it. Men need to have a bit of spunk about them. I don't mean they should be controlling, but they definitely need to know where they're going in life and lead the adventure. The only place he's heading for is prison."

"Well let's hope that he gets a change of direction. I'm glad it went well for you with your mum though. Good on you for breaking the ice. I know it's not easy handling parents sometimes. Oh... I called the registry office – we have to pop down and take in some documents. After that, it takes a few days to process but the woman said we could probably set the date within a month. D'you know where your birth certificate is?"

"I'll call Mum and get her to mail it over. She keeps all that sort of thing in a special box."

While Alice phoned Lyndsey, Kes opened his laptop. He'd been in regular communication with Taran since he'd left him in Redding. He'd kept him informed about the way his life was going and had told him all about Alice.

He sent him an email:

Hi Taran
Alice has said yes! I'm so stoked man. She's such a gem. We've decided to marry quickly. We'll whiz through all the legal stuff as soon as it can be set up. The plan is to go to the local registry office with just Alice's mum and boyfriend.
Our real wedding service will take place that night between Alice, me and our Maker. We'll say our vows and then seal them.
Taran, you'll always be my 'best man'.
Thanks a million for leading me from death to life.
You guided me to the one who has breathed life into me.

Love you bro.
Kes

He pressed 'send', stretched out on the sofa and called Alice over.

"I've arranged a little creative surprise for you – well, *us* really."

She looked excited and sat down beside him.

Taking her left hand in his, he massaged her fingers, singling out one of them with a little more pressure.

"Got a clue yet?"

"I have a pretty strong inkling, but come on, what is it?"

"I've booked us into some sessions at Laura Jones' Bespoke Jewellers. We're going to sit through an intensive two day workshop, so we can design our own wedding bands. I'll make yours, you make mine. She'll give us all the instructions but we actually produce the rings ourselves. We can then have something engraved on them. Cool, isn't it?"

Alice loved all things arty and thought it was a wonderful idea. She laughed. "What if the one I make you is wonky? You'll have to wear it for the rest of your life like that."

"Nothing's perfect, Alice. I'm not, you're not and our marriage won't be. But I'm gonna commit to you despite that. We've both found the one who is 'perfect love', and we know he delights in getting involved in all the nitty-gritty of our lives. Nothing's too dark or deep for him. He's been to hell and back for us. So he'll help us. Marriage is his idea, so we can trust him to show us how it works! Don't worry about making me a dodgy ring. I'm a dodgy guy in many ways, but what I promise you is that I'll be honest and faithful. By God's grace, I vow that to you."

Tears pricked her eyes. She knew he meant every word.

"Kes, I'm very messed up too. I know I've found the starting line and I vow to you that I'll always walk on the narrow path. I won't stray off it. I'm sure there will be many times when I'll stumble down some hole, but I promise I'll get up quickly and walk on with you. I know I've got lots of baggage. I'll be a difficult woman to live with, but I believe the love of God can mould and soften my hard, sharp edges. I'm sure you'll make me cry and I'll definitely make you cross. We'll fall out but never apart. We've both got scars, we need to respect them in each other and how they came to be there." Her mascara smudged. "I think making our wedding rings together is a beautiful idea."

She yearned to kiss him properly – full on. Her eyes washed into his.

"Not yet," he whispered, "I know what I'm like. You're a very beautiful lady and I owe it to both of us not to touch something that doesn't belong to me yet. Let's do this right."

He got out the chess set and arranged all the pieces. She happily played along, knowing full well she'd lose. Today it didn't matter. When his bishop swept her queen off the board she smiled. "I'm a winner, Kes. No matter how many pieces you take! Even in checkmate I'll always have my king."

༚

Chapter Forty-Four

A TRIP INTO TOWN

THE LONG HOURS of sunshine they'd enjoyed throughout the season began to give way to late summer. It was still very warm but the sweltering heat was subsiding.

Kes worked daily on Beulah's grounds and encouraged Alice to make the most of the pleasant weather.

"Go for walks and soak up all the peace. Be indulgent and pamper yourself."

He knew it was important for her to grasp the significance of all that had happened to her recently. Too much of her life had been robbed by mental anguish. She needed to run wild across the fields and express her new found freedom.

"You're going through a massive process of restoration. Let your hair down, do some artwork if you want. I could set up an easel in the field and bring some of my paints and brushes down from the house."

"Thanks Kes, but I'm fine just strolling along by the brook or sitting in the meadow near Vanda. I'm knitting Jimmy a sweater for the winter – my attempt at a peace offering. He probably won't like it but at least he'll see I've made an effort. It's awesome not to feel tormented anymore! I actually like being in my own company for the first time ever. I feel tranquil and full of joy. Before, I used to want to distract myself from reality all the time."

A high pressure weather system promised favourable sunny skies as their wedding day approached.

Alice struggled, wondering what to wear to the registry office.

Kes put her mind at ease. "You'll look beautiful whatever you put on. It's not that important. Your little white dress is the only thing I'm really interested in; but *that* is for my eyes only. Why don't you wear your red gypsy skirt and white blouse?"

In the end she settled for a soft, bohemian look – laced gold sandals, a red flower in her dark locks and the skirt and top that he'd suggested. She sprayed on her favourite scent and wore her usual make-up. Everything was all very easy and straightforward.

Kes looked stunningly handsome in a grey slim-fit suit. He teamed it with a penny collar shirt and no tie. His dark, choppy hair bore natural highlights from spending so much time outdoors. He'd splashed his regular fragrance of woody-peppery spice across his neck and angular face.

As he strolled out of the cottage, he called over to her sitting on the caravan step. She hurried towards him.

"Come on then," he shouted laughing, "jump into *this*!"

"Where did it come from?" she asked, climbing into the vintage sports car.

"Mum said I could take it out of the garage and give it an airing. It's hers. I've already tested it out a bit on the grounds and had it looked over by a friend of the family who specialises in classic cars. It's a beauty and drives like the wind."

They fastened their seat belts and took off down the track that led out onto the main road.

Kes raised his voice. "We've had a stack of cards arrive. We can have a read of some of them when we get back. Now listen, I've got something I need to sort this afternoon. I'm gonna have to disappear for a few hours." He winked at her. "Trust me. It'll be worth the wait."

Lyndsey and Jimmy were standing outside the registry office when the sports car pulled into the car park. They both took deep drags on their cigarettes as Alice and Kes walked over.

Kes embraced Lyndsey with a light hug and reached out to shake Jimmy's hand. The burly biker pressed his heavily ringed fingers into Kes' palm.

"Alright, mate," Kes smiled. "Thanks for doing this for us. It's good of you."

Jimmy gave a slight grin.

Lyndsey hugged Alice and started to well up.

"Don't, Mum, not yet. Your make-up will run."

Lyndsey stared at Kes and whispered into Alice's ear, "He's flippin' gorgeous, love. Good catch."

Kes drew Jimmy to one side. "Would you do me a big favour? I'm happy to drop you some cash for this, but could you come over to Beulah when we're done here and take the horse and caravan back to Melantha?"

Jimmy smiled. "Yeah, no problem, forget the money though. We came on the bike. So, when this is finished, I'll shoot back to our place and swop it for Lyndsey's car. As much as she'd like to have a go, she only rides on that baby as a passenger." He looked over at his gleaming bike with a sense of real affection.

"Thanks, mate." Kes patted him across the shoulders and led them inside.

The short ceremony was over in less than twenty minutes.

As the four of them stepped out into the glorious sunshine, Lyndsey anxiously caught hold of Alice's hand and asked if she could have a quiet word with her.

"What is it, Mum?" Alice tried not to be impatient.

"Bit weird, wasn't it, love?" she whispered. "Why weren't there any rings? And why didn't he kiss you? What kind of a wedding was that?"

"Don't worry, Mum. That was just the legal bit. Our real wedding is a private affair."

Her mum raised her eyebrows.

"Well, love, I hope you know what you're doing. It doesn't seem proper to me."

Alice held back the words that immediately surfaced, 'I don't think you're the best person to explain to me what a *proper* wedding is all about.' Instead, she managed to be gracious. "Thank you for being a witness, Mum."

They turned and went off to their respective vehicles.

Kes and Alice sped back to Beulah.

On the way, he explained to her what he'd arranged with Jimmy.

"We need to take your stuff out of the caravan before they arrive. You know what, Alice? I've been thinking... why don't you send back all those clothes to Melantha, as well? I know she gave you most of them, but you struggle wearing them now. You don't want to be reminded of the past all the time. I'll take you into town soon and you can buy a whole new wardrobe. It needn't take us long to collect up your things. Just pull out all your personal items... perhaps leave the dope in the jar?" He grinned. She hadn't smoked a joint since Darcus had left.

Alice felt relieved. Everything was new. She was delighted that the caravan was going. She didn't need a borrowed home anymore – tonight she would be sleeping with Kes!

Within an hour they had gathered her possessions and harnessed Vanda to the cart. The hardest part for Alice was letting the horse go. She leant up close to her head and stroked her nose.

Jimmy was true to his word and showed up promptly. He had cautioned Lyndsey to give her daughter plenty of space and not to linger. "They obviously don't want people hanging around, love, or they would have gone for a different style of wedding."

As Alice waved her mother off, she turned to find Kes arranging a blanket on the ground and bringing out a picnic lunch. He had sorted it all the night before. He took off his jacket, loosened his shirt and uncorked a bottle of champagne. As he toasted his beautiful bride, he kissed her hand but not her lips.

A pile of envelopes lay scattered to one side. Kes picked a few up and opened them.

"Oh, that's lovely," Alice sighed, as he passed her a card from his mum.

It was handmade with a raised heart and two doves. Inside was an elegantly written message:

To my precious son, Kes, and his lovely wife,

Welcome to the family, 'Mrs Alice Brunswick-Daniels!'

I am really looking forward to meeting you. Thank you for making my son a very happy young man. Have a blessed and wonderful day.
All my love,
Mum

The card from his dad was not so gracious.
It was humorous and crude.
Inside it read:

Hope you understand what you're letting yourselves in for, Dad and Steph.

Grandad's card contained a hefty cheque. Kes whistled at the amount and put it to one side. "You can get a whole load of pretty clothes with some of that. Let's open the rest later."

After they'd eaten, he jumped up and went over to his van.

Pointing at her, he called out, "I'll catch up with *you* in a few hours." He glanced at his watch. "I'll be back before six."

Alice packed up the remains of the picnic and went into the cottage. She cleared the dishes and tidied away the things she'd taken from the caravan. Kes' guitar rested on the sofa; she lay down beside it and ran her fingers across the strings. Memories of the first night, when he'd brought her over for a meal, passed through her mind. How could all this have happened to her? A small box lay on the coffee table. As she lifted the lid and studied the two platinum wedding bands, tears rolled down her face. A few weeks ago she had been in torment; now she knew a peace that surpassed her understanding.

Kes would return in a couple of hours; the time that lay ahead was a gift to prepare herself for the most important night of her life.

As she stepped under the shower she felt glad to be a woman. His masculinity called out the beauty of her femininity. The way he behaved towards her assured her of the immense value he placed on her. She wasn't a body for him to spend his lust on. He wanted all of her.

She glanced at her naked form in the bathroom mirror. She was pleased with what she saw. Though slender, she had plenty of soft curves. Her long, jet black hair enhanced her natural beauty. Tonight she would give herself to him without reserve.

It was incredibly fulfilling to know she was entirely desired. Soon, he would not only unlace the bodice of her dress, but also take the lid off the box deep inside of her. He had proven that he wanted to be joined to the whole of who she was, and that would arouse more than the heat of her body.

When she'd tried to seduce him, he hadn't failed the test. The strength he'd displayed to resist her had screamed out that she really meant something to him. Although he was the sexiest man she had ever seen in her life, he was also the most honest, earthy and tender-hearted.

Tonight wasn't just about Kes entering her body. It was about the completeness of him, fusing with all of her.

Chapter Forty-Five

THE REAL DEAL

WHEN KES RETURNED, there was a strange silence about him. It was as if his usual, self-assured air had been relinquished.

His vulnerability expressed itself through his eyes. They were intense and serious.

She had never seen him look so exposed and defenceless. He shot her a gentle smile and disappeared into the bathroom for half an hour. Eventually he came out dressed in a pair of jeans and grey T-shirt.

He rested back on the sofa and played his guitar.

Alice also felt frail. The thought of changing into her white dress made her feel embarrassed and self-conscious.

She couldn't imagine how she'd set herself up in the thicket that night with such bravado and fearlessness. Her courage must have been artificially stimulated.

As she went off to the bedroom to change, she sensed the two of them were mutually yielding into each other's control.

Their surrender was enabling them to be open and receptive.

Her confidence soared when she checked her appearance in the mirror. The dress fitted perfectly – its bodice shaped her figure beautifully. She loved the way the muslin skirt layers were short but not micro. The white feathers brushed her skin with their delicate softness.

Taking lots of deep breaths, she laced her sandals, walked back into the living room and sat down next to him.

His eyes swept over her. They shouted approval.

Suddenly it hit her that she was legally married, and this lovely man sitting beside her was about to become her husband in the *truest* sense.

Kes still didn't speak. Although he was mute, he wasn't uncommunicative.

He put down the guitar and reached for her hand. Picking up the box of rings he drew her up and led her out into the garden.

The evening sun was beginning to fade. Pink and violet streaks rippled through the golden sky.

Taking a silk scarf from his pocket, he blindfolded her and guided her across the meadows.

After they had walked for about fifteen minutes, he pulled her towards him and lifted her off the ground. He carried her for a short while and then placed her feet back onto the grass. Standing behind her, he held her against his chest and gently unveiled her eyes.

Their special thicket stood in front of them – the place where he had bared his soul and she had longed for him to worship her.

Ethnic fusions of chill-out music drenched the atmosphere with sensuality. The volume was carefully set, so it washed the background without being overpowering.

Alice's attempt at lighting-up the place with candles looked like child's play compared to what he had set up.

Masses of solid, beeswax pillars were all aglow. Tea-lights, in jars wrapped with wire handles, hung from branches. Various glass containers lit up the floor in patterned arrangements. A collection of vertical logs provided the table tops for starry lanterns to be displayed.

A structure had been erected directly on the spot where Alice had made herself available in her risqué outfit. Twelve rocks were piled together in a kind of rustic altar. Alongside them was a bottle of Beulah wine and something covered with a white cloth.

On the floor lay a scattering of velvet cushions.

Kes ran his hands over her bare arms and led her into the leafy cavern. Together they sat in front of his stone sculpture. Taking a lighter, he lit three cream candles. As they gently flickered, he grasped the bottle of wine, opened it and proceeded to pour it out over the stones.

Only a little remained.

An aroma of luscious berry and spice filled the air as the dark liquid trickled and dripped over the grey surface.

He carefully positioned their wedding rings on the altar
– this place where sacrifices were offered, incense was
burned and worship given.

It spoke of value and cost.

For a moment he closed his eyes, bringing to
remembrance a baby that had lost its life and a young
woman who had lost her mind.

Lifting the white cloth from a fresh loaf of bread, he took
it in his hands and ripped it in two.

His eyes were fierce with love, passion and intent.

"Jesus' body was broken so that we could be made one.
His blood was poured out as an offering so that we could go
free, both here on earth and in the next life."

He slid his hand into Alice's, searching for her wedding
finger. Placing her left hand on his thigh, he reached for the
smaller ring.

"Father, you are in heaven but you also live in us by your
Spirit. Thank you for making that possible through your
Son's sacrifice. He is the door that we have run through to
find you. You are awesome and everything you have made
is good. Thank you for creating Alice and me. Thank you
for your brilliant design. You have given us to each other
as a gift and we're stoked that we get to have the delight
of being joined together." He squeezed her hand tightly.
"Wow, the body bit will be awesome, but our hearts, minds
and spirits will unite too. We're making a commitment to
each other until our lives here on earth end. This is our
foundation for how we will care for any kids that you bless
us with. We want to model your love and faithfulness to
each other and them. That way, they'll get to know they're
treasured and wanted. It will make them feel great about

themselves too." He pulled Alice closer. "We're going to get very serious now, Father. Will you fill this moment with your presence? We don't want to be casual or selfish in what we are about to say to each other, we do it in awe of you and knowing that you see everything about us. That doesn't freak us out because we know you love us and want to help us with our weaknesses."

He held her ring between his fingers, ready to place it.

"Father, I'm taking Alice as my wife. I promise that I will love her, comfort her, honour her and be faithful to her throughout my earthly life. It starts today, and even if life gets worse or we become poor or she gets ill, I vow to love her until I die." He pushed the gleaming platinum band onto her finger and kissed her knuckle.

Alice took his ring from the altar and reached for his hand. It felt large and rough compared to hers.

She closed her eyes.

Her vows were almost whispered but full of sincerity and truth.

"Father, I'm so shocked to discover how much you love me. 'Thank you' is too small a thing to describe the gratitude I feel inside. A few weeks ago I was in pitch darkness and now I'm safe. I love Kes with all my heart. You have made him so awesomely. He's very handsome and sexy. Thank you for giving him to me." Her eyes moistened. "I'm sorry I tried to seduce him. You know why I did it. I was insecure and jealous. It wasn't out of love for him. I was just being really selfish.

"Thank you that it was *your* strength in him that resisted the ugly stuff in me. You used him to lead me away from worshipping the image of a man as my god.

"I can see now that you want us to enjoy our relationship with each other by putting you first. If you weren't first we would run out of love very quickly because we'd be rubbish at loving each other without you. You are 'love', so how could we ever hope to love one another if we're not attached to the source?"

Her beautiful face glowed with a soft radiance. She opened her eyes. They were no longer veiled in darkness, but sparkly and clear. She fixed them on Kes. "Father, I give Kes this ring as a token of my love and commitment. I pray I will always come to you when I hit up against those ugly places in my heart. I don't want to blame him for my issues and bad attitude. When he makes me mad, will you help me to be long suffering? If he annoys me will you give me patience? I want to be kind and compassionate to him. I want to support him in the things that cause him pressure. Help me to always tell him the truth and never to cheat on him. Oh and please melt the hard core of selfishness inside me, or his life will be hell once he gets to live with me."

Kes tipped his head towards her in amusement. He loved her grittiness. "Wow, I'm in for a good time, girl. If we both own our behaviour and go to God to change it, our relationship will constantly get better."

She took his hand and gently eased the wedding band onto his finger. It was chunky and solid with the word *'nissiun'* engraved around it.

With her fingers locked into his, she stood up and pulled him towards her. He was so strong he didn't budge an inch. Her eyes danced with laughter.

"Right Kes, don't you think it's time you kissed me? Kiss me long and hard. I've been waiting for this for weeks."

He rose from the ground with a huge smile on his face. Sliding his hands around her waist he drew her into him. "Listen to that!" His left hand pressed her head against his chest so firmly that his accelerated heartbeat pounded into her ear. "Can you feel what you do to me? My heart was beating like that the last time we were in this thicket! It wasn't easy for me." He tenderly kissed the side of her neck. It lit a fire.

Just beyond the altar, he'd set up a wrought iron bed. A pale muslin cloth was suspended as a canopy over the top of it. The mattress was dressed with white satin sheets and soft feathered pillows.

Drawing her along with him, he walked over to it.

He sat on the edge and peeled off his T-shirt.

"Come on then, Alice, let's rock 'n' roll." His eyes were racy and full of life.

She loosened her sandals and kicked them off. Climbing onto the mattress, she knelt beside him and placed her hands upon his shoulders.

For a moment, she closed her eyes and rested her head against his.

There was something she needed to tell him.

She'd vowed to be honest and he'd drummed it into her that she must make known what was really going on inside. For their love to flourish, it was vital that truth became the soil in which it could grow.

"Kes, I have to let you know a secret."

He turned to her. She looked such a pretty picture kneeling there in her little white dress. The delicate feathers stroked her thighs. Her lovely femininity was almost angelic. It was complemented by a warm, sugary fragrance coming from the twinkling ivory candles. The scent of cinnamon and cloves filled the thicket.

Her lustrous, jet black hair made a stunning contrast to the subtle creamy shades all around them.

Kes felt perplexed over what she was about to say, but not fearful. How could anything bad come from this beauty set before him?

He lay back on the pillows with one hand behind his head. "Nothing you've got to say would rattle me tonight, Alice. But don't tease me. What's your little surprise?"

She moved up close to his side and leant into him. "As much as Melantha taught me the fine art of seduction, I only ever tried it once and it didn't work...! I'm a virgin. I've never been with a man before. Seeing all the heartache my mum went through was a bit of a put off." She blushed and awaited his response.

He reached out towards her with his free hand and toyed with the lacing on her bustier. Absorbing her confession, a twinge of pain seared his soul. She could see it flicker through his eyes. The scar tissue was still tender with all he'd gone through with Ruby.

She knew that what she'd said would trigger a memory and touch a wound. She hadn't wanted to hurt him. Her virginity was a gift to him. She could only give it to one person and only one time.

It was hard for her, too. She almost felt guilty about telling him something that should have been received as good news. But this was the man she'd committed herself to. Though lovely, he was flawed and damaged, and that was fine by her.

She held his face and gently kissed his forehead.

"It's okay, Kes, I understand your pain. This is about *us* now. It's just a fact that I needed to let you know. It's a great thing for me, but I guess it will raise a ghost for you. I love you with all your shadows and scarred, broken bits too. I'm not Ruby, and although it's difficult, I'm not so jealous of her anymore."

He relaxed. Nothing would be a no-go area between them. The truth was a safe harbour in which they could bring anything about themselves to rest. That was the only way they would truly become one.

She smiled and stretched out alongside him. "Well come on then, the best sex is supposed to be with someone you respect, that you feel completely free with and who you know is committed to you. I'm totally secure with you, so show me heaven."

There was a lot of laughter that came out of the thicket that night. Alice soon received the kiss she'd been longing for. When his mouth finally met hers, it was well worth the wait.

As the sunset faded and darkness fell, the magical array of lanterns mingled with the stars to create a perfect setting for their marriage to be finalised.

All holy covenants are sealed in blood, and as her hymen broke, the spiritual bond between them was fully entered into.

Their Father in heaven viewed the satin sheets that enveloped them as gift wrap. Underneath, they lay immersed in the heat of each other's bodies.

By midnight, all but one of the many candles that surrounded them had burnt out. As Kes and Alice slept, all but one of the many seeds he'd released into her body gave up the fight. The champion that made it through buried itself into its target, and Inara Brunswick-Daniels was conceived.

After that wonderful day, they made love frequently and in some very interesting places. The circular chamber in Beulah was Alice's favourite location because it oozed romance. A summer house in the formal gardens was good for when she dropped off his lunch. There was a lovely spot down by the brook where she had first spoken to him, and their tiny bedroom at the cottage was also very accommodating. It saw lots of early bedtimes and long lie-ins.

Chapter Forty-Six

CLOTHES

K ES STUDIED HER one morning as she lay naked in his arms. "I know you don't spend much time in them, but d'you want to go off and buy a load of clothes soon? I hate shopping but I'm willing to endure it if it will make you happy."

"Oh yeah, that would be great. Can we drive around some of the boutiques in the local villages? They're bound to have some interesting and unique things."

The following weekend they took off. As they drove through the country lanes, signs of autumn were all around. The leaves were turning and there was a slight chill in the air.

Within a twenty-five mile radius, there were several villages that had small, exclusive shops. Kes was surprised to discover that he quite enjoyed himself. Art and craft seemed to thrive in these sorts of places and he found much to interest him.

He had almost given Alice an open bank card.

Although he was wise with money, he wanted to be extravagant. When he told her to spend up to three grand, she looked worried.

"Alice, we paid out next to nothing on our wedding. The most expense went on the rings. I earn good money at Beulah and Grandad gave us a packet. Have fun. Buy stuff you wouldn't normally think you could afford. That's why I drove the van today – the boot in the sports car is too small!"

She kissed his lips and sent him into a coffee shop. "Okay, if I'm going to have that much pleasure I'll need time. I'll be distracted if I drag you into every shop. Knowing you're hanging around getting bored will make me feel guilty; I won't want to try anything on. So you go and get some lunch. I don't need food, I'm too excited."

She had a wonderful day. They didn't have time to visit all the villages but they managed three. The van soon overflowed with carrier bags of varying shades and sizes. Most of the things that she bought had a bit of a hippy edge to them, but the colours were softer than her previous wardrobe.

She gazed at him in awe as they drove home. Her hand rested on his leg. "Are you the perfect guy, or what?"

"Unfortunately, my parents set me a really bad example of how to do relationships. Dad taught me how *not* to treat a woman! My mum would have been very proud of me today…! Oh, by the way, she called. She wants us both to get in touch as soon as possible. Let's set it up on the internet."

Alice looked concerned. "I'm really nervous about that. What if she doesn't like me?"

"She'll love you. Honestly, don't worry about that. She's really sweet. She just carries a lot of rejection from my dad, so sometimes she's a bit cuckoo. His emotional neglect pushed her over the edge. He's very detached and uses women as objects for his pleasure. He can't go any deeper than the surface. I know, because I was a chip off the old block! I'd love to have it out with him, but I know that I need to forgive him. That's the only way I'm going to be able to move on from some of the things I get stuck with. Taran wrestled it through with me once. He said, 'holding onto bitterness is like taking poison while you wait for the other person to die.' You end up in the prison of your own unforgiveness."

Alice thought deeply about what he was saying. So much of it applied to her also. "I remember you sharing about what your dad said to you when he was coming back to Trevanna Bay. You were pretty angry, hey?"

"When my dad called, after Blake's death, I got in touch with a rage inside of me; it could have easily spilled out all over Taran, but he hadn't done anything wrong. I wanted to hit him so hard. Later I realised it was my dad I really wanted to punch. I can feel it in me sometimes. When I think of him, I get angry and frustrated. I remember how I reacted when I found out he'd been cheating on my mum. My heart grew hard and I built a strong defence. I lost all respect and trust, not only for him, but nearly everyone else. When your own flesh and blood backstabs you, why would you ever put your confidence in other people? You just become independent and isolated inside, even when you're with a bunch of mates; you keep certain areas off limits.

"Taran was different because I could tell from how he lived his life that he wasn't faking it. It was only when I began to see my own shortcomings and failures, that I realised I should try to give my dad a break. It would be great if he could come and say sorry, but I don't think he understands he's done anything wrong. It's either that or he's harder hearted than I can imagine and doesn't care anyway."

Alice ran her fingers through his hair and held his neck firmly. "Well, we're both smashed up in the fathering area, aren't we, Kes? We're like a couple of orphans, but at least we've found our true Father now. He'll never leave us or be unfaithful to us."

They pulled up outside the cottage and he helped her in with her shopping – it took a couple of trips.

She enjoyed hanging up all her lovely things. The small wardrobe soon bulged and the set of drawers overflowed with delicate lingerie. As he made the tea, she kept popping out and showing him bits and pieces. He passed the odd comment but like a lot of guys, didn't understand her attention to the detail.

"Yeah, Alice, it's all very pretty, but if you wanna know the truth, my favourite thing is when you're wearing nothing at all."

❧

Chapter Forty-Seven

BEAUTIFUL DESTINATION

A UTUMN CONTINUED, and they woke one Sunday morning to a cold day. Alice eased herself up and sat on the edge of the bed. Her head was bent over and she felt terrible. A wave of nausea swept through her stomach. She ran to the bathroom, urged, and vomited up some yellow bile.

"Are you alright?" Kes called from the bed.

"Yeah, I think so. I've just been feeling weird the past few days. I was exhausted yesterday and I didn't do much. Maybe I've picked up a bug."She walked back into the bedroom.

Kes sat up. "Either that or you're pregnant," he grinned, "wouldn't that be amazing?"

She stared at him and considered the possibility. Her period *was* a bit overdue.

"Flip, Kes, I think I probably am. In fact, the way things have been between us, I'd be surprised if I wasn't."

The following day they popped out and picked up a testing kit. The result was positive.

"Bet it happened on our wedding night," he laughed, "I felt something in my spirit. It was like a light went on. If we have a little girl let's call her Inara."

"What does it mean?"

"A ray of light that is heaven-sent."

She gasped. "Oh I love that, and it would be true. Yeah, I'm happy to call her Inara. What if we're having a boy?"

"I don't believe we are."

They were happy days. Winter fast approached. Alice got over her morning sickness and spent lots of her time curled up by the fire knitting tiny jumpers, shawls and booties. They were both glad to be living in the small cottage rather than Beulah. It was cosier and easier to keep.

Kes continued to work on the estate; there was always something to do. His grandad only wanted general oversight of the place and he wasn't interested in having more workers involved unless a specialised job came up.

They often made internet calls to Italy. Cara loved Alice and was overjoyed to see how content Kes had become. She'd agonised over him when his father had left, knowing that the break-up lay at the root of a lot of his problems.

He shared with her about his faith and she respected it. She could tell there had been a massive change in him and knew it wasn't just down to him having found a lovely wife. "Mum, I'm serious. I would have committed suicide at Trevanna Bay. I got so desperate over the way I was living my life and how it was hurting the people around me. Selfishness wrecks lives."

Alice had been honest with her also. She told her if it hadn't have been for her spiritual breakthrough, she would still have been very oppressed and lost.

Cara offered them a winter holiday in the mountains. "Why don't you take the key to the chalet and go up for Christmas? You used to love it there, Kes. We had some good times in that little place when Grandma was alive, didn't we? Take Alice up and show her."

"I don't know, Mum. We're really happy here and I'm not sure I want the hassle. Christmas can get a bit hectic with all the running around."

"Yes, but it would be just as quiet as the cottage, up there. You wouldn't be overlooked and there would probably be a powdering of snow. Anyway, think about it. You're very welcome if you want to."

He talked it over with Alice and although they were content where they were, she thought it might be a good idea to visit somewhere new. "It will get you away from Beulah for a while. I guess you could do with a break."

Over the next few days she slowly assembled some of their clothes and prepared for their winter retreat. They didn't need much because the chalet was fully equipped. The plan was to go for the main Christmas weekend. They'd pad it out either side and get to spend five days away.

Kes decided to take the sports car; their medium holdall fitted snugly into the boot.

It was a cold afternoon as they pulled out of Beulah. The winter sun was bright in the sky. Their holiday home was a three hour drive to the north.

Kes was looking forward to seeing the old wooden chalet. Childhood memories of being with his grandparents filled his mind. He wondered if the decorations were still kept in a box under the stairs.

They stopped off at a supermarket to pick up some supplies. "I'll get it, Alice. Why don't you grab a drink in the cafe?" He was so attentive and caring. She wandered off and got a latte while he braved the crowds.

Within an hour, the shopping was crammed onto the tiny rear seat and they were back on the road. As the early darkness descended, he turned his headlights to full beam. The winding country road led them towards their beautiful destination.

The Last Chapter...

Chapter Forty-Eight

DARKNESS AND SUNSHINE

PC NIGEL THORPE spewed into a bush. He had been the first to arrive on the scene. Two mangled bodies lay lifeless. The green sports car had taken the full impact of a head on collision. It had spun onto its side and hurtled into a tree.

It hadn't been Kes' fault. A drunken driver had overtaken on a bend. They stood no chance of avoiding the crash.

As the road traffic cop assessed the situation, he marvelled at how young these two dead bodies were.

Snatched, harvested, in seconds.

One moment Alice had been resting her head on Kes' shoulder. He'd been listening to his favourite music thinking he was the most fortunate man alive.

A single act of selfish disregard for others had taken three people from this earth in the twinkling of an eye.

As the fire and ambulance crew arrived to assist the police, they absorbed the solemnity of the horrific accident. What could be a worse scenario than this abrupt, cruel end?

For Kes, Alice and Inara it was a completely different story. They had stepped into eternity that night.

It was only their dead bodies that lay battered and broken. Death couldn't keep its evil grip on them. Their souls and spirits were alive. They had passed through the door that every man must face and were ecstatic. Their hearts had already been prepared for this moment, death held no sting.

For those who knew and loved them, the news was devastating.

It sent such a shock wave through their family and friends, that many people spent their Christmas in deep grief and mental anguish.

Cara was inconsolable and blamed herself entirely.

Grandad's heart raced uncontrollably. He had to be admitted to hospital; he wanted to die, such was his mourning.

Kes' father, Justin, got so drunk that he fell down the stairs and needed stitches.

Lyndsey went into complete shock and had to be sedated.

Jimmy was surprisingly soft-hearted. He showed genuine grief. He had really liked Kes and had been looking forward to getting to know him.

Taran went off by himself. He refused to be in anyone's company for several days and hardly ate a thing over the whole festive period. On hearing the date of the funeral, he jumped on the first flight out of California, hired a car and headed for Beulah.

Cara had already arrived and met him at the cottage. They were numb and in a state of disbelief.

Although it seemed surreal, they managed to talk over the fine details of the solemn day that lay ahead.

Taran begged her to let him give the main address. She was only too glad for him to do it. "Taran, you knew him so well. Kes would have wanted that. If you feel you can be strong enough, go ahead. Oh, and Taran, there's something else…" Her eyes filled with tears and she lowered her voice. "…Kes and Alice recently told me that they were expecting a baby. They were convinced it was a little girl. Her name was Inara." She held him in a tight embrace and then left him alone to reflect.

It was therapeutic for Taran to sit and write about his best friend. It would have been more damaging if he had kept his thoughts and feelings inside. To think of Kes and all he meant to him, brought the beginning of his healing. He wrote long into the night.

ॐ

Attached to Beulah was a private family chapel. Although small, it displayed magnificent architecture and decoration. It had originally been built for the family and servants of the house to worship in.

Several graves, statues and memorial stones stood in its walled garden.

The chapel was laid out in a traditional style. Tapestries hung on white walls and wooden pews stood in rows.

The main focal point was a simple altar on which a cross was placed. Next to it, three candles awaited lighting. The lectern, where Taran would stand to give his talk, was shaped like an eagle. A baptismal font, symbolic of welcoming new-born babies into the church, stood near the entrance.

Cara went to prepare the chapel for the following day's events. A local florist accompanied her and placed a sweet-scented bouquet of lilies on the altar.

The service was to be short. Taran would bear the full weight of the address to those gathered. A group of young musicians had been asked to lead a few simple songs.

After the time in the chapel, the bodies of Kes, Alice and Inara would be laid to rest in the earth. A large grave had been prepared to receive their coffins.

The morning came quickly. Taran hadn't slept. He didn't care. There was steel in him that would keep him alert and focussed for what lay ahead.

Getting up to address the mourners, he walked to the lectern and unfolded his notes.

He glanced down for a moment. Cara wondered if he would be able to start.

Clearing his throat, he lifted his head and spoke with strength and clarity.

"It's a good thing to embrace our emotion. None of us should attempt to minimise our feelings today. We all share a deep sorrow for the sudden and violent passing of people that we loved and cherished."

Kes' dad shuffled his feet and looked down.

"We can't avoid facing the fact that mankind is mortal. Mortality is written on all of creation. As much as we would love to think that we are masters of our own destiny, to do as we please, when we please, there is one event that we must all attend – our own death.

"Against death we are helpless. These seventy years or so, which we are given as a gift down here, are nothing compared to eternity. If we consider eternity it will influence the way we live out our short lives on earth. It will affect our values. We will live purposefully and respect that the breath within us comes from our Creator.

"We spend so much of our lives concerned about our bodies. There's nothing wrong with that in one sense. To nourish them, look after them and try to keep them well, is good, but they are only our 'temporary tents'. They are the house that contains the real us… It's good to paint the outside of your house and present it well. We identify each other by our physical appearance, but our true identity lies within."

Justin's new wife Steph glanced down at her cleavage. She adjusted her dress to maximise her husband's view of her breast implants. The tight bodice was as low cut as she could get away with. She'd recently gone under the knife and wanted *everybody* to share her joy at being two sizes bigger.

Her enhancements had set her back a few thousand pounds, but the large investment couldn't secure her husband's fidelity.

His eyes still wandered.

He ran them over every other attractive woman in the room. When Cara had walked in, he'd been startled by his ex-wife's beauty. Somewhere he felt he'd been robbed, even though he'd been the one who'd discarded her.

Steph continued listening to Taran.

"I'm sure, like me, you are struggling to come to terms with the trauma and shock of three precious lives taken so recklessly. It seems pointless – wrong. How could they be taken in their prime – in their first few months of marriage and with Alice pregnant with a much desired baby?

"Kes was my best friend. I considered him to be like a brother. I loved him. I'm completely devastated. The pain I feel would be unbearable if it weren't for the fact that I'm certain I'll see him again. I'll spend eternity with him. I had the joy and struggle of sharing some of my life with him. We lived in a house together a few years back. Then we both moved out to California. During that time I got to know him really well.

"Kes was not perfect. He had his issues. I had the privilege of helping him when his failures became too much for him to bear. I know he went through a deep spiritual experience. There was a time in California when he said a prayer on the beach with me and some other mates. It went something like this: 'Jesus, I've got nothing but a load of broken pieces. Please forgive me for my selfishness and come into my heart and change me.' He was totally sincere."

Justin muttered to Steph, "What the hell's he talking about, my son wasn't religious!"

Taran didn't hear what he said but looked straight at him.

"Whether Kes or Alice lived or died, they knew who they belonged to. Their earthly bodies were formed out of the dust and they will now return to the dust. But their spirits and souls are with Christ for all eternity. They were prepared for the tragedy that stole them from us. They had already entered through the door marked Yeshua Ha'Mashiach. The other night they passed into another dimension. They weren't afraid of death anymore. During their short lives on earth they had both faced deep agony in their souls. For both of them, suicide would have seemed less painful. They overcame it by understanding that many of their own failures and choices had led them to such desperation. As they turned from their independence, they accepted God's help to change their hearts. Today they are with Christ in paradise."

Melantha spat on the floor – her dark countenance personified unveiled evil. She hated being in the hallowed chapel. She got up and went out for a cigarette.

Undeterred by the disturbance, Taran carried on. He knew that Melantha had company that hated all things holy.

"Those of us who are left behind know that one day we will die. Life is a battle. The last enemy that all of us will face is death.

"We have seen how it can come suddenly, when we least expect it. It is no respecter of persons, even if you're a billionaire you will still have to face it and leave this earth with nothing except your relationship with God.

343

"Kes and Alice fell asleep but have woken up in the presence of Jesus. They loved Him. They knew he was their best friend – the one who loved them despite their failures and mistakes. His sacrifice on the cross led them to their heavenly Father. They were already living with him on earth.

"Kes sent me an email recently. He was stoked that Alice had been freed from the fears within her. He told me that he comforted her by saying, 'Alice, you can be sure that when you die you'll step into heaven, because heaven has already stepped into you.'

"We are wise to evaluate our lives. We need to measure our days and understand our frailty.

"Kes was a strapping, handsome and healthy guy. He was either surfing, in the gym, or working hard at something. But in his human state he was weak, vulnerable and unable to preserve himself."

Jimmy choked up.

"One day we must give an account of our lives to our Creator. Through Jesus' death, he destroyed the evil one who has the power of death."

A text came through on Jimmy's phone. One of the guys he dealt drugs with had been fatally stabbed. Although he felt a surge of despair, it made him all the more eager to hear the rest of what Taran had to say.

"Most of us are so full of self-importance that we don't easily accept our mortality. We are really like a blade of grass that grows, wilts, and blows away in the wind. Our lives here are like a vapour.

"Kes and Alice set out on a journey. They left their little cottage in the woods to go to another home. While they were in their bodies they were absent from their heavenly home. Their loving Father opened a door and welcomed them in." Melantha overheard his talk from the chapel porch. She went back to the Three Castles scowling.

"Many of you will be asking, 'if Kes and Alice loved their heavenly Father so much, why were they taken? Why were their lives cut short? Why didn't God intervene?'

"Some things remain a mystery, but we can be sure of this. Their Father did intervene. He didn't abandon Kes and Alice. He wasn't lacking in power. Two thousand years ago, he sent his Son to die for them to open up the kingdom of heaven for them. He made a way for them to know life down here and beyond the grave. So as you say good-bye to them today, remember that because of the resurrection they are very much alive."

He folded his notes, stuffed them in his pocket and went and sat down. Cara squeezed his hand and gave him a tearful smile. "Thank you Taran, that was beautiful," she whispered.

He buried his head in his sleeve and sobbed. Although he believed every word that had come from his lips, he couldn't bear to see the two coffins lying in front of him. He wanted to rip off the lid, scoop Kes into his arms and never give him up. He pictured himself holding him so hard that life rushed back into his cold body and his heart began to beat again. He didn't want that box to go into the earth. It was too final. Please God could this be a bad dream? Could he suddenly wake up and find himself fooling around again with his best friend?

He didn't hear the musicians play their songs. It was just some background sound that his thoughts shut out.

345

As the coffins were carried away to be laid in the ground, people started to file out.

Steph confidently strode ahead. Of all the mourners, she was the least emotionally attached to the three who had died. She was more interested in what everyone thought of her figure than the proceedings.

Justin followed after her. He stared over at a pretty blonde sitting on the back row. Although he didn't know who she was, he winked at her. He couldn't help himself. It was as if his eye was a camera and in dropping the shutter he could snap up the image for future meditation.

Taran was one of the last to leave the chapel. He sat in silence watching the three candles flicker on the altar. The beauty of the flowers offered some comfort. A soft hand rested gently on his shoulder. He thought it was probably Cara. When it persisted he looked up.

Ruby slid into the pew beside him. Her face was distorted with grief. They didn't say anything. They just wept together.

After a short while, they walked out into the graveyard and stood next to each other as the coffins were lowered into the ground.

He turned to her. "D'you want to go for a coffee?" When she nodded, he went over to Cara.

"Cara, please can you excuse me from the refreshments? I…"

She looked at his pained expression. She could see his heart was broken.

"It's okay, Taran. You don't need to explain anything. You're always looking after everyone else. You go and get some time for yourself. Thank you so much for everything you've done. Keep in touch, won't you? If you ever want to come out to Italy let me know. You're always welcome." She kissed his cheek.

He led Ruby around to the front of the house where his car was parked. As they stood on the gravel, he loosened his tie and undid the top button of his shirt. "Do you mind if it's a long drive to the coffee shop?"

She shook her head. Her eyes glazed over with tears.

They drove off, and the minutes gave way to hours.

They didn't need to say a word to each other. They both knew where they were going – where they had to be.

It was instinctive, like returning swallows.

They travelled in silence for two and a half hours. The long journey provided the time for them to dwell on their private thoughts about Kes.

Just as the winter sun was beginning to fade, they pulled into the empty car park on the beach front of Trevanna Bay. As they stepped onto the sand, they gave each other the space to reflect on the enormity of their loss.

The modern house to their left stood as a witness to all the memories their souls couldn't conceal.

Ruby lingered on the dunes where Kes had first kissed her. Her eyes traced the path where they had made their passionate flight back to his bedroom.

She slipped off her shoes and followed Taran down to the water's edge. He stood on the spot where Kes had created his sculptured woman. He could barely contain his grief as he relived the moment he'd discovered his best friend so close to death.

As Ruby joined him, her haunted, pretty eyes searched his for answers.

He spoke softly and slowly, letting her hold on to every word.

"He *did* love you, Ruby. Not just for your body or what he could get out of you. In the end he came to know what true love was all about. He was *devastated* at what he'd done to you. He would have made a great husband and brilliant dad. But you need to understand something really important. The agony of losing you and his baby became the door for his salvation."

His words wrenched off the lid. The well of grief and sorrow that had never known release, came up in great, racking sobs. It poured out of her.

"Taran, how can I ever be forgiven for what I did? I think about my baby every day of my life. I'm hooked on anti-depressants so I can take a detour from the track my conscience takes me on. But I'm always led back to a pit of guilt. I drink to try to cover the agony – I loved Kes so much. I couldn't bear to be without him. The thought of having his baby as a constant reminder of him was hell. I couldn't have coped with seeing him arrive at my home to share time with our child, knowing he had some other girl sitting in his car. I would have died of jealousy.

"It seemed a simple thing for me to do – to cut my baby out of our lives completely. It might have been quick, but it didn't turn out to be easy. After I did it, I knew I'd done the wrong thing – I love children really – I can't live with myself. I hate the silence of my own company. I want to tear out my conscience. I have to take sleeping tablets because I fixate on what I did all the time."

Taran pulled her close and caressed her fragile frame.

"Ruby, you *can* be forgiven. You can have this weight of guilt taken off your back. You're not beyond saving; nobody is, no matter what they've done. We've all messed up. I need to tell you what happened to Kes in California. He went through a massive change. I'd love to try to share all the details with you. There's much more to it than what you heard at the funeral today. He would have wanted you to know that he took full responsibility for what happened. He hated the way he'd treated you and his child. He'd have loved to have told you himself."

As he held her in his arms, he knew two things – her inner soul was as delicate as her body, and one day he was going to marry her.

When the last vestige of sorrow came out, he lifted her head and tenderly kissed her lips. It was the sweetest of kisses, pure and healing.

He held her hand and led her back up the beach. "How did you find out about Kes?"

"Jett called me... Occasionally, he checks up on how I'm doing. One of the DJ's, who used to work at the club with Kes, heard the news and told him. Although he was worried about telling me, he thought I would want to know."

Darkness was closing in and there was a bitter chill in the wind. Taran was both shattered and famished. "Shall we go and check out the restaurant and see if Jett's around?"

"I'd love to. It would be so good to see him again. He's a lovely guy and he's always watched out for me."

స్

Exit Darcus is also available on Kindle.

The Purple Veil artbook
that is featured in Exit Darcus
is also written by K L Cole.
It is available as
a hard back full-colour book on Amazon.co.uk
and as an eBook on Kindle.

The Purple Veil

To view the gallery of images or to contact the author
visit www.thepurpleveil.com

Printed in Great Britain
by Amazon.co.uk, Ltd.,
Marston Gate.